W9-CLK-608

FIND HIM

FIND HIM

JAKE HINKSON

The following is a work of fiction. Names, characters, places, events and incidents are either the product of the author's imagination or used in an entirely fictitious manner. Any resemblance to actual persons, living or dead, is entirely coincidental.

Cover and jacket design by 2FacedDesign

ISBN 978-1-951709-75-4

Library of Congress Control Number: available upon request

An imprint of Polis Books, LLC
62 Ottowa Road S
Marlboro, NJ
www.PolisBooks.com

for my mother

Susan Paschal Hinkson

Even the young
are known by their deeds

Proverbs 20:11

PROLOGUE

When someone knocks on the door of room 15, the girl wakes up first. Still groggy, she rubs at her bleary eyes in the darkness, and, for a moment, can't remember where she is. A sliver of red neon stabbing through the motel curtains is the room's only illumination. Another knock, louder than before, makes her jump. The lighter and charred soda can roll off the bedspread and fall to the carpet. A chemical stink still fills the air, like a burning plastic bag, the lingering odor of meth.

She curses and grabs the boy next to her in bed.

Another knock.

A man's voice. "Front desk. I need to talk to you two." The door's so close to the bed, it feels like the man is already inside the room.

The girl shakes the boy awake.

"The guy from the front desk is at the door," she whispers.

"What?" the boys asks, his eyes half closed.

"The guy from the—"

She's interrupted by hard knuckles rapping on the room's big windowpane. The hollow reverberation of glass makes the whole wall seem wobbly.

The girl stumbles to her feet, nearly tripping over her suitcase on the floor, and peers through the cracked peephole. The man outside is off center, his face indistinct in the dull red glow.

As if he can see her peeking out at him, the man pounds the glass harder.

"Front. Desk. Don't make me use the key."

"You better answer it before he gets pissed," she tells the boy.

The boy climbs to his feet wearing a white t-shirt and black boxer briefs. Rubbing his face, he flips on the bathroom light to help him get his bearings. Then he staggers over and looks through the peephole. Seeing the same half-silhouette the girl saw, he eases open the door with the chain on.

He's about to say something when a bolt cutter catches the taut little chain and snips it in half. It sounds like fingers snapping.

Two men shove their way into the room, leaving the door open to the parking lot. The younger of the two men swings the heavy bolt cutter with both hands and hits the boy in the face. The crack of bone beneath steel is loud enough to hear. Tumbling over a chair, the boy falls to the floor. When the girl starts to yell, the older man grabs her throat and shoves her onto the bed, straddling her chest and lifting a machete above his head, choking her scream into a cough.

"Be quiet," he tells her.

Behind them, the younger man beats the boy with the bolt cutter until he curls into a bloody ball in the corner with his hands covering his head.

The older man drags the girl off the mattress by her throat and drops her on the floor between the window and the bed. The door of the room is still ajar, bathing her in the red neon of the motel's vacancy sign.

"Take him into the bathroom," the older man says over his shoulder.

The younger man wipes his sweaty face with the back of his forearm. "To the bathroom?"

"Yeah," the older man says. Then, picking up on the younger man's trepidation, he turns and nods at the bathroom, saying, "Go on now. It's okay. Take him on in there and keep him quiet."

The younger man pulls the boy to his feet and pushes him toward the orange glow of the bathroom.

The older man stands over the girl on the floor.

She's staring up at him, scared but trying to stay calm. She gathers her breath. "I'm sorry, Eli."

"What for?" Eli asks. He taps the side of her head with the flat black blade of the machete. "Hm? What exactly you sorry for?"

She opens her mouth to plead with him, but as she looks up at his face in the dim neon glow, her own face changes. With her mouth shaking, she's not staring anymore. She's glaring.

She swallows.

In a defiant rush of words she tells him, "I'm sorry I ever met you."

Eli closes his eyes. Sighs. Nods at some old thought, some old suspicion now confirmed.

He crouches down next to her with the machete laid across his thigh. Looking into her drowning eyes, he tells her, "Girl, you ain't even met the real me yet."

She tries to say something else, but her teeth are chattering. She clamps her mouth shut.

He yanks her up by her thin bare arm. "You wanna be with him so bad," he tells her, "be with him now." He shoves her toward the bathroom.

The younger man pushes her inside, then wipes more sweat from his face and asks, "What now?"

Eli walks back to the front doorway. He surveys the motel parking lot aglow in moonlight and neon, and then, satisfied with the stillness and silence he finds there, he shuts and locks the door to room 15.

"Let's start with the boy," he says.

CHAPTER 1

Lily Stevens marches into the police station from the cold September rain and walks up to the man behind the front desk. He's wearing a black uniform, and the overhead lights give his high and tight blond hair a fluorescent shine, but he's young, barely out of his teens himself.

Wiping her dripping face, Lily says, "I'd like to speak to the sheriff."

On the walk here from the bus stop, she was caught by a sudden downpour, and now the braided hair hanging to her hips is beginning to unravel. If church doctrine permitted her to wear makeup, her face would be streaked and messy; instead, her skin is slick and pink. Even with her coat on, her maternity shirt is stuck to her rounded belly.

"We ain't got a sheriff," the young officer says. "Got a chief."

She shifts from one soaked sneaker to the other, the damp hem of her denim skirt slapping at her ankles. "Okay, then, may I speak to the chief?"

Lily watches him look her over. She's used to it by now. The quick way someone takes in her too-long hair and her too-long skirt, the absence of any makeup or jewelry, her unpierced ears. And then, of course, her swollen belly and her bare ring finger.

He says, "May I ask what you want to speak to the chief about?"

A silver-haired man steps into the doorway at the other end of the room. He wears a crisp white shirt with dark slacks and has a badge pinned on his belt next to a holstered gun. With both hands, he cradles a steaming coffee mug.

"My fiancé is missing."

The young officer says, "You don't need the chief for a missing boyfriend. You can talk to me about that."

"Fiancé."

"What?"

"You said 'boyfriend.' He's my fiancé."

"Got it."

The silver-haired man in the doorway blows some steam off his coffee and takes a sip.

Lily calls to him, "Excuse me, sir, are you the chief?"

The young officer leans forward. "Hey, girl, you can't—"

"It's okay, Jason," the silver-haired man says. "Miss, you want to step back here with me?"

Lily gives the young officer a terse glance—*lotta help you were*—and follows the chief down a bright hallway with bare white walls and lacquered concrete floors.

He leads her to an open office door and says, "Have a seat. Can I get you a towel or something?"

"No, thank you," Lily says, slipping out of her coat. "I'm not that wet. Rain just caught me outside." She takes a seat in one of the black cushioned guest chairs across from his desk, bare except for a computer and a telephone. "So, what I'm here about—"

"Hold on a sec, before you get started," he says without sitting down, "you're Lily Stevens, aren't you?"

Lily stares at him. Beneath her wet lashes, her eyes are iron-gray. "Yes. Do you know me?"

"It's my business to know who people are in Conway, Lily. I don't know everybody in the city, of course, but I know most of them. Your daddy's a preacher, right? David Stevens. You all are Pentecostals, got that little church over on Azalea."

"Yes, sir. That's right."

"How old are you? Seventeen?"

"I just turned eighteen."

"I see. Your momma and daddy know you're here?"

"No."

"Is there any reason for that?"

"What do you mean?"

"I just mean that usually if I'm talking to somebody your age without a parent or guardian present, it's because there's something bad happening at home. Is there anything you'd like to tell me?"

Lily sits up straight. "No. It's nothing like that at all. This isn't about my parents."

"Okay, then." He regards his coffee. "Excuse me a second. Need a refill."

When he leaves the office, Lily lets out a ragged breath and rubs her belly. She allows herself to slump forward, rotating her shoulders, trying to untwist the knot of muscles in the center of her back.

When the chief walks back in, though, she sits up as straight as a church pew.

He takes a seat behind his desk. "Okay, then. Tell me all about it."

"You know who I am. You know Peter Cutchin, too?"

"Sure, I know Peter. Works at the Corinthian. His momma, Cynthia, works at the flower shop."

"He's missing," Lily says.

"How long?"

"Over a week."

"He's been missing over a week, why am I just now hearing about it?"

"People don't think he's missing."

"Where do people think he is?"

"Everybody thinks he just ran off."

The chief scratches his ear. "I see." He gestures at her belly. "Peter's the daddy?"

"Of course."

"And, correct me if I'm wrong, but weren't y'all all set to be married last week?"

"Yes, we were."

"And he didn't show up…"

"I know how it looks," she says, "but that's not how it is."

"Uh-huh. What's Peter's momma say?"

"She says he ran off because he doesn't want to see me anymore."

The chief grins sadly. "But you don't want to think that's true."

"It isn't true. Not that it matters to her. She never wanted us to get married, anyway."

"How come?"

"She blames me, that's how come. First, she made a big fuss about 'how do we know it's Peter's baby?' like I was some…like I was out running around. That led to a big fight. Then once that finally cooled down, she made a big fuss about where Peter and I are going to live after we get married. We wanted to stay with my parents, so my mother could help me when the baby comes, but Cynthia wouldn't have it. Said I needed a 'stronger guiding hand' than my mother could give me. So, of course, *that* led to a huge fight. Not just in our families, but in our church. Gossip, people taking sides, just a big mess all around. We could have gotten married two months ago if it wasn't for all the fighting and hurt feelings."

"And now?"

"Now he's gone, and she blames me for that, too. But something's wrong. Peter wouldn't just up and leave without telling anybody."

"He might. It's been done." The chief leans forward. "Excuse my bluntness, Lily, but it's been done quite a bit. Boy gets a girl pregnant and runs off before she can get a ring on his finger—that's a story as old as time. And Peter, if you'll excuse my bluntness, well, he ain't a bad kid. But he's always been a little directionless."

"That was true before," Lily says. "But we're going to get married and raise our baby in the church. That's plenty of direction."

"Except…now he's gone," the chief says.

Lily looks down at her bare hands.

"You see my point?" the chief says.

"Yes," she says, raising her eyes to meet his, "but he didn't even tell his mother where he was going. His own mama. They're so close. He wouldn't leave without telling her where he was going."

"That's been done before, too," the chief says. "'Course, the other possibility is that maybe she knows, and she just doesn't want to tell you. That's also been known to happen."

"You could ask her," Lily suggests. "She won't hardly speak to me anymore, but if you asked her…"

The chief almost says something, but he catches himself. He leans forward and touches his phone. "Actually… She works just up the street here, doesn't she?"

"Yes, sir."

He picks up his phone and turns to the computer on his desk. With one hand, he types a quick Google search for the phone number of Ye Olde Thyme Flower Shoppe. When he has it, he calls the store.

"Sandy! Jeff Reid here. How're you this morning? Good…good to hear. Say, is Cynthia Cutchin working this morning? Good. May I speak to her, please? And say, Sandy, I may ask her to step over to the station for just a quick sec. Be mighty obliged if you could spare her for a little bit."

Why would this only take a little bit? Lily wonders.

The chief says, "Hi, Cynthia. Jeff Reid. How are you this morning? Oh, I'm fine. Listen, I wonder if you wouldn't mind coming over to the station for just a second. It's not a big deal, but I got a little matter to discuss with you… Yes, ma'am… No, I think it'd better keep until you get here. I promise there's nothing to be alarmed about. I just need to ask you a couple of questions. Only take a minute… Okay, then. See you in a sec. Thank you."

He hangs up. "Okay, then. She'll be over in a minute."

Without touching her chest, Lily can feel her heartbeat. Sister Cynthia is coming.

"When's the last time you saw Peter?" the chief asks.

"Last Friday, after school."

"Y'all have a fight?"

"No, not exactly."

"What's 'not exactly' mean?"

"We didn't have a fight, but he was being quiet. I tried to get him to talk about whatever was on his mind, but he didn't want to talk. And when I told him he should come in and visit with my family, he didn't want to."

"Was that out of the ordinary?"

She shifts in the chair. "Well, lately, things have been really tense. You know, with the problems with his mother and everything. But when he dropped me off, he didn't even want to come in and say hi to my mom. I told him that would only make him look bad."

"What'd he say to that?"

"Nothing. Just got quiet."

"Where'd he go after he dropped you off?"

"To work. I called his house the next morning."

"Not his cell?"

"He doesn't have a cellphone. Sister Cynthia doesn't believe in them."

"Really?"

"Yeah."

"There something in the Bible against cellphones?"

"No. Most adults in our church have them. But Sister Cynthia's got her own interpretation of scripture. She thinks cellphones are gateways to sin."

"Hard to argue with that," the chief says.

"She's...strict. Stricter than most Pentecostals even. She's got her own way of doing."

"Peter's nineteen, though, isn't he? He always do what she tells him?"

"Well, no, not always. Like you said, he did some running around when he first got out of high school, but he still lives with her and it's her house, her rules. That's another reason I thought we should live with my parents."

"Do you have a cellphone?"

"No, in our house only my parents have cellphones."

"But you and Peter both have landlines?"

"Yes."

"Okay. So, you called his house Saturday morning..."

"And there was no answer. Which was weird. I knew Sister Cynthia was out of town. She was with some of the women from our church who went to a big Ladies' Revival Conference in St. Paul last week. But it was weird that Peter didn't answer, because I called pretty early. I called all day, and then that night Sister Cynthia finally got home and answered the phone. She said his bed hadn't been slept in, and his car and suitcase were gone."

"He leave her a note or anything like that?"

"She won't tell me anything. Aside from the fact that he's gone and it's all my fault."

The chief scratches his ear again. "I see," he says. "Well, let's hear what she has to say when she gets here, okay?"

He picks up his coffee, finds that it has gone cold, and places the cup back on his desk. Then he turns to the computer on his desk and begins deleting spam messages from his email. Without turning back to her, he asks, "How are your folks?"

"They're good," she lies.

"Uh-huh. Things better at the church?"

"Yeah," she lies.

"I don't know much about the Pentecostals," he says, his finger clicking the mouse. "The women in your church can't wear pants or makeup, right? And y'all don't cut your hair?"

"No."

He nods like she said something interesting. "Got an officer on the force who goes to the Assembly of God. That's some kind of Pentecostal, I think. But his wife wears pants..."

"They're different than us. They're kind of mainstream. We're Oneness Pentecostals. Apostolic."

"What's that mean?"

She checks the door. She hates the idea of Sister Cynthia walking in while she's fumbling through an explanation of their church for an outsider. "We...we just try to do exactly what the original apostles did in the Bible."

He turns to look at her.

She can see this is lost on him. "We're kind of strict," she says, just to say something.

In fact, clothing and hair styles are just surface details. The things that really set the Oneness church apart from other Christians are deeper, more theologically complicated. These distinctions are not minor matters to her church, nor are they minor matters to Lily. And if she were of the mind to explain the theological implications of Oneness doctrine to him, she could. But now is not the time. Right now, she has other, more pressing concerns.

"Are you going to look for Peter?" she asks.

"Let's wait and see what his momma says." The chief keeps clicking his mouse and staring at the computer. In the same offhanded way as before he says, "Never saw your daddy preach, but I hear y'all's services get pretty wild. Jumping around and speaking in tongues and all that."

She doesn't know how to respond to that—and never knows, really, how to respond when outsiders act like a real worship service is a circus act.

She's still searching for something else to say when the young blond officer walks in, leading Sister Cynthia.

A pale woman under the best of circumstances, under these harsh lights Sister Cynthia is as blank as a wall. Her hair, brown in her youth, has long since faded into colorlessness and is balanced high atop her head, held in place by bobby pins and Aqua Net. Her dough-white face pinkens when she sees Lily.

The chief turns toward her. "It's okay, Cynthia. Please have a seat."

There is one chair next to Lily. Cynthia sits down and places her purse on her lap. Even sitting down, her long denim skirt nearly covers her feet.

Clearly bracing herself, she asks, "Did something happen?"

With a paternal air, the chief assures her, "No, no. It's just that Lily here is trying to find Peter, and we're wondering if you know where he is."

Sister Cynthia's body collapses forward, and she clutches the purse like a floatation device. "Oh, Lord! You scared me. I thought you were going to tell me something had happened to him." She rubs her face and wipes a tear from the corner of one eye. "You ought not to have done that to me, Jeff. You like to have given me a heart attack."

The chief doesn't apologize for his thoughtlessness, but he nods to show her that he understands her worry. "I'm sure there's nothing to be alarmed about, Cynthia. We're just here this morning because Lily got a little concerned. She hasn't talked to Peter in a few days."

Sister Cynthia sits back up and loosens her grip on her purse. She breaths deeply. Then she says, "Well, he's down in Little Rock somewheres, but I'm ashamed to say that I don't know exactly where he's staying. He's got some…people he visits down there." She rubs her face. "A mother should know her son's friends, but I never got to meet any of his Little Rock friends."

"Well, Peter's not exactly a boy anymore."

"No…"

"He's gonna know folks you don't know."

"I expect."

"But you haven't heard from him in a while? Is that normal?"

"Didn't used to be." Sister Cynthia looks down at her hands, pressing her short, stubby thumbnails together. "But I guess you could say that 'normal' has changed a lot over the last few months." She pulls a small packet of Kleenex from her purse and peels off a single tissue. "He run off while I was out of town at a conference. Packed a bag and drove away without word one to me."

"If he left without a word, how do you know he's in Little Rock?" the chief asks.

"Well, there's nowhere else he could be. The only folks he knows that don't live here are the…people he knows down there. And he's been spending more and more time down there." She folds the tissue in half. "He just wanted to get away from things here. I'm ashamed to say it, but I half expected this to happen."

"Well, heaven knows this kind of thing has happened before in situations like this one," the chief reassures her.

Sister Cynthia only raises her eyebrows in affirmation, pointedly refusing to lower herself to comment on situations like this one.

The chief asks, "Peter take his stuff?"

"Just his car, our little roller suitcase, some of his clothes."

"Okay." The chief stands. "Cynthia, I'd appreciate it if you'd let me know when he contacts you. Matter of fact, please have him call me. I'd like to have a talk with him. You can tell him that it's unofficial. Just a man-to-man talk. It won't be a pleasant conversation, but I want him to call me."

"Thank you, Jeff. The boy could use that kind of talk from a man, the sterner the better as far as I'm concerned."

"Okay, then."

"I gotta be getting back to work. We're fixing to open."

"Of course," the chief says, standing up to walk her to the door. "Thank you for coming in to help us resolve this."

"That's it?" Lily asks him.

"I think," the chief says, his voice shading into irritation, "we've wasted enough time on this for one morning. A nineteen-year-old boy who gets a girl pregnant, then packs his suitcase and drives away ain't missing. He's running away."

Lily lowers her head, unable to make eye contact with either the police officer or Peter's mother. "I just want to know he's okay."

Sister Cynthia blows her nose and balls up the tissue. "Me too." She takes a deep breath and says, "Lily, look at me, dear. No one loves that boy more than me. No one ever could. And this ain't harder on anyone than it is on me. This ain't how I raised him to be. You know that. If his father was still alive, Peter wouldn't be acting this way. I blame myself for the way he's turned out. It's always on the mother. Especially when she's a widow. But I did my best." She tosses the tissue in the small plastic trash can next to the chief's desk. "But now Peter has to figure things out for himself, and he has to make his own decision. Me and you can't make it for him. We just need to pray on it. I can promise you that as soon as I talk to him, I'll make him call you."

When she stands up, Sister Cynthia's gentle Christian face is so blandly placid, the chief completely misses the quiet rage in her eyes. But Lily can see it, can glimpse the imminent fury coming her way, and she knows there will be consequences for bringing a member of the church here today.

As the chief shows Sister Cynthia out, Lily doesn't move. She can't believe this is happening. They're not going to look for him. They think it's her fault he left, and that's that.

Her vision blurs, her brain scrambled by shame, embarrassment, and rage. It's hard to think.

Except for one thing, one thought that remains clear in her mind.

Peter didn't just run away.

CHAPTER 2

The rain-pimpled doors of the station release her back into a day gone grayer and colder than before. Above her, a damp Arkansas flag flutters in the wind. Walking down the front steps in the drizzle, she flinches when she looks across the street and sees her father getting out of their car.

David Stevens is dressed in a white shirt and charcoal slacks with his good black shoes. Since she revealed her pregnancy, he's more or less stopped eating and has shed ten pounds off his already lean frame. He isn't wearing a coat, and he looks frail in the biting wind.

With raindrops stippling puddles on the concrete around them, he walks over and hands her the keys.

"Go wait for me," David says.

"Yes, sir."

He climbs the steps to the station, and she walks to the car and settles into the passenger seat. Though she knows he's furious, she can't bring herself to regret coming here. She looks back at the station. The chief must have called him. Of course. When he excused himself, and he was out of the room for a minute, he went and called her father.

She pulls her hair around. It's too wet and tangled to run her fingers through, so she clutches it like a rope in her cold fists.

When David Stevens finally walks back from the station, she takes a breath. He opens the door and gets in but doesn't start the car.

With his eyes closed, he asks, "What on earth did you think you were doing?"

"They need to look for Peter."

He turns to her. "Is that for you to decide?"

She bows her head. David has never been a harsh father. When he's not preaching in the Spirit, he's relaxed and reserved. He has the quiet, thoughtful air of a bookish man, an unusual quality for a preacher, especially a Pentecostal. She knows he would rather be in his office compiling a timeline of Paul's missionary journey to Rome in 61 AD than arguing with her. Yet it is precisely because he's always been gentle with her that she finds his quiet admonitions worse than a whipping. She feels like she's betrayed his trust.

Softly, he says, "Lily, one day you need to realize that the root of stubbornness is pride. That's the reason you won't let this go. Pride. You just don't want to be wrong. Even though it's clear to everyone that you are."

She stares at her clenched fists.

"Your poor momma…" he says. "You know how upset she's going to be?"

"Daddy—"

"Just stop. Please. Don't say anything. These days I never know what's about to come out of your mouth."

Lily sinks into herself.

They stop at a light. Across the street at the fire department, little kids are filing off a school bus. Lily remembers when they took her class to the fire station when she was in elementary. That seems like a long time ago, but she realizes it was only about seven or eight years ago.

Her father doesn't seem to notice the bus, but he's lost in the past, too. "You used to be smart. Good grades. Good head on your shoulders. And now…" He lifts an open palm like all her promise has just floated out of his hand.

They pass by the campus of UCA, and she watches a couple of girls with umbrellas and backpacks walking across the glistening green lawn.

David tells her, "The only thing worse than getting in trouble with that boy in the first place is what you're doing now. He's run off, and you're up here making sure everybody in town keeps talking about it. Is that what you want?"

"No, sir."

"Chief Reid called me to come get you."

"I figured."

"He just did that out of courtesy to me. You realize that?"

"Yes, sir."

"What happened at the police station?"

"They asked Sister Cynthia about Peter."

"You had them drag her up there…"

"She came in to talk. Just for a few minutes."

"You know there are going to be consequences for that, don't you? At the church? Once she tells everyone that you had her dragged into the police station, what do you think will happen?"

Lily doesn't move, doesn't respond.

"This," he says. "This thing you did here today. What do you think this says about me?"

"It doesn't say anything about you."

"Everything you do says something about me, Lily. I can't believe a girl as bright as you could've forgotten that."

She lowers her head again.

"All the teenage girls running around pregnant these days," he says, "and nobody cares. Nobody bats an eyelash. But you they look at. And do you know why?"

"Because I'm your daughter."

"Because you're my daughter, that's right. Maybe that isn't fair, Lily, but that's the way it is. The preacher's daughter can still be a scandal, even in this day and age. Do you understand that?"

"Yes, sir."

"What'd Sister Cynthia say when they dragged her in there?"

"That Peter went down to Little Rock."

"Doesn't everybody know that?"

"I don't," she says.

David groans. After a while, he pulls off the road and puts the car in park and covers his eyes with his hand.

He doesn't cry, but Lily feels the shame on her skin like a burn. Her whole body hurts with it. She turns away from him and looks out the window.

When they get home, her mother is waiting at the door.

Her father says, "She went up to the police station to ask them to find Peter."

Her mother's face turns ashen. "No, she didn't."

"Yes. She did."

Her mother looks like she's been slapped. "This whole town, Lily… This whole town is gonna talk."

Lily can already feel her mother beginning to come untied. Peggy Stevens can lose hold of herself, especially when the problem has to do with disappointing or angering other people. This fear comes from Peggy's own childhood, when her father, himself a Pentecostal preacher, was forced out of his ministry. The reasons for the loss of her grandfather's church have never been explained to Lily. Like so many workings of the world, they've been promised as a secret to be revealed in due time. Whatever happened back there, however, the effect of it is that other people's expectations are like a slow burning flame for Peggy Stevens, as if their disapproval could flare up at any moment and burn her house to the ground.

Lily walks past her and goes to the couch and sits down. As her gentle father confers with her timid mother, she holds her belly and waits to be scolded.

Peggy asks her husband, "What did the police say?"

"Jeff Reid was nice about it," David says. "Told me he wanted to spare me the embarrassment. But he's not the one to worry about. She had them drag Sister Cynthia in there."

Peggy puts her hand to her mouth and turns to her daughter. "Oh, Lily..."

Lily nods at her mother, almost as if she's sympathizing. Peggy doesn't cry, just stares at her like she's trying to come to terms with a tragedy. "He's just no good, Lily," she says. "Can't you see that? He's just no good."

"Him being good has nothing to do with it," she says.

"What's that supposed to mean?" David asks.

"He's the father of my child. Why am I the only one who cares about that? You, Cynthia, the police. No one cares that the father of my baby just disappeared one day. Something's happened to him."

"What do you think happened to him? He packed a bag and left town two days before he was supposed to marry you. You can't figure out what that means?"

"I know what everybody else thinks it means. I'm not blind. I know how it looks. And it's not like I'm so lovesick I think he could never leave me. I was only lovesick long enough to get pregnant. I've been cured of that sickness. But I also know something that nobody else seems to understand. Peter wouldn't leave his baby. After what happened with his own daddy, he would never just abandon his son.

He would not do that. Something's wrong."

Exasperated, Peggy turns to David and raises her hands. *Will you talk some sense into her?*

"What if you're wrong?" he asks their daughter. "Just for a moment, consider that possibility. What if the simplest answer is the correct one? What if this boy just got cold feet and ran off, inconceivable as that may be, then what?"

Lily rubs her belly. "Then we need to find him before the baby comes," she says. "He made a promise to me, and he made a promise to his son. Maybe nobody else cares about that, but I do. I intend to make him honor his promise. I'm not just sitting around here waiting to be another unmarried teenage mother."

Later, her mother starts dinner while her father goes next door to the church to meet with Brother Josiah Williams. Josiah is thinking of going to the Apostolic Bible Institute in St. Paul, and he wants to seek the preacher's counsel about it. Peggy makes him promise to be back for dinner, but Lily knows he'll probably stay at the church until bedtime.

She goes to her room and shuts her door. Her bedroom looks the same as it has for a long time, yet everything seems a little odd to her at this moment, as if she's showing it to a stranger. A bed with a mint green bedspread. A desk with her schoolbooks. A dresser with her combs and hair clips and bobby pins. She knows that a lot of girls have jewelry and makeup on their dressers, and while she also knows that many of her church friends secretly wish they could wear makeup and earrings and such ostentatious effects, she's always told herself that she's lucky she doesn't have to fool with any of it. In this way, she's always been the perfect model of the pious Pentecostal teenager. She's never cared what anyone thought of her. She's always worn her long hair proudly, like Christian armor, as a way to tell the world *I am not afraid of you. I am not afraid of being different.*

She pulls her hair around and brushes it out.

I like your hair, he told her. It was the first thing he had ever said to her that indicated that he liked her. They'd known each other for years, but one night after church he stared too long at her and said, *I like your hair.*

She tosses her brush back on the dresser. She's angry. Angry at herself for ever letting that idiot boy turn her head. Angry at him for being too weak to stand up to his mother. They could have been married two months ago if not for Sister Cynthia's intransigence. And now the police chief is being as pigheaded as everyone else around here…

She knows she should pray, but she's even a little angry at the Lord these days for staying silent. She wants to pray, to talk to the Lord and ask him to help her find Peter, but she can't. It's like with Daddy. She can't really talk to her father anymore, and she can't pray.

But she knows she should. She knows Jesus is waiting to hear from her. She gets down on her knees, elbows on the bed, and clutches her hands together.

She begins "Please, Lord Jesus," but then someone knocks on her door.

Looking up, she asks, "Who is it?"

"Me," her brother says.

"Go away."

"Let me in, I got to talk to you."

She climbs to her feet, one hand on her belly, and opens the door.

Adam looks over her shoulder like he wants to see if someone is in her room.

"Who you talking to?"

"I was praying, brainless. What do you want?"

"Why are you biting my head off?" he says. "I didn't do nothing."

"Anything. 'I didn't do *anything*.'"

"Whatever. Can I come in?"

"Why?"

"Because I want to talk to you."

"Since when?"

Her little brother hasn't asked to come to her room to talk in a few years. He is small and thin, even for fifteen, and his narrow face is dark and brooding. He's been in a bad mood since he hit puberty. Before that, they had been friends, and he'd always looked up to her. She was the one in their family who taught him how to tie his shoes and how to whistle. They used to play together, to wrestle in their bedrooms. Once her body started to develop, though, he recoiled in disgust. If he glimpsed her bra strap, he would get uncomfortable. And then when his own voice changed, when his own body began to develop, that same day he seemed to decide she was no longer fit to have a conversation with. Looking back on it, she thinks that maybe she teased him too much about it when it happened.

"Just let me in for a second," he says. "I got to talk to you."

She moves out of the way and he comes into the room. He's wearing a white dress shirt, and his hands are in the pockets of his khakis. Oneness boys tend not to be great dressers in the first place, but Adam gets teased more than most. He just stands out everywhere, seems awkward everywhere.

He glances around her room like he's from the Department of Human Services. "What are you doing?"

"I told you, I was praying. I interrupted a conversation with Jesus to talk to you. So far, it's feeling like a big mistake."

He nods. "You've made bigger mistakes."

"Why don't you get out of my room before I punch you in your big mistake of a face?"

He nods again. "Okay, but I heard something that I thought I should tell you."

"What?"

"Something about Peter."

"What? What about Peter?"

"Oh, now you're interested."

"Stop it, Adam. Don't mess with me."

"I'm not messing with you."

"Then what're you talking about?"

"You know Chance Berryman?"

"Chance Berryman, not really. Why?"

"But you know him a little?"

"I mean, he was a senior when I was a freshman. We know each other by sight, but we never said more than a word or two to each other. He was always kind of rough, so I steered clear of him. Especially after he almost killed Greg Hughes."

That was a few years ago. One day after school, Lily had followed the swarm of students rushing to the edge of the parking lot. Peering over the shoulders of the kids in front of her, she saw Chance Berryman knocking a boy named Greg Hughes to the ground. A couple of girls screamed as Chance climbed on top of Greg and began slamming his bloody face into the blacktop. School security finally ran outside and dragged Chance away, but not before he'd permanently blinded the other boy in one eye. Chance was kicked out of school and spent some time in juvenile detention for that. Lily's unaware of what's become of him since then.

"Him and Peter are friends," Adam says.

"No, they're not. Where'd you hear that?"

"Chance told me."

"What? When?"

"This afternoon. He was with some other man, an older guy. Chance has that big red Ford Raptor? They saw me walking home and pulled up beside me and asked me if I was your brother. When I said yes, they asked me if I'd seen Peter."

"What'd you say?"

"What do you think I said? I said no."

"What'd they want?"

"They wanted to know where Peter was. Chance said he needed to talk to him. Told me to tell Peter to call him."

"Then what?"

"Then nothing. They drove off."

Lily sits down on her bed.

"That doesn't mean they're friends," she says. "Just means they know each other. A lot of people know each other. Maybe Chance just wanted to borrow something from him."

Adam watches her with a slight smile on his thin, downy lips.

"Why are you smiling?" she asks.

"I'm not," he says.

"Yes, you are. Why are you smiling? You think this is funny?"

"Kind of."

"Why are you being hateful?"

"I'm not being hateful. That would be un-Christlike. I'm just reflecting that one reaps what one sows."

"You're weird, Adam. You know that? You're just a hateful little weirdo."

"At least I'm not a fornicator."

Lily feels like he's pitched water in her face, but before she can say anything, he turns and leaves, strolling down the hall to ask his mother what they're having for dinner. She stares at the empty doorway for a moment, knowing that she should be mad at him for his taunts and insults. But right now, she doesn't really care about that.

Right now, she just wants to know why Chance Berryman wants to talk to Peter.

CHAPTER 3

One week earlier.

Friday night at the Corinthian Inn.

By ten, the parking lot sits half empty. Only the occasional swoosh of a passing semi out on the interstate breaks the silence.

Peter Cutchin is wandering aimlessly through the halls of the inn. Business is slow tonight. The back annex is empty. In the main section of the inn, with fifty rooms and suites available, there are fewer than two dozen guest rooms occupied. Peter stops to pick up an empty Reese's Pieces bag off the industrial gray carpet and throws it in the trash. That's as much work as he's really done tonight.

He drifts past the long glass window looking in on the empty swimming pool area, which is closed this late. He should drain the water and refill it before the morning shift, but that can wait. The pool doesn't get much use these days, anyway. The Corinthian Inn was built by some ambitious dreamer back in the 1980s who hoped that Conway, Arkansas was going to become a destination location. Today, though, few people come here to come here, so most of the people who stay at the inn are passing through on their way to somewhere else, up to the Ozarks maybe, or down to Mississippi or Texas. By the time the Corinthian came into the possession of its current owner, Mr. Baker, the original dream had already given way to a harder set of realities.

Peter heads up to the front desk to talk to the only other employee working the late shift. Although they're both dressed in the standard Corinthian uniform of white dress shirt and blue slacks with black shoes, they present a striking contrast. Allan—tall, middle-aged, rotund, bald—has been standing behind the front desk for an hour reading a thick book titled *Modernism: The Lure of Heresy*. Peter—shorter, younger, thinner, amply-haired—has already walked through the entire inn three times.

Peter slouches against the wall and watches Allan reading.

"Good book?" he asks.

"Yes."

"What's it about?"

"It's about not bothering people while they're reading. I'll loan it to you."

"Thanks."

"No problem."

Peter sits down. After a moment, he begins to gently rock in the chair, his knee bouncing.

"Hey," he says, "can I ask a question?"

"With the best of them."

"Huh?"

"I'm trying to read this treatise on modernism, Peter…"

"I know, but can the treatise on modernism wait? I wanted to ask you something about Lily."

Allan marks his page with a bookmark.

"Lily?" he says.

"Yeah."

"What about her?"

"You think I'm doing the right thing, marrying her?"

"You getting cold feet?"

"No, but the wedding's in a couple of days. Kinda focuses your attention, you know?"

"I bet."

"So, do you think I'm doing the right thing?"

"Jesus, man, how the hell should I know?"

"Because you're a man of the world. You been around. You're, like, what, fifty?"

"Fifty? I will murder you where you sit."

"Just kidding."

"I'm a well-preserved forty-two, thank you very much. And I've been told I don't look a day over thirty-five."

"Who told you that?"

"Various gentlemen across a spectrum of dating apps. *Moving on…*"

"You're about the same age as my mom."

"Shut up. Do you love Lily?"

"Yeah. Of course."

"You want to marry her?"

"It's the right thing to do. It's the right thing for the kid."

"Well, that's a separate issue. You could still be a father to the kid without being married to Lily."

"That ain't the way Lily sees it."

"Maybe she could change her mind."

"Lily doesn't change her mind."

"No?"

"No. Arguing with her is like arguing with the weather. There's no point."

"Well, the bottom line is, do you *want* to marry her?"

Peter thinks about it. Finally, he nods. "Yes," he says. "I want to marry her."

"Okay, then, what's the problem?"

"Everything. Aside from how much I love Lily, literally everything is a problem. My mother won't even speak her name. We want to get married in the church, right? Not a big service. Private. Just me and Lily and her family and my mom. You know. A quiet little ceremony with the families, to heal the wounds from the last couple months. But my mom just up and left town to go to this Pentecostal woman's conference for two nights. She'll be back in time to come to the wedding if she wants, but she won't commit to it. She just keeps saying, 'I don't know. I need to pray on it.' It's awful. Lily and her mother are both furious."

"Will you still go through with the ceremony if your mom's not there?"

"I mean, I don't want to get married without her there, but at this point I guess I have to. Of course, Lily's parents are going to hate me no matter what I do. Especially Sister Peggy. She's already mad at me, and her shit list is chiseled in stone like the ten commandments. She'll never forgive me if my mom insults Lily by not showing up. I'll hear about that for the rest of my damn life."

"Peggy Stevens?"

"Yeah."

"Lily's mother is Peggy Stevens?"

"Yeah. Why? You know her?"

Allan looks out one of the big windows in the foyer at the mostly empty parking lot. "We've never met. But I've seen her around. Never put two and two together that Lily was her daughter." He tugs at his earlobe, something he often does when he's thinking. "It's a small world," he says.

Peter runs his fingers through his hair and says nothing to that. He leans forward and rubs the back of his neck, swiveling his head around as if trying to unloosen a knot. "I've made so many mistakes."

"We all make mistakes."

"Maybe, but I've made more than my share."

"Hey," Allan says, trying to lighten the mood "if we didn't make mistakes, we wouldn't be working here."

"Yeah." Peter shakes his head again and stands up. He sticks his hands in his pockets and mutters, "This shithole. That's another big mistake."

Allan says nothing to that. Bitching about the Corinthian and Mr. Baker is a natural part of the job, but lately, Peter, usually a good-natured kid, has been given more and more to these dark mood swings. Allan tries not to contribute to this one.

The phone rings.

Allan picks it up.

"Corinthian Inn, Allan speaking. May I help you?" He listens for a minute, saying nothing. He writes nothing down. Finally, he simply says, "Okay," and hangs up the phone.

Peter asks, "Mr. Baker?"

"Yeah."

"Chance and Eli are driving up?"

Allan spreads his palms, as if to say, *What can you do.*

Peter is quiet for a while, staring down the hallway toward the back annex. "You ever think that what we're doing here is wrong?" he asks.

Allan looks away from the younger man, out the sliding glass doors of the Corinthian, at the frenzy of phototactic bugs swarming beneath the lamplight in the empty portico.

"I try not to think about it," he says. "Just do your job. Don't worry yourself about things that aren't your business."

The kid doesn't respond at all.

"You okay?" Allan asks.

Peter leans forward and presses the heels of his hands against his eyes.

"No."

"You still worrying about the wedding?"

"The wedding. The baby." He rubs his face. "Everything."

Allan says, "It'll be okay."

"I'm not sure that's true. People always say that kind of thing. 'It'll be okay.' But it doesn't have to be."

"No, I guess not."

Peter's vision has moved to some middle distance. More to himself than to Allan, he says, "The more I see of the world, the more I think my mother's right. Seems like everything she ever told me about the world is true."

Allan, harboring a strong suspicion of where he fits into the worldview of Peter's mother, just says, "Yeah?"

"She said we were born in sin and in need of grace."

Allan shrugs. "Well, I don't know about the *born in sin* part," he says, "but the world could do with a little more grace. I'll grant her that."

He looks over at Peter, but the kid is still staring at the floor. Does he even hear him? Allan is trying to be a little positive, but the kid doesn't seem receptive to it.

Peter pushes himself away from the desk. "Gonna pop outside and get some air. I'll be back in a second, and you can go on your break."

"Okay," Allan says. He wants to add something else like, "You'll be fine." But he doesn't. Instead, he watches as the kid wanders out through the sliding glass doors to stand in the portico and stare up at the moon.

He picks up his book and opens to his bookmark. He'd been reading about Gustave Caillebotte and Impressionism. The book has a picture of Caillebotte's best canvas, *Paris, a Rainy Day*, which Allan saw once on display at the Art Institute of Chicago. That was years ago, when he was in college. A lifetime ago, it seems to Allan. He'd been about Peter's age then.

He's still reflecting on that, on the way the painting in person is a larger, more powerful experience than can be conveyed by a reproduction in a book, and he's starting to wonder if he will ever go back to Chicago, go back to that enormous museum and stand there again in front of the painting now as an older, sadder man, when he looks up and sees headlights turn into the parking lot and drive toward the back annex. Soon they're followed by another pair of headlights.

He returns to his book, but a few minutes later, he looks up again and realizes that Peter isn't in the portico anymore. Kid should be back by now.

Allan puts down the book. He strolls toward the sliding glass doors, his hands in his pockets. He's going to step outside, see where the kid is, maybe take a peek at the back annex. As he steps into the cool night air, however, he hears an engine start in the employee parking lot on the other side of the hotel.

Peter's car blows past the portico. It barely slows down to make the turn out of the parking lot, its tires screaming as it skids across the service road and swerves into a ditch. Kicking up dust and spitting out gravel, the car rights itself at the last second and swings back onto the road. Allan's mouth is open as he watches Peter's taillights disappear into the dark.

For a moment he can still hear its engine roaring in the distance, but then even that fades away. The silence feels final. Allan doesn't think he and Peter will be continuing their conversation any time soon. As he stands there under the portico light, staring out into the dark, there's nothing left but the anonymous whoosh of passing cars out on the interstate, the sound of people headed somewhere, anywhere, else.

CHAPTER 4

Sunday.

Her family has already left for church when Lily gets out of the shower and dresses. She blow dries her hair as much as she can, but there's too much of it, and there's no way to get it all dry in time. It's still dripping as she grabs her Bible and hurries next door.

Services haven't started yet, and as she crosses the yard in the cool morning air, everyone is still outside the church. Car and trucks, none very new, fill the gravel parking lot. Children chase each other across the lawn while their parents pause on the front steps to greet each other. The men wear old suits with scuffed shoes, carrying their Bibles in callused hands. The boys have short, slicked down hair and button-up shirts tucked into clean blue jeans. The women all wear long floral print dresses. The older women have their hair done up in sculpted beehives, while the younger women wear it down, sprayed to immobile poofs in the front and cascading waist-length in the back.

Their church has almost sixty members. Now, compared to the big Baptist or Methodist churches across town, sixty isn't an impressive number, but as David Stevens tells his daughter, it's easy to pack the pews when all you do is promise casserole and Jesus loves you.

Oneness preachers have a harder task. First, they have to convince people to break themselves before Christ in order to receive his Holy Ghost and speak in tongues. That's hard enough, but Oneness Pentecostals also reject the doctrine of the Trinity—the idea that God is contained in three Persons: Father, Son, and Holy Ghost. Oneness Pentecostals preach instead that Jesus Christ is a singular deity who takes the symbolic *titles* of Father, Son, and Holy Ghost but remains always and forever one Person. As David Stevens explained it to his daughter when she was a young girl, "One equals one. One doesn't equal three. Pretty simple math." Because of this doctrine, Oneness believers are often denounced as heretics. And that's before you even get to the prohibition on women cutting their hair, wearing pants, or putting on makeup. When you think about all of *that*, Lily would argue, sixty members seems pretty miraculous.

The building itself is humble. It was originally built as a Baptist church, and when the Baptists outgrew it and moved somewhere bigger and nicer, they sold it to the Pentecostals. The sanctuary has a vaulted wooden ceiling and pew space for about a hundred people. There is a small office in the back for the pastor, three classrooms for Sunday school, and a dining hall.

As Lily walks up, her father is talking to some of the men. Adam is at his side, watching and listening to the men talk. Lily did something similar when she was his age. She would stand by her mother and listen to the women talk their talk, studying them, studying the way they held themselves in relation to their men and to the outside world, and, especially, how they held themselves in relation to each other.

Lily passes by the men. Her father glances at her and then back to the conversation. Usually, the talk of the men before church is light and given to storytelling and good-natured joking, but today they all seem quiet and serious. Brother Stark stands with his arms crossed, and Brother Drinkwater taps his Bible against his leg. Her father is staring at the ground now.

She notices that her mother is in a similarly quiet conference with some of the women. As usual, Sister Drinkwater, tall and loud, is doing most of the talking. Whatever she's saying, Sister Stark at her side is nodding and murmuring assent. Peggy, holding her Bible to her chest, isn't saying anything.

Lily looks around for Sister Cynthia. She's nowhere to be seen.

When the time comes for everyone to go inside, Lily finally finds her. Cynthia is sitting in her usual place, the fourth pew from the back, on the end, by the aisle. Her hair is perfectly shaped high on her head, her clothes clean and ironed. She is reading—or at least she is pretending to read—her Bible. As people drift in, everyone stops to greet her, and Cynthia makes a show of looking up from her Bible to return the greeting. *Oh, good morning, Sister Drinkwater. Oh, good morning, Sister Stark.*

Lily slips in as quietly as she can and takes the last pew in the back. A few gentle souls wave hello to her, but every person in the church turns around at some point to *look* at her, to take note of her round belly and wet hair. Lily notices that Sister Cynthia, however, does not turn around.

She's acting innocent, Lily thinks. *As if she wasn't on the phone with Brenda Drinkwater all night. Something's going on...*

Walking up to the pulpit, David Stevens looks down at his Bible, as if he's unsure how to start. Lily's always loved to hear her father preach. He was preaching the first time she ever received the Holy Ghost. He was the one who baptized her, the one who has guided her to the Lord time and time again. But now, he's looking down, not really searching the book, just sort of staring at it.

Pews creak. Feet shuffle. The fidgeting church waits for him to speak, but it won't wait much longer.

The preacher raises his head.

"We have some serious things to talk about this morning," he tells the congregation.

No one responds. The creaking and the shuffling stops. The silence of the room startles Lily. For a church where people usually shout their praises to God, the room is almost oppressively quiet. Pentecostals believe in worshipping. In crying out to Jesus from the pews, in shouting encouragement and assent to the preacher. Now, the sanctuary is as quiet as a roomful of Baptists.

David Stevens says, "I understand that some people have some things they'd like to say to me, to the church. I'd like to invite those people to stand up now and speak."

People glance around to see who will stand up. From the back pew, Lily can watch everyone. Raymond Wise, the oldest man in church, adjusts his hearing aid. Sitting next to his parents, seminary-bound Josiah Williams bows his head as if he's saying a silent prayer. Dale Overstreet, one of the newest members of the congregation, puts his arm around his wife Bethany as if they're about to watch a movie. On the other side of the church, Denise Stark squirms in the pew next to her husband and her daughters. A stone-faced woman with dark eyes that match her hair, Sister Stark never says much to anyone outside of her family, but during worship she's the loudest person in church. She always screams, a terrified and terrifying shriek, as if someone were attempting to rape her. Right now, though, she's as quiet as everyone else. When she glances over her shoulder at Lily, Lily stares back at her until Sister Stark looks away.

Sitting by herself, just a few pews in front of Lily, Cynthia Cutchin is as still as a statue.

Finally, Brenda Drinkwater stands up to speak. No one is surprised. Sister Drinkwater is a prominent member of the congregation. She stands six-feet tall but wears her hair in a graying beehive that gives her three more inches. Her husband is a quiet man by nature; even during worship, he mostly just mumbles his prayers and praises. Sister

Drinkwater, by contrast, is a woman who always speaks as if she's trying to be heard over a vacuum cleaner. She comes by it naturally. Her great-grandfather was the Reverend O. M. Tyler, one of the key organizers of the first general assembly of Oneness Pentecostals back in 1917. Being related to Tyler is as close to being royalty as one can get in a Oneness church, but Sister Drinkwater hasn't done much with the family connection. About twenty years ago, she talked Brother Drinkwater into putting all their money and sweat and prayers into opening a store that sold window blinds. Within two years, Fine Blinds went out of business and left them bankrupt. Now Brother Drinkwater works for his brother-in-law, and vigorous Sister Drinkwater stays at home and collects disability for some vague old injury that has not stopped her from doing anything except working. Her main preoccupation is church.

She is also, as it just so happens, Sister Cynthia's best friend.

"Well, Brother David," Sister Drinkwater announces in her big voice, "probably best to get right to it. Nobody wants to cause you or your family any pain at this difficult time, but some people are starting to feel like this congregation is a flock without a shepherd."

From the murmuring congregation, there are a couple of *amens* of support.

"Go on, Sister Drinkwater," David tells her. "Say what you need to say."

"You know we all love you, and we all love your family, but scripture says to abstain from all appearance of evil. Can you say that your house has done that? When the world looks to your house, looks to your house as the representatives of this church, what does it see?"

Every time Sister Drinkwater says *your house*, Lily feels like she's been slapped across the face.

Sister Drinkwater goes on, telling the preacher, "You know it better than any of us. You preached it to us yourself. We got to be separate from the world. We got to be separate from the world so that the world will see the reflection of the Lord Jesus in us rather than a reflection of itself."

David says, "If you're rebuking me, Sister, then I thank you for your rebuke."

From his pew, Brother Drinkwater, to support his wife, quotes scripture, "'Better is an open rebuke than hidden love.'"

"Amen," someone calls out in support.

"That's right," David Stevens tells them. "'Better is an open rebuke than hidden love.' Proverbs 27:5. And I want you all to know that I count this rebuke as a blessing."

Sister Drinkwater says, "I'm glad to hear that, Brother David, but I'm afraid that's not going to be enough. Some in the church think there ought to be a vote put to the people next week. A vote to seek new leadership."

David clears his throat. "I see," he says with the gravity of a martyr.

"It's not personal, Brother. But it's got to be done. Forgive me for being blunt, but we can't say we're holding ourselves to a different standard than the world when our pastor has an unmarried pregnant teenager sitting in the back pew."

There are murmurs of support, but someone in the congregation, finding this last statement to be a bit over the line, calls out, "'Judge not lest ye be judged,' Brenda."

Someone else adds an *amen* to that.

Sister Drinkwater doesn't turn around to answer to her critics, but Brother Drinkwater stands up beside his wife. "No one here can judge," he tells the church quietly. "We all know that only the Lord Jesus himself can judge. And no one here wants a fight." He turns to face the preacher. "But, Brother David, many of us just think it might be best for you to concentrate on your family for a while. It's for your own good, and for the good of the church, and for the good of your whole family."

More people *amen* to that.

In the back, Lily stands up. The blood beating in her head makes her dizzy. "May I say something?" she calls out, steadying herself against the pew.

The entire church turns around to look at her.

Lily sets her feet and stands straight. She says, "I just want you all to know that as soon as Peter comes back, we're going through with the wedding."

People avert their gaze. Her father twists his hands together. Her mother rubs her eyes. Standing beside his wife, Brother Drinkwater looks down at the Bible in his hands.

Sister Drinkwater is the only one still looking Lily in the eye. She says, "It don't seem like that's gonna happen, Lily. You gotta know it, too. Just yesterday, you was up at the police station asking for a statewide manhunt to track him down and bring him back here."

"I didn't ask for a statewide manhunt," Lily snaps.

"Fact remains," Sister Drinkwater snaps back, "you had them drag in poor Sister Cynthia from her job, embarrassing her in front of her coworkers, and bringing even more negative attention to this church." She turns to the people around her and says, "I mean, how long are we supposed to let this go on? Facts is facts, and it don't take long for a congregation to become known for the actions of one person." She turns to address Lily's mother. "I know you understand that from personal experience, Sister Peggy."

Peggy Stevens lowers her face like she's at a funeral.

Lily scowls. *What does* that *mean?* She sees a similar look of surprise on her brother's face.

From his pulpit, his own face turning red, David's voice betrays anger for the first time when he says, "That's enough, Sister Drinkwater."

Sister Drinkwater, sensing that she's overstepped a line, exchanges a look with her husband, prompting him to answer for her.

Brother Drinkwater takes a deep breath and says calmly, "When people get passionate, they're apt to say things they don't mean." He shakes his head and addresses the rest of the congregation, "But the fact remains that this church has a problem it needs to deal with. We can't just wish it away. The Stevens family might be waiting for Peter to come back and marry Lily, but the rest of us need to move on. We need to move on with the business of the church. That is why we're here, after all. We need to be about the Lord's work. And the first step is to decide if we need new leadership."

There are many nods and *amen*s, and Lily can feel the quiet assent of the rest of the room gathering force. Whatever else the congregation thinks about sin and forgiveness, everyone here agrees that the personal drama of the Stevens family has taken up too much of the church's time.

As Lily and the Drinkwaters sit down, David Stevens closes his Bible and tells his congregation, "Clearly, we need to put these questions of no-confidence and new leadership to a vote. In deference to members of the congregation who aren't with us today, I suggest we schedule a special business meeting, that way everyone who wants to be here can be here. If we schedule it for this Friday night, that should give everyone time to pray on it. Are we agreed?"

As one, the church says *Amen.*

Only Lily Stevens and Cynthia Cutchin, alone in their separate pews, say nothing.

With the atmosphere for a worship service ruined, David Stevens releases the church early. People hug each other, shake their heads sadly, say they're going to pray hard about it. The adults all make sure to shake hands with the Stevens family before they leave. Some of the women cry. It's all so upsetting. A lot of people hug Lily, to show her that they still love her, still care about her. Heading for the door with Cynthia, Sister Drinkwater leaves without addressing Lily at all, but her husband stops to give her a hug. His suit is tight, his thin body all muscle and bone.

"God bless you, dear," Brother Drinkwater says gravely. "I'll be praying for you."

She receives the hug limply, and then she says, "Could you tell your wife and her friend something for me?"

"What's that, dear?"

"Tell them that when Peter and I walk in here married on Friday night, we'll all be able to get back to doing the Lord's work."

Brother Drinkwater seems so pained by her words, he looks ready to cry. He takes a deep breath and tells her, "Just trust the Lord, Lily. Whatever happens, you just trust the Lord."

"I trust the Lord that Peter and I will be here Friday night," she says.

His eyes are almost glassy as he pats her shoulder with his rough hand. Then he walks outside to join his wife, still shaking his head.

CHAPTER 5

The next day, after school, Lily decides to break into Cynthia's house.

She spends most of the day with her head down, quieter than usual. Hurrying from class to class without making eye contact with her classmates or her teachers, she only has one thing on her mind, one problem she has to solve. The trouble is, she's not sure where she should even start to solve it.

When she gets home, she finds that Adam has gone to a friend's house, and her parents are about to leave.

"Sister Powell is back in the hospital with her hip," Peggy tells her. "Apparently the replacement they put in last year has come loose, and they have to do some kind of adjustment."

"So y'all are going up there to pray with her?"

"Well, I'm still the pastor," her father says, adding, with a small dark smile, "for the next few days, anyway. Still gotta do the job."

"Okay," Lily says, unsure if she should smile back.

"Do you need anything?" her mother asks as they're about to step out the door. "We'll only be gone a couple of hours or so."

"No, I'm fine," Lily says. "I'm just going to rest."

As she stands at the window, however, watching her father's car disappear down the street, she thinks, *I only have a few days left to find him.*

But she's already talked to everyone she can think to talk to. She's already talked to the police. That was a dead end. Now what?

The answer comes to her as suddenly as if it were a prompting of the Holy Ghost.

Begin at the beginning.

Okay. Begin at the beginning. But where is that? Where would the police start? They'd talk to his mother most likely, get as many details as possible. They'd probably go out to the house to see his room, see what he took with him and what he left behind.

It occurs to her that she hasn't been to his house since he disappeared. She's not exactly welcome there. She's had to just take Cynthia's word about everything.

But Cynthia is probably at work right now.

Once she has the thought, she's seized by it. She actually can go to Cynthia's house, right now, this minute. *To find what, though?* She doesn't know. But she doesn't know what else to do. Maybe some small part of her suspects that she's going to walk in and find Peter sitting on his bed, hiding from her.

She turns and goes to her room. She closes the door and opens the bottom drawer of her bureau. From beneath three neatly folded jean skirts, she retrieves a key.

She stares at the duplicate of the Cutchin house key in her palm. After they found out she was pregnant, Peter had it made for her. He was afraid that her parents would throw her out once she told them she was having a baby. Lily told him that her parents would never do such a thing, but he insisted she take it, just to be safe. Since it was a gesture of love, an attempt to show her that he would take care of her, she took the key. She didn't have the heart to point out to him that it was *his* mother who was more likely to be the one to overreact.

She squeezes the key in her fist and nods. "Got to," she says.

It's turned warm outside, so she dresses in a jean skirt over thin stockings, with a lime-green maternity shirt that's actually a little too large. She pulls her hair back in a banana clip, puts on some tennis shoes, and goes out to her mother's car.

Traffic is light as she drives over to the Olde Thyme Flower Shoppe, slows down, and cruises by just to be sure that Sister Cynthia's car is still parked in the back lot with the other employee vehicles.

It is.

Lily follows 65 out of town until she passes the big Assembly of God church on the hill, and then just before the Pickles Gap Gun Shop, she turns up a red gravel road with no sign. There's a cluster of old homes along this road, including a few owned by members of the church. Elderly Brother Wise lives at the top of the hill with his daughter, and the Drinkwaters live just over the ridge. Below the Wises on the road are a couple of younger families Lily doesn't know. And nestled into the trees at the bottom of the hill is Sister Cynthia's house.

Peter has lived in this same house all his life. His father, Danny Cutchin, built the house right after he married Cynthia, built it with his brother, just the two of them, with only a one-day assist from the men at church to help raise and set the trusses. It's fairly big, with tall windows and a little porch in the front, but Cynthia hasn't been able to afford to keep up repairs, and a couple of hard winters, with a nasty tornado season in between, have left the place with missing shingles on the roof and a six-foot gap in the siding.

Not long after Danny and his brother finished the house, Peter was born. But then, one year later, a plague of sorrow befell the family.

Danny's brother died in a head-on collision when his truck hydroplaned out on 65 during a winter storm. Danny Cutchin, still reeling from the grief, was informed the following spring that a swelling under his jawbone was lymphoma. He hung on through years of chemotherapy, years that bankrupted the family. His hair fell out like ashes and surgery disfigured his jaw. He died holding his son's tiny hand when Peter was barely five.

Only one of the neighbors seems to be home, Brother Wise. Peter always liked Brother Wise and used to mow the old man's lawn and then sit on his porch drinking Mountain Dew and listening to Brother Wise's stories of being on a ship in the Philippines in World War II. At ninety-three, Brother Wise lives with his daughter, but right now the daughter's car is gone and Brother Wise is sitting alone by the living room window, watching the trees grow. He doesn't turn in Lily's direction when she gets out of her car and hurries up to Sister Cynthia's front door. He just gazes off, his attention lost in the trees.

Lily takes out the key, unlocks the door, and goes inside.

She pauses inside the foyer, squeezing the key in her palm, listening to the silence of the house. She takes a step and the creak of the floor seems loud enough to echo up the street.

Up the street. Will Brother Wise mention her visit to Cynthia? He's half blind and probably can't see beyond the trees in his own yard. Still...

She can't worry about that now. She steadies herself and moves on.

The house is well kept, Sister Cynthia being a devout believer in the precept that cleanliness is next to godliness. The foyer smells freshly mopped. The den is tidy, vacuumed, and dusted. *She has nothing else to do*, Lily thinks. *She comes home from work and cleans the house.* Maybe she talks on the phone to her cousins in Texas or some of her friends from church. But there are no televisions or computers in the house. No cellphones, no electronic tablets, no video games. No books besides the Bible. There's one small radio in the den. Sister Cynthia used to listen to an AM channel that picked up a Oneness preacher out of Texarkana, but for some reason the station stopped carrying the preacher and now Cynthia doesn't even listen to the radio except to check the weather. With Peter gone, she just sits here alone in her spotless house. It's as though she's afraid to have any personality at all for fear of offending the Lord. The only thing she believes in, other than God and Lysol, is the sanctity of motherhood, but she's as rigid on that subject as she is on the others.

Walking down the hallway hung with family photos, Lily finds the door to Peter's room open. His bed is made, the floor vacuumed, the shelves dusted. The centerpiece of the wall space is a framed poster of the 1994 Arkansas Razorback championship basketball team, a family heirloom which had once belonged to Peter's father. Tacked up over his bed are football pennants from his senior year of high school. In the corner, a desk, bare except for a lamp, a cup of pens, and Peter's Bible.

Being in this room again is a bit dizzying. The bed, with its hunter-green comforter and soft pillows is a place of deep sensual memory for her, the place, five months ago, where they made their child.

Lily shakes her head and goes to the dresser by the bed and opens the top drawer, which is full of socks balled up in pairs. She feels underneath them. Nothing. She goes through the rest of the drawers of underwear, shirts, jeans, slacks. She walks over to the desk and sifts through its drawers. Most of them are crammed with papers, old tests and graded homework from years past, shoved here after class and forgotten. Then, in the bottom drawer, she finds what she's looking for.

Her letters to him, bound together with a rubber band. She taps the bundle of letters against her chin and shuts her eyes and tries to decide what this means. *He wouldn't leave without these*, she thinks. They're not salacious, but they are deeply intimate, not the kind of thing he would leave behind for his mother to find. If he were planning to leave, he would take the letters with him, right? Opening her eyes and staring at them, she thinks, *Or maybe not. Maybe he doesn't care.*

Maybe he just ran off like everybody's been saying.

She doesn't believe that, but she doesn't know what else to think. She's still pondering the meaning of the abandoned letters when she hears the front door open.

CHAPTER 6

Lily doesn't move, doesn't breathe.

She waits for Cynthia's voice. Cynthia knows the car parked outside and she must know it's not Peggy Stevens back here poking around in Peter's room.

But Lily doesn't hear Cynthia's voice.

Instead, she hears footsteps. Heavy. Booted. More than one pair.

"Anybody home?" a man asks.

It's not Peter. The voice is older, raspier. She steps toward the window over Peter's desk and sees a blood-red Ford Raptor with fancy rims and suspension lift parked in the driveway next to her mother's car.

Chance Berryman's truck, she is almost sure.

She puts the letters back in the desk drawer and closes it quietly.

"Hello," she calls out.

She steps into the doorway. At the end of the carpeted hallway stands a stranger. He's older than her father, maybe in his fifties, with rough skin and shaggy hair that's gray-over-black like cigarette ashes. He's wearing a snap-button black cowboy shirt and dirty blue jeans.

Standing behind this man, looking over his shoulder, is Chance Berryman.

He's put on weight since she last saw him, smashing Greg Hughes's face into the pavement of the high school parking lot. Chance always had a thick chest and shoulders, but now his gut strains against a gray Razorback t-shirt. When he sees her, he adjusts a Dallas Cowboy's cap over his sweaty hair and says awkwardly, "Oh, hey, Lily."

The older man turns around and looks at Chance, "Lily?"

"Yeah, this is his little girlfriend."

She asks, "What are y'all doing in here, Chance?"

It's the older man who answers. "Oh, we were just in the neighborhood," he says. "Thought we'd drop by and check on Pete. He home?"

"Y'all never seen a doorbell before?"

The two men are out of place in Cynthia's sterile Christian home. With a dirty hand, the older man pushes open the door of the hallway bathroom and glances inside.

"Sometimes people get nervous when they hear a doorbell in the middle of the day," he explains. "The easily alarmed have even been known to start unholstering instruments of home defense before a man can properly announce himself."

Chance smiles at that. "Instruments of home defense," he chuckles. "That's a good one, Eli."

Eli nods. "Besides, the door was open, so we just come on in."

Lily grimaces. She didn't think to lock the door behind her.

"At any rate," Eli tells her, "we didn't want to alarm Pete. Is he around?"

"No."

"Do you know where he is?"

"No, as a matter of fact, I don't."

He walks toward her. "You sure he ain't back there with you?"

"What? No."

"You sure?"

"Of course, I'm sure."

She has to back into the room as he steps into the doorway. When she backs up, he follows her into the room. Behind him, Chance fills the doorway. The back of Lily's legs hit the bed.

Since she knows Chance, however slightly, she turns to him. "See? I told you, he ain't here."

He ignores her, watching the older man like a dog waiting on its master.

Eli is looking around the small, tidy room, thinking.

"He's not here," Lily tells him. "Hasn't been here in a while. So y'all can just leave."

He's so close to her she can smell the mildew on his clothes, as if they were left damp in a washing machine too long. When he reaches for the blinds over the desk, she can see his knuckles, as hard as hickory knobs, can see the stout cord of veins climbing his hairy arm and disappearing under the sleeve of his shirt. He closes the blinds.

"Where is he?" Eli asks.

"I told you, I don't know. He's missing. Been missing about a week. No one's heard from him."

"So, what, he run off and left you?"

"It looks that way. At least to other people."

"How does it look to you?"

"I don't know." She has to swallow before she says, "For all I know, maybe he was trying to get away from you two."

Eli takes a deep breath like he's just heard disappointing news.

Chance asks her, "The fuck does that mean?"

"Nothing."

"He say something about us?"

"No."

"For you to say that, he must have said something..."

"No, he didn't. But I mean, here y'all are, looking for him. Don't take a genius to put one and one together and get two. What am I supposed to think?"

The older man says, "You'd be better off not to think about us at all, darlin'."

She tastes sweat on her lips, feels it on her chest and belly. She peels the maternity shirt away from her skin. She wants to get them out of here, get them outside where other people might see what's happening, but on some innate level, Lily also believes that if one does not acknowledge fear or react to it, the source of the fear loses its power. She is wrong about this, but it gives her the confidence to gather her courage, cross her arms, and say, "I'll leave the not thinking up to you two." She turns to Chance and says firmly, "Now y'all better go."

She's still looking at Chance when Eli smashes into her. She sees the surprise on the younger man's face before she sees Eli move at all, but by then Eli's already sent her tumbling back onto the bed. He climbs on top of her, ignoring her belly, and straddles her hips. He twists a fistful of her hair in his fist and jerks her head back. When she yelps, he slaps her. It's like a balloon popping in her ear. Her vision goes liquid. His fingers twist her hair tighter, his knuckles scraping against her scalp.

He pulls her face close to his.

"Watch your mouth when you talk to me, cunt."

He jerks her head back and forth like he's trying to pull it off her neck. Then he slaps her again so hard her eyes clear up.

"You understand?"

"Yes, sir. Yes, sir, I understand."

"Now you tell me where that sack of shit run off to."

"I swear I don't know, sir."

"You don't got no way to get a hold of him? Don't lie to me."

She shakes her head.

He twists her hair until she's afraid it's going to rip out of her scalp.

"Don't shake your head at me, bitch. Answer."

"I don't have any idea. Please. I swear to God. No one knows how to find him."

With another jerk of her hair, he releases her, like he's shoving her away. But he doesn't move. Still straddling her hips, he tells her, more calmly now, "If I find out you're lying to me, I'm gonna come back here. And I ain't going to be looking for Peter anymore. I'm going to be looking for you."

"I'm not lying to you."

He stares at her a while, his cigarette breath hot against her skin. Then his face changes. From a scowl of rage, his lips slip into a leathery smile. Still inches from her face, in a softer voice he says, "Good. That's good. And I guess you realize that our little visit here today is just between us, right?"

"Yes, sir."

"Good." He pats her smooth face, still red from his slap. "I like it better when you're nice. It allows me to be nice." He pats her face again.

He climbs off of her, standing up again, and says, "Okay, Chance, let's go."

Chance's eyes are wide, almost as if he'd been slapped, too. He steps out of the doorway as Eli goes down the hall. As she pushes herself up on the bed, he turns back to Lily for a moment. Avoiding her eyes, he nods like one of them has said something, then he hurries after Eli.

When she hears the front door close, Lily gets up and goes to the window. The two men climb into the truck, and Chance backs out. She watches them drive away until they disappear.

Her face, numb at first, starts to sizzle. She doesn't touch her cheek, and she doesn't lift her hand to her temple, though she feels the first dull tremor of a headache. She just stands in the center of Peter's room, her arms wrapped around the baby in her belly.

Finally, it occurs to her that she must leave. Quietly, she straightens the sheets on the bed, erasing the indentions of two bodies. She walks down the hall and goes outside, locking the door behind her. Then she drives home.

When she gets to her house, she goes to her room without saying anything to anyone. She just sits on her bed for some time, staring in the mirror over her dresser, rubbing her face.

CHAPTER 7

What could people like that want with Peter?

She's looking in her bedroom mirror at the red mark on her cheek. She brushes her fingertip across it. Her face doesn't hurt, though she definitely has a small headache now.

Peter's never mentioned Chance or Eli. How does he know them? Clearly he's mixed up in something bad, but what? *Drugs?* It seems like the obvious answer. Doesn't everything involve drugs these days? But he doesn't use drugs—at least not as far as she knows—so, what, he got mixed up with them to make some money? It's not like he cares about cars or speakers or clothes or anything like that, so maybe the money was for Lily and the baby. But then something happened, something went wrong between them, and now Peter's run away.

It's a harrowing speculation, and it makes her afraid not just for Peter but for herself and for the baby. If he's running from a man like Eli, there's no telling how far he'll go to get away.

FIND HIM

Peggy calls her to dinner.

When she walks into the dining room, Peggy asks, "What happened to your cheek?"

"What? Oh, nothing. I just bent over to get socks out of my drawer and smacked my face on the dresser like an idiot."

"Looks like it might bruise. At least you didn't cut the skin. Did it hurt?"

"Yes."

"You might should put some ice on it after dinner."

"Okay," she says. Then she asks, "Where's Daddy?"

Peggy puts a bowl of green beans on the table next to the brisket leftovers from Sunday. "He's working tonight," she says.

"Oh, right."

Four nights a week, Lily's father packs ice in a little shed on the other side of town. His pay from the church, dependent on the inconsistent tithes and offerings of his small congregation, has never been enough to cover the family expenses. Since it would look wrong for his wife to work outside the home, he's taken a job working for a man who sells bags of ice to football concession stands and gas stations across the state. There are members of the church who would be happy to offer Brother Stevens a job in management or sales, but he doesn't want a job that would require him to interact with the public. He feels it would diminish his standing as a preacher to be seen as just another employee greeting customers and peddling goods or services.

Instead, four nights a week, David Stevens drives over to a small, nondescript building in the woods. There, a large, loud machine freezes water into chopped ice and feeds it into ten- and forty-pound plastic bags that he loads onto a metal dolly cart and stacks in a walk-in freezer. It is a one-man job, and he's there alone. The machine churns out dozens of bags of ice an hour, but a large part of the job is simply waiting for the water to freeze. Lily suspects that her father rather likes all the free time. While the machine clangs and grinds away, he sits and reads his Bible and thinks his thoughts.

Lily imagines him there alone tonight. *Does he prefer to be alone?*

Peggy sits down. "Adam," she says, "will you say the blessing?"

"Yes, Momma."

They bow over the meal and Adam prays. When he's done, they start eating and Peggy asks him about his day. He begins to tell her about the dumb things the dumb kids at school said or did. He often does this, reporting to his mother about the druggies, whores, and blasphemers who apparently comprise the entire student body of their school. His mother eggs him on. Her mother's only real vice, Lily thinks, is offering herself as a hungry audience for the secondhand gossip of teenagers.

Lily stabs at her brisket.

While part of her wants to interrupt Adam's report to tell Peggy about what happened at Cynthia's house, she knows better than to give in to the temptation. In a sense, she's protecting her mother. Lily entered Cynthia's house illegally herself, after all. It's better for Peggy not to know about that, to be able to say honestly she had no idea it had occurred. And if Peggy knew about Eli and Chance, her heart would only harden more toward Peter. No, Lily decides, for the time being it's better to keep this afternoon, as Eli said, just between them.

"Are you alright, Lily?"

She looks up from her plate to realize that her mother is staring at her with concern.

"I'm fine."

"You sure? Not eating. And you look worried."

Lily shrugs.

Her mother nods. "Are you worried about the vote?"

"Sure," Lily says.

"Trust the Lord," Peggy says, turning to include Adam. "Both of you."

Adam nods, but Lily looks at her mother now more closely than before. The mention of the vote makes her think about yesterday's disaster at the church. She says, "Can I ask a question, Momma?"

"Of course."

"I don't know if you'll like it."

"Okay..."

"What did Sister Drinkwater mean? When she said that you know about people judging the church from personal experience?"

Adam sits back a bit in his chair. "I was wondering the same thing," he says in a rare bit of sibling solidarity. "That was a weird thing for her to say."

Their mother puts down her fork and lowers her head for a moment. She nods to herself and leans back in her chair. "It's just like Brenda to throw that in my face in front of the whole church." She draws a long breath and says, "But that's not the point, I guess."

Her children stare at her, waiting.

She takes another long breath. "You know my daddy was a preacher before I was born," she says. "And you know he lost his church. Well, he lost his church because he had an affair. I was only a couple of years old when it happened, so I don't remember it. I don't remember him ever being a preacher, ever having the church. It was always something that had been lost. Something that broke my momma's heart. I don't think she ever got over it." Peggy picks up her water, takes a sip, and puts the water back down. "Anything else? Any other questions? Better ask them now because I'm not going to want to have this conversation again."

"Who was the woman?" Lily asks.

Peggy pats at her hair and then crosses her arms. "She was a woman who was hired to do the books for the church. A married woman. Not a member of the church, not a Holy Ghost-filled woman."

"Do you know her name?" Adam asks.

"Alice Woodson," Peggy says. She says it like she resents the question, like she's mad at them for wanting to know, mad at them for making her say the name. "Anything else?"

"How did people find out about the affair?" Lily asks.

"Alice Woodson got pregnant."

Lily and Adam look at each other across the table.

"Did she have the baby?" Adam asks his mother.

"Yes. A boy."

"Do you know him?" Lily asks.

"Well, we've never met for coffee, if that's what you mean."

"But you know who he is?"

"Of course. He still lives in town."

Adam gestures *c'mon already* and asks, "Well, who is he?"

Peggy sits up straighter and stares at her son. "Don't speak to me like that, Adam."

Adam lowers his head. "Yes, ma'am."

"But who is he, Momma?" Lily asks, prodding more gently than her brother.

Peggy Stevens says flatly, "His name is Allan."

Lily is knocked back. "Woodson," she says, registering the name. "Allan Woodson. The Allan Woodson who works at the Corinthian?"

Her mother nods. "Yes."

"The Allan who works with Peter. He's my uncle?"

"I don't think I want to discuss this any further."

"Isn't he some kind of homosexual?" Adam asks.

"Are there different kinds?" Lily asks.

Adam shrugs.

"I said I don't want to discuss this further," their mother says.

She picks up her fork, looks down at her plate, then puts her fork down again. She gets up from the table, says, "Excuse me," and goes back to her bedroom.

Lily stares at her brother. He's still blinking, shaking his head. She's about to say something, when their mother walks back in and sits down again.

"We're going to finish our dinner," Peggy announces. "And then you both have homework to do. I don't want you to say anything about this to your father."

"Why not?" Adam asks.

"Don't talk back to me," his mother snaps. "Your father has enough on his mind that he doesn't need to deal with this old mess. I'll tell him we discussed it when he gets home. It was a shameful thing that happened over forty years ago. It's nobody's business except the people it happened to, and they're all gone. So now it's nobody's business, and it will be a *very* long time before I am going to be able to forgive Sister Brenda for bringing it up in the middle of church. A very long time. Now eat."

After dinner, Lily sprawls across her bed, staring at the ceiling and thinking about the secrets that adults keep. It increasingly seems to her that the world of adults is a world of hidden knowledge. And at the center of that knowledge always seems to be sex.

In her family and in her church, sex is never discussed except to be forbidden, a secret meant to be revealed within the adult world of marriage. But marriage itself is a mystery that mostly transpires behind closed doors. Private conversations kept low so the children can't hear. Sex kept so discreet that Lily has no idea if her parents even touch each other anymore. And while she's been taught that the Bible is supposed to illuminate these things, it rarely does. Between Solomon's thousand wives and Jesus's perpetual virginity, she was never sure what she was supposed to actually think about sex.

Adults and their secrets. Her grandfather had his, apparently. Lily had her own, but now her secret is as public as her swollen belly.

Adults and their secrets…

She gets up and walks down the hall and knocks gently on her mother's door. "Momma?"

"Yes," Peggy says from behind the door.

"I need to run up to the store to buy that body pillow the doctor told me to get."

"Okay," Peggy says. "Do you want me to come with you?"

"No, I'm fine. Do you want me to get you anything?"

"No, thank you. There's gas in the car and money for the pillow in my purse on the counter."

As she pulls out of the driveway, Lily's happy to be free of her family for a while. And she actually does need to buy a pillow to offset the discomfort in her right hip when she tries to sleep.

Before she gets it, though, she has another stop she wants to make.

CHAPTER 8

When Lily arrives at the house, the yard is dark, so she pulls up close. She wants Sister Cynthia to know she's there, doesn't want to surprise her too much when she knocks on the door.

But Lily is barely out of the car before Sister Cynthia is on the porch, a dark silhouette standing against the light from the front hallway.

"I need to talk to you," Lily says.

Sister Cynthia stares at her from the darkness for a moment, then reaches into the house to turn on the porch light.

In the electric glow, she looks tired and sad, still wearing the white turtleneck and light green cardigan she wore to work today. Now that she's home, though, her hair is unpinned, and, thus loosened, hangs almost to her knees.

"Okay, then," she says. "You say your piece, and then you be on your way."

Lily nods. Apparently, Cynthia's unaware that people were in her house this afternoon. Or, at the very least, she's unaware that Lily was in her house this afternoon.

"Can we go inside?" she asks.

"I don't really want you coming inside my house, Lily. Excuse me for being rude, but it's too much to expect me to put out tea for you."

"Don't worry, Cynthia, I don't expect you to start being kind to me now."

"You got an awful smart mouth for someone so young, girl."

"And you talk an awful lot of foolishness for someone so old."

Cynthia crosses her arms. "That all you came up here for? To disrespect me?"

"No." Lily walks up the steps of the porch. "Look, I know you're mad at me—"

"For what? What do you think I'm mad at you about?"

"You blame me for getting into trouble with your son."

"Did my boy force himself on you?"

"Sister Cynthia..."

"Oh, I'm *Sister* Cynthia now."

"You want me to call you Sister Cutchin? Or Mrs. Cutchin?"

She shrugs. "I don't care what you call me, Lily. But you didn't answer my question. Did my son force himself on you?"

"Of course not."

"No, of course not. My boy doesn't force himself on girls. So then whose fault is it?"

"You act like I forced myself on him."

"He's a man. Barely that, he's just a boy. They'll do whatever girls will let them do. Didn't your momma teach you that?"

Lily grips the wooden handrailing of the porch like she's squeezing a throat. "Just stop right there. Cynthia. Don't say another word against my mother."

Nodding, confirmed in some old suspicion, Cynthia says, "See what I mean? We ain't ready to talk. I don't know what you thought you come up here to say to me, but I don't want to hear it. Far as I'm concerned, you're the worst thing ever happened to my son. You might wear your hair long and shout on Sunday, but you ruined Peter's life. It's going to take me a lot of prayer and a lot of years before I can even think about forgiving you for that."

Lily wants to reply, to defend herself, but Cynthia stares at her with an anger so deep and permanent it seems almost peaceful, less like an emotion and more like a final state of being. This woman will never forgive her. Better to get down to business and get out of here.

She asks, "Do you know who Chance Berryman is?"

"What? Who's that?"

"Peter never mentioned him? Or a guy named Eli?"

"What are you talking about?"

"He ever act worried about anything at work or…?"

"Peter has enough to worry about."

Lily lets go of the handrailing. "Okay, Sister Cynthia." Careful of the steps in the dark, she walks back to the car, but before she gets in, she says, "I'm having his child. You can hate me if you really think that's the right thing to do, the Christlike thing to do. But I'm having his baby. And to me, that seems like a good reason for us to try to get along at some point."

In answer to this olive branch, Cynthia turns around, goes back in her house, and shuts the door.

Where would Peter have met someone like Eli?

She pulls onto 65 and drives home without the radio on, letting passing headlights on the highway flash over her in silence.

He would have had to meet Eli through someone else. When Peter first disappeared, she sought out all his friends to see if anyone had any idea where he could have gone. The problem was, Peter didn't really have many friends. Most of the people he had been friendly with in high school had drifted away or gone to college. So, eliminating his friends, the people at church, and his mother, there is only one place left to go.

The Corinthian. She could drive up there tomorrow and try talking to some of his coworkers.

Or she could reach out to one person in particular.

CHAPTER 9

The next morning, at a sprawling complex called The Fairways, Lily knocks on the apartment door of Allan Woodson. As she waits, she looks over the railing of the second-floor balcony, watching a man wandering around the empty communal swimming pool talking on his cell phone, his face lifted to the cool sunlight. Somewhere, a car alarm beeps five times and goes silent. Downstairs, a baby cries. Lily knocks again.

She feels odd being here. She feels odd not being in school. This morning she lied and told her parents she felt sick. As they were heading out the door to take food to Sister Platt, an elderly shut-in member of their congregation, Lily was still sitting on the couch. As soon as her father pulled out of the driveway, however, she dressed and grabbed her mother's car keys off the kitchen counter. She's not happy with how easily lying seems to come to her these days.

The door opens and a man's head—large, bald, and high above her—peeks out.

"Yes?"

"Hi. Are you Allan?"

He looks her up and down and says, "And you're Lily."

"Yes. May I talk to you for a minute?"

"About what?"

"About Peter."

"Peter..."

"Yes, sir."

"Please, you don't have to *sir* me. I'm not so old."

Lily smiles. "Okay, then. Can we talk for a minute? I'd really appreciate it."

Allan nods. "Of course," he says.

The door opens wider, and although Peter had told her that Allan was big, Lily is shocked by the size of the man who stands in the doorway. Allan Woodson is mountainous. He wears a tarp-like black t-shirt that barely covers an enormous belly that hangs past the belt on his baggy gray jeans. Even if he was thin, however, Allan would still be large. His head nearly scrapes the doorway, and his broad shoulders give way to powerful arms and thick hands that could palm Lily's skull.

"Why don't you come on in, darlin'?" he says.

She nods and walks past him. The front door opens directly into a small den crowded with four large, overflowing bookshelves. Lily's never seen so many books in a person's home before. She remembers Peter telling her once that Allan always brings a book to work so he can read during the downtime. "Allan's a man with theories," Peter said. "About everything."

On the other side of the room, through an open bedroom door, she sees an old man in a wheelchair parked in front of a television.

The old man calls out, "Al, who is that?"

"Nobody," Allan calls back. "Just a friend."

"I'm sorry if I'm bothering you," Lily says.

Allan frowns and shakes his head, as if to indicate that there's no problem.

"*Who* is it?" the old man asks.

Allan walks to the bedroom and says, "I told you it's nobody. Just somebody I need to talk to for a second."

"How can she be nobody and somebody at the same time?"

"That's an ontological mystery we'll have to sort out later. Right now, can you just watch TV for a while?"

"You said you was gonna make me a sandwich."

"And I'll make it. Jesus H. Christ. Hold your horses."

Allan closes the door and rolls his eyes. "Lucky for us, *Fox & Friends* is on."

He walks over and turns on a floor lamp next to one of the bookshelves. The light splashes into a single corner, illuminating the room without resolving its dimness. Then he goes to the kitchen, leaving her to look around for a moment.

Lily scans the bookshelves. She doesn't see anything she's read, but Allan's taste seems eclectic. She spies thick tomes of science-fiction, slender volumes of poetry and plays, and many novels she's never heard of. There are some biographies of actors and musicians whose names she recognizes. On one shelf she counts at least three biographies of the country singer Reba McEntire. Outside his bookshelves, Allan's ramshackle décor is antique but inexpensive, with lamps, end tables, and chairs in different styles from different eras. The walls are covered in carefully spaced movie posters, old print ads and playbills, and photographs. She looks at them like she's in a museum. A tour poster of a band she's never heard of called the Eurythmics, a short-haired woman and a long-haired man. Another poster of a '50s movie called *Two-Gun Lady* with a woman wearing jeans, boots, and six-shooters. Some of the framed photographs are pictures of famous people Lily vaguely recognizes but can't name, although she does spy one glossy eight by ten, clearly from the 1990s, of Reba McEntire, signed *To Allan, Love Reba.*

The rest of the framed photographs look like they're vintage, pictures of family ancestors from long ago. Among them, there is only one family photo, the kind taken for a church directory. Allan and his parents. Allan is a teenager, much thinner but still pudgy, with a head of wispy brown hair. His father is large, imposing, and bored.

But Lily stares the longest at Allan's mother—a heavyset woman in makeup, gold hoop earrings, and a blue church dress. In the photograph, she has an awkward mouth that cannot fully commit to a smile. *This woman had an affair with Grandpa Tackett?*

From the kitchen, Allan asks, "Would you like something? I was about to make my dad a PB and J. I'm just going to have a glass of water."

She walks over to the doorway. "No, thank you. I'm fine."

Allan smiles and nods. "Polite." He places bread, a jar of chunky peanut butter, and a jar of blackberry jelly on the counter and pulls a plate from the drying rack next to the sink.

He's making the sandwich when the bedroom door opens, and the old man rolls out and stops in front of Lily. He is a large man who has aged into smallness. His shoulders droop and his head hangs low, as if he's imploding. His long, atrophied limbs curl around a torso as hard and round as a melon. Peering out at Lily from beneath the thrust of unruly gray eyebrows, he says, "Herman Woodson. My son's too rude to introduce us, so I have to do it myself. Who are you?"

"Dad…" Allan says.

"I'm Lily."

"Lily? Lily who?"

"Lily Stevens, sir."

The old man stares at her.

Lily says, "Nice to meet you, sir."

"Your momma wouldn't happen to be Peggy Tackett, would she?"

"Yes, sir. Tackett was her maiden name."

The old man turns to his son. Gruffly, he asks, "You know who her momma is?"

Allan looks Lily up and down. "Yeah, I know," he says. He turns back to his father. "But she's not here about that. She's here about my work, at the hotel."

The old man glares up at Lily, breathing through his mouth. She tries to smile politely at him, but he just squints at her, as if peering into the sun. She looks down and smooths out a wrinkle in the maternity shirt against her belly.

Finally, Allan mumbles something and picks up the sandwich and milk. "C'mon, Dad, I think Doocy's back on…"

"It was nice to meet you, sir," Lily tells the old man.

He regards her a moment longer. Then, saying nothing, he starts back to his room, with his son following behind him with his lunch and a folding dinner tray.

Lily wanders into the den, looking concerned when Allan steps out of the bedroom and closes the door behind him.

"I hope I didn't upset him," she says.

Walking back to the kitchen, Allan shrugs. "He's been upset for forty-two years," he says. He pours himself a glass of water and calls to her, "Please, have a seat."

When he comes back in and sits down across from her, Lily says, "So, you know who my mother is."

"Unless I'm mistaken, your mother is Peggy Stevens, née Tackett, my long-lost half-sister. Which makes you my niece."

"Yes," she says.

He nods and waits for her to find her next words. He has a way of coolly regarding her that makes Lily feel judged. It's not hostile, but it's not charitable either.

She says, "I'm not really here about any of that."

"You don't say."

"No. I'm looking for Peter."

"Peter's gone, darlin'."

"I know. That's why I'm looking for him."

"That's a bad idea."

"Why?"

"Because chasing around after some boy is no way to spend a life."

"I'm not chasing around after him. I'm trying to find him."

Allan sips his water. "That sounds like a distinction without a difference."

"Did he talk to you before he left?"

"No," he says. "He just tore ass out of the parking lot in the middle of his shift one night and didn't show up to work the next time he was supposed to."

"You don't think that's odd?"

Allan shrugs. "Not showing up to work is a very popular way to quit. I've done it myself on occasion."

"But you two were friends. Why would he leave without saying goodbye to you?"

"Well, look, we're friendly at work, but, on the other hand, it's not like we're *friend* friends in real life. We don't hang out or anything. It was definitely rude, but it's also not like he owes me a goodbye."

"Didn't he help you move something one time?"

"Yeah, he helped me carry up my dad's Tempur-Pedic. Like three months ago?"

"That's right," Lily says with a nod. "That's how I found you. I remember Peter telling me you lived here."

"Okay, but that still doesn't make us boon companions or anything. Why come see me? I don't know where he is."

"Well, you and I *are* kin. I mean, sort of. I guess I hoped you would help me."

Allan laughs at that and puts his glass on the coffee table. "I'm not sure what to say, Lily. The idea that you're coming to me because we're kin is a little rich. Your family never claimed me as kin before—"

"I just found out about you. My mother just told me."

"That only proves my point. Your mother acts like I don't exist, but now that you need help, suddenly we're kinfolk?"

"My mother didn't do anything to you. You don't have to be like that."

"I'm not being like anything, Lily. I'm just stating some facts. And as for Peter, I really can't help you anyway because I don't know where he went."

"Do you have any idea *why* he ran off?"

Allan raises his eyebrows and glances down at Lily's round belly.

"I have," he says, "an idea."

She ignores that. "Are you sure it didn't have something to do with Eli?"

Allan sits up. "What'd you say?"

"Eli. You know him? I…ran into him and Chance Berryman yesterday."

"What do you mean you ran into them?"

"I went to Peter's house. They were there looking for him."

Now Allan notices the tiny bruise on Lily's cheek. "What happened?"

"Eli attacked me, trying to get me to tell him where Peter is."

Allan shakes his head. "That motherfucker. Are you okay?"

"Yes, but now I'm worried. Why are they looking for him?"

Allan frowns. "I'm not exactly sure."

"Well, who are they? They don't work up there, right? So how do you know them?"

Allan stares at her, stares at her bruise. He tugs at his earlobe for a moment while he thinks.

"Lily," he says finally, "I think maybe you should go home."

"What? Why? What's wrong?"

"What's wrong is this has nothing to do with you."

"That man slapped me around because he was trying to find the father of my child. So it concerns me quite a bit."

Allan stands up. "I understand, and I can see why you'd feel that way, but you should probably go anyway, okay? I can't really help you."

Lily stands up. "Why are you suddenly throwing me out? What's wrong?"

"I'm not throwing you out. I'm just telling you that I can't help you."

"I'm not afraid of those guys. I'm not afraid of bullies."

"These aren't mean kids at school, Lily," Allan says, going to the front door. "Forget about all this. I know that's not what you want to hear, but I promise it'll be easier on you in the long run. Just go home and have your baby. Maybe Peter will come back around."

Lily stays planted in the middle of the room. "What does *that* mean? '*Maybe* he'll come back'?"

Allan won't look at her. He opens the door. "I'm sorry, Lily. Really. But it's time for you to go."

Allan's father, hearing the door, calls out, "What's going on, Allan?"

"Nothing," Allan calls back. "Lily's just leaving."

Lily stares at him, but she doesn't know what else to do. She walks past him and turns around to say something, but the door gently shuts behind her as soon as her shoes touch the balcony.

She stares at the door. She thinks about kicking it. She decides not to.

Instead, she walks downstairs to her mother's car and drives home.

CHAPTER 10

Later that afternoon when her parents come home, her mother goes to their bedroom and shuts the door while her father retreats to the church. Adam is at a friend's house. Silence, which Lily had not noticed when she was home alone, now seems to possess the house. Her mother's quiet presence in the bedroom—the barely perceptible creak of floorboard and bedspring—serves only to amplify her father's absence, to make the emptiness of their home a solid, immovable object.

In her own room, Lily's mind is turning. She keeps going back to the men at Peter's house. Who is Eli? Why does a guy as big as Allan seem leery of him? And what does he have to do with Peter?

She puts on her shoes and coat and walks next door to talk to her father.

The entrance to the church is unlocked. Through long, slender windows, the soft light of dusk slants across empty pews in the sanctuary. When the Baptists still owned the building, the windows in the sanctuary had been stained-glass representations of different biblical figures—Moses, John the Baptist, a long-haired Jesus—but her father doesn't approve of such ornamentation, nor of the way Christ was portrayed, and so he dismantled the colorful glass plates and sold the pieces to a local artist. Now the church windows are clear panes that Adam is charged with washing every Saturday.

Lily walks down the aisle, passes the stage, and opens the door leading back to the classrooms. "Daddy," she calls, but his office is empty. She searches down the hall for him and finds him in the woman's bathroom, the door open, standing over the toilet with a plunger.

"Hello, my daughter," David Stevens says.

"What are you doing, Daddy?" she asks.

"Toiling in the Lord's service, my child."

"Such glamorous work."

"I know. It's the inevitable downside to all the fame and fortune we enjoy. I was trying to work on Sunday's sermon, when suddenly I realized that I'll probably be out of a job by Friday night. That's when I remembered that this thing is on the fritz again." He wipes some sweat from his face. "Figured I'd come in here and do some actual work."

Lily only stares back at him. He's always had a biting sense of humor, but she's never heard him be caustic, especially about his job. If he was anyone else, she'd say he seems angry.

He wipes sweat from his brow. "Did you want something, sweetie?"

She hesitates. She wanted to talk to him, to tell him everything that's happened. But now she feels like she shouldn't. "No," she says. "Just restless, I guess."

"You feeling better?"

"What?"

"You felt sick today?"

"Oh. Yeah. I'm feeling a lot better."

He nods. "Good. Well, I need to run to my office and call Aztec Jim, see if he'll let me borrow his plumbing snake. If I can't snake this thing out, we may have to call in the professionals."

She just nods. "Okay. I'll leave you to it."

She walks a few steps down the hall, stops, and goes back. "Daddy, can I ask you a question?"

"Of course."

"Are you worried?"

"About the vote on Friday?"

"Yes."

He straightens up and wipes more sweat away. "The Lord told us to trust in Him. That's all I know to do."

"But are you scared?"

"Well, we wouldn't need faith if life was nothing but a pat on the back. Fear is the chasm; faith is the bridge. That's the way I think of it. And now, if you'll excuse me," he says, holding up the plunger, "I need to get back to the Lord's work." Returning his attention to the toilet, he mutters, "If I get this thing fixed, maybe I'll go into business as a plumber and we won't have to worry ourselves with what anybody thinks anymore."

Lily stares at the top of his head for a moment, unsure what to say.

She wanders back through the sanctuary and, on an impulse, sits down in a pew. As always happens when her mind is still for more than a moment, she can't help but worry about Peter. When she thinks about a man like Eli looking for him…

She takes a deep breath in the quiet sanctuary and tries to reassure herself. God will protect him. She's seen many movements of the Holy Ghost in this room, and Peter's salvation was the most glorious she's ever beheld. She has to believe in that, if nothing else. It bound them together at the very moment of his redemption. It was the moment she fell in love with him.

Like all miracles, it was a surprise. After high school, Peter had drifted away from church. He tried college, but he flunked out after a semester. Sister Cynthia seemed happy about that because she considers universities to be nests of atheists and homosexuals—and expensive nests, at that. But after he flunked out of school, he didn't immediately return to church. He started working at the Corinthian Inn. He stayed out late. He started spending more time down in Little Rock, which his mother considered one step up from Sodom and Gomorrah. He begged off going to church, claiming he had to work on Sundays and Wednesdays. When his mother prayed during altar calls, everyone knew what she was praying about.

Then the most inexplicable thing of all had happened. One Sunday night, he came back to church, and right off Lily could see the need for the Holy Ghost in his eyes. His polite smiles couldn't hide why he was there.

People come into a Pentecostal church for many different reasons. Occasionally, curiosity seekers wander in, spiritual tourists who stay just long enough to collect the sight of fanatics twirling in circles and screaming the name of Jesus, and then they disappear, never to be heard from again. Other people come out of politeness; they come because someone—a relative or a friend—has begged or badgered them into coming. But others walk in with a need, a burden they must lay at the altar. That was Peter.

He arrived alone, without his mother. She was home sick that night, and Peter had walked in by himself, a peculiar figure still wearing his uniform from the Corinthian, a white dress shirt tucked into blue slacks. He was taller than Lily, though still on the shorter side for a guy, and his hair had grown somewhat shaggy by the standards of their congregation. David greeted him warmly, followed by other members of the church, but Lily held back. They'd known each other most of their lives, but he was a couple of years older, and when they were children, those years had made them largely invisible to each other.

That night, however, she could see that his face was darkened with worry. He exchanged greetings and shook hands with people, but he did not return their smiles. He took a seat, and when the service began, he stayed in his seat even when the rest of the church took to their feet to shout their praises and call for a movement of the Holy Ghost.

David Stevens preached hard that night, right from the start. Oftentimes he eases into the worship tentatively—feeling out where the congregation is—but other times, unable to contain himself, he seizes control of them. That night, he *led* them to worship. His own need for the Lord's presence almost seemed like a physical yearning. This was not theological or philosophical. This was closer to hunger or lust. As he spurred the crowd to worship, people shouted and clapped and sang. Feet stomped. Sister Drinkwater swayed and moaned. Sister Stark slapped her hands to her ears and screamed and spun in circles. Peter, still sitting with his eyes closed, began to rock back and forth.

Lily was at the front with almost everyone else, clapping and singing, when she saw him finally rise and start for the aisle. He dropped to his knees at the altar. David laid a palm on his forehead and prayed. The men of the church gathered around—Brother Drinkwater, Brother Stark, Aztec Jim, and the others. They put their thick, working hands on his shoulders, on his back, on his arms, and they prayed for him. The women formed a circle around the men. Lily joined them, lifting her hands and her voice, praying for the blessing to fall on him.

Peter shook. He lowered his head to hide his face. His cheeks turned pink and he put his hand to his eyes to try to stop the tears. His mouth opened and spit fell down his chin. Then he threw his head back. He called out the name of Jesus and sounds erupted from him, a volcanic expulsion of grief and fear and sadness. It was as if the Holy Ghost was emptying out the boy's heart to make room for Himself.

When it was done and he collapsed, Peter opened his eyes and Lily saw him revealed in a kind of spiritual nakedness that only the Ghost-filled can ever know. She is not a romantic by nature. She does not indulge fairy tales or countenance the kind of nonsense written about in secular love songs. But what she does believe in, and what she trusts above all other things, is the Holy Ghost moment. And when Peter's eyes opened that night, wet and half crazy with emotional exhaustion, she saw him stripped of his ego and defenses, saw him exposed in all his human need and wonder, and she approved of the man she saw.

After the service, her father had met privately with Peter in his office, where they talked and prayed together for a while. Lily had lurked around, hoping to see Peter before he left. When he returned from the back with David, they were smiling. Peter looked as calm as a man out for a stroll on a spring evening.

"Peter's come back to us," David Stevens told his daughter.

"I'm glad," she told Peter. She gave him a hug.

"Thanks." He smiled, looking at her in a way he never had before. "You know, Lily," he said, "I really like your hair."

She shakes her head now to remember it. *I really like your hair*. He looked in her eyes and said those words to her, and she went home and thought about him all night.

The next time they saw each other at church, they walked right to one another, laughing at their own directness.

"Well, hello," he said.

"Well, hello yourself."

People in church smiled to see it, the clear attraction, the drawing together of good kids. Everyone had the same idea of it: Peter was a nice boy who needed direction. Lily was the kind of girl who would show him the way. Her parents were pleased with the pairing. "She's going to boss you," David told Peter with a smile and a shake of his head. "Lord help you, is she going to boss you around."

The only one who wasn't happy was Cynthia. She had always assumed she was all the boss that Peter would ever need, and she made clear to him that his responsibility to her outweighed his courtship of Lily. Girlfriends come and go. A boy only has one mother. Lily recognized right off that if she was going to be with Peter, she would have to find a way to deal with Cynthia. She saw that challenge coming, and she felt up to it.

What surprised her was the pull of sin. She'd always viewed sex from the safe distance of religious judgment. The body and its functions were worldly, but Christ had called his followers to the higher plane of spiritual ecstasy, to the movements of the Holy Ghost. When Peter kissed Lily for the first time, however, she felt her body come alive.

At first, she wasn't worried. She still trusted her own commitment to the Lord. She trusted Peter's commitment, too. They never *decided* to have sex. They never would have made that decision. And yet the escalation toward sex was as inexorable as it was gradual. Kisses that lingered, hands that drifted, the touch and taste and smell of skin. Eventually, she realized she'd always been quick to judge other people's sexual sins because she'd never actually experienced her own body before. Because she'd always viewed premarital sex as unholy, she'd also unknowingly viewed it as unnatural. It had never occurred to her that when temptation came, it would feel as natural as turning her face to the sun, as instinctive as eating. She tried to make sure she and Peter were never alone long enough for temptation to meet opportunity.

But then one evening, she went over to his house to have dinner with him and Cynthia, and he opened the door with a strange look on his face. His mother had been forced to stay late at work to help with the store inventory, he told her. And then Lily knew why he looked so strange. He was afraid. He knew what was going to happen.

They shouldn't have stayed there that night, she thinks. They should have left, gone over to her house to be with her parents. But they didn't. From the moment he told her they were alone that night she stopped thinking clearly.

She rubs her belly to calm the baby.

Her mind is clear now, though.

CHAPTER 11

Lily stays home from school the next day because she has her monthly doctor's appointment. For a while now, her blood work has been showing that she's low on iron and folic acid, so in addition to the usual checkup and ultrasound, Dr. Eljerary also wants to see how she's been handling the new prenatal vitamins he has her taking. She had been taking vitamin gummies, which she preferred, but he's made her switch to "real food ones" that supposedly absorb better. All she knows is the pills are enormous and smell like wet dog hair.

Normally, her mother takes her to her appointments, but this morning her parents are driving an elderly couple in the church, Brother and Sister Satterwhite, to Brother Satterwhite's AFib checkup at the Arkansas Heart Hospital down in Little Rock. Her parents' weekday ministry, it sometimes seems to Lily, largely consists of hospital visits.

She doesn't mind being alone today, though. After her own doctor's appointment, she plans to make another stop.

FIND HIM

When she gets to the Corinthian Inn that afternoon, she pulls into the Guest Only parking by the front entrance, gets out of the car, and walks through the sliding glass doors.

Allan Woodson looks up from the computer at the front desk. When he sees Lily striding across the giant blue C adorning the buffed white floor of the lobby, he hangs his head.

"I'd like to speak to Mr. Baker," she says.

"What do you mean?"

"Mr. Baker. The owner. I'd like to speak to him."

She nods past him at a closed office door marked MANAGEMENT. "Is that his office?"

"He's not here right now. Why do you want to talk to him, anyway?"

"I want to know what he can tell me about Eli."

Allan hangs his head again. Before she can speak, he holds up a finger. He picks up the desk phone beside him, dials a number, and stares at Lily while he waits for an answer. Lily starts to say something else, but Allan shakes his head.

"Hey, Dillard," Allan says into the phone, "could you come watch the front for me for a sec? …C'mon, man…just do it. Try not to be a dick for once in your life. Just come watch the front… Yes, as soon as you can. Thank you *so much*."

He hangs up and points down a carpeted hallway. "Down there."

"What?"

"Go wait for me down there. By the pool."

Lily follows the hallway to a bank of windows looking in on an empty blue swimming pool. The inn is large, but it's getting old. It's been here as long as she can remember, and the years of competition with budget motels on one hand and deep-pocketed chain hotels on the other haven't been kind. The place needs new carpeting, updated fixtures, a bright paintjob. The Corinthian Inn feels exhausted.

She leans against the cool glass and stares back up the hall. She can see the lip of the front desk jutting out, but she can't see Allan.

Soon, a small man appears in the lobby. He's dressed in a variation on the same Corinthian uniform: a blue vest over a white button-up, dark blue slacks, and scuffed brown shoes. He glances down the hallway at Lily and says something to Allan that Lily can't hear.

Allan comes around the desk. Despite being dressed in the same blue and white as the little man, his clothes look different on him. They don't fit right. With his outsized proportions, Lily wonders if any clothes fit him right. He waves the little man toward the desk, but the man doesn't move. He watches Allan walk down the hall to Lily.

When Allan gets to her, Lily tells him, "That man's still watching us."

With a shake of his big head, but without looking back at the man, Allan takes Lily by the elbow and leads her further down the bright hallway. When they come to an intersecting corridor, he pulls Lily to the left. At a room marked 1004, he opens the door with a swipe of a card attached to a lanyard on his wrist and tells Lily to go inside.

Allan reaches for a wall switch as the door shuts behind them. The room is hotel clean, with a big window facing the parking lot, ugly brown carpet, and twin beds with sheets pulled drumhead tight.

Allan says, "Okay, what do you want?"

The smell of industrial cleaning agents makes Lily's stomach turn, but she ignores it and says, "I want to talk to Mr. Baker."

"To ask him about Eli," Allan says, as if the idea itself is ludicrous.

"Yeah. Nobody else will tell me anything. Who else is there to talk to?"

Allan wipes sweat from his face. "Don't you see that I'm trying to help you?"

"Not really. The way I see it, you haven't done anything but tell me to shut up and go home. Why don't you want me to talk to Mr. Baker?"

"Because you don't want to talk to Mr. Baker."

"Why not?"

"Because Mr. Baker is unpleasant. He's an unpleasant man."

"Well, let's go back out there, and I'll talk to him and find out how unpleasant he is."

"I told you, he's not here today. Besides, he's not the one to talk to about Peter. He doesn't know where Peter went."

"How do you know?"

"Because if he knew, then Eli would know."

That stops her for a moment. "Mr. Baker and Eli are mixed up in something? Is that what you're telling me?"

"I'm not…" Allan shakes his head. "Go home. I'm telling you to go home. You don't want to be up here asking questions about Eli. Just trust me on this."

"Why should I trust you?"

"Because, despite everything, I'm noble at heart."

"What?"

Allan shakes his head again. "I'm advising you not to talk to Mr. Baker."

"Then tell me why Peter left."

"I don't know why he left, Lily."

She stares at him.

"I don't."

"It's obvious you know something you're not telling me."

Allan holds up a finger and steps to the door. He peers through the peephole, twisting his neck to see as much as he can. When he's satisfied, he steps back to Lily.

"I think you should leave," he says. "You should get out of here. I need to get back to work."

"You know," Lily says. "I could just take what I know to the police chief. Chief Jeff Reid. I met him a few days ago. I could go there right now, and he'd make you answer my questions."

"Maybe he would, Lily, and maybe he wouldn't."

"What does that mean?"

Allan digs out his cell phone, looks at the time, and sighs. "It means

I have to go, Lily. I have to go back up to the front desk. I ate up my whole break in here whispering with you, and now I owe a favor to that fucking creep I'm working with today. What *you* should do is get out of here. Go home and cry your heart out, and then put that boy behind you before you get yourself in trouble."

He opens the door.

Lily follows him back to the lobby where they expect to see the little man behind the front desk, but he's not there. The phone is ringing.

"Son of a bitch," Allan mutters.

He walks through a door to the right of the desk, and, reaching for the phone, tells Lily, "Go home and think about what I said." Then he answers the phone in a voice exuding professional calm and competence, "Corinthian Inn. This is Allan. How may I help you?"

Slightly dazed, as if she's lost, Lily wanders outside. She's almost to the car when she hears footsteps behind her.

The little man dressed in Corinthian blue and white. He is eye to eye with her and as slight as a boy. His eyes are big, and though he can't be more than thirty years old, his hair has already retreated back to the middle of his skull.

"You're Lily, right?" he asks.

"Yes," she says.

He looks back at the front doors. Turning back to her, he asks, "You looking for Peter?"

"Yes," she says.

"That's what I figured. Everybody up here knew about you. Me, Allan, all the rest of 'em. When he up and left, I figured you'd get the picture."

"What picture?"

"That he done moved on and don't care nothing about you, girl."

She steps toward him. "What are you talking about?"

In a voice that's little more than a whisper, his big blue eyes welling up with tears like water balloons, the little man says, "He done tolt me he was tired of having sex with you, Lily. Said you weren't no good. Said he had to go to Little Rock to get the kind of thing he wanted. Said you was too much of a good girl. Said down there he could get—"

She hears no more. She's fumbling with her keys, climbing into the car. She can't hear more of this, can't see more of these people. She drives away with her skin buzzing and her face turning scarlet. Halfway home, she swings the car off the road, throws it in park, and screams.

CHAPTER 12

That night as Allan is leaving work, Chance Berryman stops him just outside the sliding glass doors.

"Eli wants to talk to you," Chance says.

"Oh…hey," Allan says. He glances back toward the foyer, but Dillard, who was manning the front desk only a moment ago, has conveniently slipped away to the manager's office. Allan turns back to Chance. "No one told me y'all were coming up tonight."

"We come up just to see you."

"Me? Why?"

Chance doesn't respond. Instead, he follows Allan to the parking lot where his Raptor is parked next to Allan's large electric-blue Silverado.

Eli is leaning against Allan's truck smoking a cigarette.

"Didn't figure you for a truck guy," he tells Allan.

"I need plenty of room."

Eli looks Allan up and down. Craning his neck to look at Chance, he says, "Goddamn, he *is* a big one, ain't he?"

"I told you," Chance says.

Allan glances back at Chance, who has stopped a few steps behind him. Slowly balling up his fists, he asks Eli, "What can I do for you?"

Eli places his burning cigarette on the hood of Allan's truck. He's shorter than Allan or Chance, but he's leaner and harder than either, with scraped knuckles and dirty jeans. Stepping forward, he asks, "You have a visitor today?"

"What do you mean?"

"You know what I mean. You know *who* I mean. What'd she want?"

Allan casually steps past Eli and swipes the cigarette off the truck. He can't tell if his heart is thumping from fear or anger, but either way, it doesn't show. He steps on the cigarette and leans against the truck so he can keep both of the men in front of him.

"She wanted to know where Peter went."

"Why'd she ask you?"

Allan waves at the hotel. "'Cause I work with him."

"So does Dillard."

"Yeah, well, Dillard's a couple chromosomes short of a full gene pool."

"Nah, there's more to it than that. You and her had a private talk. What's that about?"

"How do you know we had a private talk?"

"Little birdie told me."

Allan sighs. "We're kind of related. I wanted to talk to her in private because this isn't the kind of thing you talk about in public. Besides, this is a place of business. Won't exactly do to have some knocked-up teenager crying in the lobby about her boyfriend."

"Awful considerate of you. What's 'kind of related' mean?"

Allan shrugs. "I'm her uncle. Sort of. Her family doesn't exactly claim me, let's leave it at that."

"So, she just come up here to ask you if you seen Pete?"

"Yeah. He knocked her up and ran off. She's out looking for him.

She knows I work with him, so she came up here to ask me if I knew where he went."

"What'd you tell her?"

"I told her I don't have the slightest fucking idea where Peter went. Which I don't."

"She ask anything about us?"

"About you? No. Why would she ask about you?"

"She ask about this place?"

"Why would she ask about this place?"

"She didn't say anything about the annex?"

"No, man. I don't think she knows anything about any of that. All she knows is her boyfriend used to work here. She's looking for him. That's it."

Eli rubs his mouth and shakes his head. "I still don't like her coming up here."

"Why do you care if she's looking for Peter?" Allan asks. "You looking for him, too?"

Eli smiles. "That ain't none of your business, big 'un."

"Hey, I was minding my own business 'til you guys accosted me in the parking lot."

Something about the way he says it, or perhaps just the choice of the word *accosted* itself, makes Eli and Chance laugh.

Then Eli squints, looks him up and down again, and says, "Holy fuck. I just realized. You're so damn big, I guess I didn't realize it before. You're a queer, ain't you?"

These words have never signaled a pleasant turn in a conversation in his experience, so Allan has to swallow hard before he can answer, but when he does answer, his voice doesn't crack. "I'm gay, yeah."

"I didn't know they grew 'em as big as you."

"My parents won a ribbon at the county fair."

Eli grins at that. "Hey, man, whatever floats your boat. Hell, I got a cousin who's queer. Fact is, if you wanna know the truth, he's the only one on that side of the family who ain't a complete piece of shit."

"Is he single?"

Eli and Chance both laugh at that, and Eli says, "You're okay. You're alright." He walks over to Allan and leans against the truck as genially as if they're tailgating. "Listen, I didn't come up here to start shit with you. I'm a reasonable man. If I can solve a problem with an ass kicking or a polite conversation, well, hell, I'll take the polite conversation any day of the week. And you, you're just the desk man. You worked your shift today, and now all you want to do is go home, right? That's understandable. You didn't figure on a couple assholes like me and Chance driving up here and *accosting* you in the parking lot. So, hey, you just go on home, and don't worry about none of this.

"But now listen," Eli says, inching closer to him, "if that little pregnant girl is any kind of kinfolk to you, you should have a talk with her. You should tell her to stay home and mind her own business. 'Cause I already had a polite conversation with her, and it don't seem to have worked."

"Okay."

"You get what I'm saying?"

"I do."

"Good," Eli says. "And if you hear anything from Peter, I want you to let me know."

"Sure. Okay."

Eli stares at Allan for a moment. Then he says, "Okay, Chance, let's go." As Chance heads back to his truck, Eli tells Allan, "See you next time we're up here. And when I do," he says, smiling at the mashed butt on the ground, "you owe me a cigarette."

Allan watches them drive away. For a moment, he can't really move, relieved that they're gone, and ashamed that he's relieved. He can still feel the gulp he had to take before he answered Eli, that small humiliating swallow. In a flash, he can remember similar humiliations in schoolyards and hallways. Closeted or not, the big effete boy who wouldn't fight back was always a good target. He'd finally had to shove a few heads into a few lockers to get that bullshit to end, and now here he is, a grown man, again feeling this way.

He turns and walks back to the inn. He finds Dillard sitting behind the front desk trying to look innocent. He pulls him to his feet.

"Wha—" Dillard tries to say.

Allan lifts him off the ground by his neck, and Dillard has to grasp the big man's forearms to keep from choking.

"You called Eli, didn't you?" Allan demands.

"Aaggg."

Carrying him down the hall, Allan says, "You ever talk to Eli about me again—you ever talk to *anybody* about me again—and I'm gonna beat the inbred out of you. You understand me?"

"Yaggg," Dillard tries to say.

Allan kicks open the door to the swimming area, shoves aside a couple of rickety old beach chairs, and throws Dillard in the pool.

On his way home, he stops at Walmart to pick up some groceries. He's still pumping with adrenaline, but the shopping's got to get done. He buys some chicken thighs, a bag of frozen mixed vegetables, some rolls that are on sale, and two bottles of Diet Pepsi because they're buy one, get one free. As he watches for the discount at the register, he's reminded of his mother doing the same thing, standing eagle-eyed in the checkout line with her accordion folder full of carefully organized coupons in her hands. It's not lost on him that he's become his father's caretaker. He does all the shopping, prepares all the meals, pays all the bills, and makes sure the old man takes his daily medications. He does allow some indulgences, however, that his mother never would have permitted. The last thing he buys is a chocolate birthday cake. It's no one's birthday. He and his father just like to eat birthday cake.

He doesn't buy alcohol. He has wine at home. His father doesn't drink, never did. What did Herman Woodson ever do, in fact? Although he attended the occasional service at the Baptist church with his wife and son, his true religion was sheetrock, his only dogma the proper way to cut and hang drywall. He worked six days a week, eight or ten or twelve hours a day, putting up walls. He started bringing his son along as soon as the boy was old enough to be of help, so Allan grew up hanging sheetrock after school, on weekends, and during the summer. Today, he's forgotten most of what his father taught him about the job, but those memories of working are, ironically, the best memories he has of the old man.

Of course, Allan can't imagine what he would have had in common with his "real" father. His mother rarely spoke of the man, and certainly Herman never wanted to discuss it.

Over the years, however, Allan deduced certain facts about the affair that produced him. His mother was an accountant, and she'd met the Reverend William Tackett when he hired her to go over the books of his church. Their affair was brief, but it was impossible to keep completely undetected, and once Allan was born, it became public. Though damaged, both marriages survived the scandal, and now, forty-two years later, most of the people who ever really cared about it are gone, including Alice and both of the Tacketts. The only ones left to deal with the consequences of the affair are Allan and Herman, who have still never discussed it.

And, of course, there's Peggy Stevens, a woman he's never met. He's always wondered about her, his half-sister. He's seen her around town over the years, but she's never glanced in his direction. After a while, that began to seem deliberate, so Allan kept his distance.

But now he's met her daughter. His niece. A girl careening toward disaster.

He's not sure what he should do about that.

"When's dinner?" his father asks, rolling into the den as Allan carries in the groceries.

"Good to see you too, old man."

The apartment is warm, the way his father likes it. The lights are low, also the way he likes it. From the old man's bedroom, Allan can hear fevered warnings emanating from Fox News.

His father follows him into the kitchen.

"What's new in the world?" Allan asks.

"Same old thing. Liberals still jumping all over Trump."

"Trump still putting kids in cages?"

The old man grumbles, "All them books you read, you'd think you'd be smarter."

"I know," Allan says, putting the groceries away. "I wonder about that myself."

"Well, that's the problem with you intellectuals. You're so smart you work your way back around to being stupid again."

"We need to give you your pm pills," he tells his father.

"Okay," the old man says.

"Then I'll make the chicken."

"Okay."

"How's the back?"

"Same old piece of shit."

After decades of almost Calvinist devotion to hard work, one day about twenty years ago, Herman Woodson bent down to pick up a big sheet of drywall and never stood up right again. He'd had injuries before, but he'd always worked through them. Working through pain, exhaustion, and injury had, in fact, been one of the defining principles of his life. But after his back injury, age performed its dark alchemy. The harder he worked, the worse things got. Then the morning finally came when he couldn't get out of bed without help. Now he's in a wheelchair, with nothing left but his attitude.

"Let's get your pills," Allan says.

"Don't know why I can't get my own pills."

"You know why."

"Maybe you should worry about yourself, and let me take care of myself."

"Okay, I'll do that, right after I give you your dope and fix you dinner."

His father follows him to the bathroom. Allan keeps the drugs locked up on a high shelf. He gives the old man his pills and a cup of water. As he watches his father, sitting in his wheelchair swallowing his oxy, it occurs to him that his mother never saw him like this, never saw him as an old man. He's happy for that small mercy at least.

His father asks him, "Ever feel like you're back in the hospital?"

"What?"

"Back when you worked at that prison hospital, whatever it was, that nuthouse for teenagers."

"Home For Youth. What made you think about that?"

"Don't know. Giving me them pills, you look like a nurse. Made me think about how you used to do that for a living, before you got into the hotel business."

"I was a youth counselor. Not a nurse."

"Yeah. Still, made me think of it." His father finishes the water.

Taking the cup, Allan says, "I think I hear Hannity, Dad. Go on, and I'll go fix dinner."

After he sets up the old man's dinner tray in front of his bedroom television, Allan takes to the living room couch. He goes to his DVR and scrolls over the movies he's recorded off of TCM, but he can't focus on the menu.

"Goddamn it," he mutters.

He lays down on the couch, his long, hairy legs hanging off the end, and shuts his eyes.

He thinks about Lily.

She's not going to stop looking for that shithead, is she?

As soon as he asks himself the question, he knows the answer.

Of course she won't. At least not until the baby comes. He ruined her life, and she probably thinks if she can find him, he'll somehow unruin it. She'll look for him until she has to drop out of school and get a job.

Normally, it wouldn't matter. She could run all over town asking people if they've heard from him. It's embarrassing, but it wouldn't really matter…

Except now she's coming up to the Corinthian. Which means she's putting herself in danger. And she doesn't even realize what that means.

The worst part is, he knows how he could help her. When he told Lily—and Eli—that he didn't know where Peter is, that was, of course, the truth.

But he does have an idea of where to look.

CHAPTER 13

"Been calling you for days," Fiona says. "Thought you'd up and died or something."

Everyone is milling about in the morning light on the lawn and the steps of the school, bags slung over shoulders or dropped at feet, laughing or flirting or screaming or complaining, waiting for the first bell to summon them inside. Fiona and Lily are in their usual spot, near a side entrance facing the parking lot.

"Sorry," Lily says.

"Been leaving messages with your family."

Fiona Stark is the only other Oneness girl who attends her high school. She's the youngest daughter of the stone-faced Starks, who have taught Fiona to look with grave suspicion upon any book that isn't the Bible. This suspicion is rather common among the Oneness, but Fiona's father is fanatical even by those standards. He's a proud illiterate who, in his youth, memorized the entire New Testament from a set of books-on-tape read by Johnny Cash. During church services,

Lily's father can request any verse and Brother Stark will recite the New King James version of that verse back to him. Given that example at home, Fiona's constantly asking Lily why they're being forced to learn one thing or another at school. She regards science as atheist propaganda and thinks literature is the boring gibberish of drunks and perverts. The loneliest Lily ever feels is when she's with Fiona, walking the hallways of their school, listening to her complain. They are both outsiders because of their religion, but they regard this outsider status in pointedly different ways. Lily loves to read and do well on tests, and she secretly knows which girls in her classes she'd like to be friends with. Fiona, on the other hand, relishes being an outsider and draws palpable comfort from her belief that her teachers and classmates will all go to hell one day.

Because theirs is a friendship of necessity, Lily sometimes feels bad that she doesn't really like Fiona. Her guilt is assuaged, in part, by the fact that she suspects Fiona feels much the same way about her.

"Sorry," Lily says. "I've been busy with baby stuff."

"I bet. I'm surprised you came back to school at all."

"What do you mean?"

Like her mother and her older sisters, Fiona is short, broad-shouldered, and thick-hipped. Unlike Lily, she always wears her hair up in a braided bun that she continually pokes with the tips of her fingers, as if tucking it back into place. She jabs at it now and says, "I figured you just quit."

"Why would I do that? I have to come to school."

Fiona swats in the direction of the school building like it's a giant gnat. "What good does it do you to come up here and listen to this nonsense all day? I mean, really. Better off getting a job. Make some money. Get ready for the baby. My cousin works at the bus factory. She might could get you on there. You know what we had to do in biology yesterday? Wanna hear about the big educational breakthrough you missed? We cut up a frog. Sliced him open and pulled out his freaking guts. Now, where's that gonna get you? At least at the bus factory, you'd be learning a skill you can use. My cousin installs seats there. She might could get you on."

Lily ponders that for a moment. She doesn't countenance Fiona's brief diatribe against education, but she does wonder if she should quit school early and get a job. Her parents have so little money. And why would she stay in school? At one time, she thought maybe she'd like to be an English teacher, like her favorite teacher, Ms. Crockett. Now, however, the thought of one day being a teacher seems like another silly dream. Few people in her church pursue any higher education. In the Oneness church, going to college usually means going to the Apostolic Bible Institute in St. Paul. The men go to be preachers. The women go to be preacher's wives. But for Lily, unmarried with a baby on the way, even that thought of college is gone.

The first bell rings. Around them, the migration of students into the school building begins, but glancing over Fiona's shoulder at the parking lot, Lily sees Allan Woodson walking toward her.

He's wearing baggy jeans and a black button-up shirt. He has on large black sneakers. Compared to the two girls, he seems even more enormous than before, and despite the early morning chill in the air, his bald head is bare and sweaty. Without looking at Fiona, he tells Lily, "I need to talk to you."

Fiona looks from Allan to Lily. *What on earth is this about?*

Lily tells Allan, "The bell just rang. I have to go to class."

"Is that a joke?" Allan says. "You came up to my work but now—"

"Okay," Lily says. "Okay. Let's go talk. Over by your truck." She turns to Fiona. "I'll see you in class."

Lily follows Allan to his Silverado in the parking lot.

Allan nods over her shoulder. "What's her deal?" he asks. "She looks insane."

"What?"

Lily glances back. Fiona hasn't moved. Standing rock steady in her long skirt and braided bun, she's still watching them from the front steps of the school, chewing on her lips.

"She's… She doesn't… She's pretty sheltered."

"Coming from you, that's saying a lot."

"Well, trust me, it's true."

The second bell rings. Fiona doesn't move.

"I'm already late for class," Lily says. "What do you want?"

"Are you still looking for Peter?"

"Of course, I am."

"That's what I figured."

"So why are you here?"

"I came to tell you that if you still want to see him, I might know where to look for him. Emphasis on the *might*."

She grabs his arm. "Are you serious? You know where he is?"

"I have an idea of where to look."

"Let's go."

That takes him aback. "Now?"

"What, I'm supposed to go sit through social studies? Yes, let's go now."

"Okay, but what about Lizzie Borden?"

"What do you—?" Lily turns around. Fiona is still there, glaring at them. "Oh Lord." She tells Allan, "Hold on a second."

She walks back to Fiona. "I have to go…"

"What are you talking about? Go where?"

She doesn't want to tell Fiona, but she can't just ride off with a stranger in a truck without telling her something.

"I… Listen, maybe he knows where Peter is. Maybe."

"Oh my gosh, are you serious?"

"Yes."

"That's amazing. But who is this guy?"

"He's my uncle." She warms to the word's authoritative sheen. "My uncle Allan. He works at the Corinthian with Peter. I went up there to see him the other day to ask about Peter." She neglects to mention the visit to Allan's apartment. "Look, don't worry about it. You should really go to class before you get in trouble. I'll call you later. But listen, you can't tell anybody, okay? Somebody up here asks you about me, like one of the teachers or something, the principal, whoever, you just tell them I went home because I was feeling nauseous."

"What if they call your house?"

"I don't think they will," Lily says. "They might ask me for a doctor's note tomorrow or something, but I doubt they'd call to check up on me today. But if they do, then they do. I'll deal with that when I get home."

"Okay..."

"Please don't tell anybody, Fiona. I really need to do this without my parents worrying about me."

"Why do you think I'd tell anybody? Ain't like you're the only topic of conversation, you know."

"I know. Just...I just need you to keep this quiet." Lily leans in, goes for the kill. "You're the only one I can trust, my only real friend. And I'll tell you everything that happens if you can just keep this quiet. Okay?"

Fiona's eyes widen as if to receive all of the secret. "Okay, yeah, of course," she says. "I didn't know it was like that. You know you can trust me."

Lily doesn't know if that's true, but to seal the pact, she does something she rarely does with Fiona. She gives her a hug. "Thank you," she says.

CHAPTER 14

"You okay in that seat?" Allan asks. "You can push it back."

"Thanks," Lily says, getting comfortable. "Where are we going?"

"Little Rock."

"Where in Little Rock?"

"Southwest," he says. "Off of Geyer Springs Road. Do you know much about the city?"

"Not really."

"Ever been there?"

"Of course I have. I'm not a complete hick, you know."

This is only partially true. She's been to Little Rock a few times over the years, mostly to attend services at various churches, but she's never gone there without her family. She's never driven the streets herself, and she's certainly never been there alone. Little Rock is only about thirty miles south of Conway, but it might as well be in another country. Many of the adults she knows fled there during the white flight of the '90s, and today when the adults around her speak of Little Rock, they speak of it almost exclusively in terms of crime and moral decay. If her parents knew she was headed there right now, both of them would panic.

Allan pulls out of the parking lot. When they come to a traffic circle, he turns onto Farris Road.

"I don't think you're a hick, by the way," he tells her.

"Well, that's a load off my mind," she says.

At the next red light, Allan stops and looks down at the girl beside him, as if appraising her sarcasm visually. "Did you just get sassy with me?" he asks.

"I'm sick of people treating me like a dumb little country girl."

"All I asked was if you've ever been to Little Rock."

"Well, I have."

The light turns green.

"Well, okay, hooray for you. You know, I'm the one who's entitled to get pissy here. I'm driving you down to Little Rock on my day off to look for your idiot boyfriend. I don't have to do that."

As they merge onto I-40, Lily says, "I know. I appreciate you doing this. I really do."

Allan glances at her, then back at the road. "It's okay."

"Good," she says. "So tell me why we're going to Little Rock."

"We're going to see someone who used to work at the Corinthian. Maybe Peter is staying with them."

"Who?"

"Just someone who used to work there."

Lily stares at Allan a moment, and then turns to look out the window. She closes her eyes. When she opens them, she asks, "Is this someone a girl?"

"Yes."

They pass billboards for a fishing boat manufacturer and a gas station, and then the trees take over and there's not much to look at aside from the verdant blur of passing evergreens.

Lily asks, "What's her name?"

"Ciara."

"What'd you say?"

"Ciara."

"What kind of name is that?"

"It's just a name, Lily."

"Who is she?"

"Just a girl who used to work at the Corinthian."

Lily sees a break in the trees revealing a portion of wire fencing and a little sign stuck to a post displaying a message she can't read.

"So is this Ciara his girlfriend?" she asks.

"Not as far as I know."

The indistinctness of the reply makes Lily a little sick to her stomach. "Why would he be with her if she's not his girlfriend?" she asks.

Allan searches for the right words.

"She's his girlfriend," Lily says, answering her own question, smiling a furious smile. "He has another girlfriend."

"I didn't say that, Lily."

"Then what are you saying?"

"Ciara worked at the Corinthian before you and Peter even got together. Once y'all started dating, she quit and went to work at another hotel down in Little Rock. But after she quit, I know they kept in some kind of touch because occasionally she'd call up to the Corinthian to talk to him. He never said much about it, but I always wondered if something was up. So when I ask myself, 'Where could Peter have run off to?' my first thought is Ciara. Call it a hunch."

Lily doesn't respond to that. She just faces the window, thinking. Her desire not to find Peter with another woman is eclipsed by her desire to know the truth. If she can find the truth, then she'll know how to act. She can yell at him, beg him, guilt him, hit him if she has to. The not knowing is the problem.

As upset as it makes her to think about Peter running off with another girl, she's also clearheaded enough to recognize that it makes a certain amount of sense. From the beginning, from the day he disappeared, she's wondered if there could be someone else. The idea of Peter running away by himself always seemed unlikely to her. It's part of the reason she doesn't believe he simply skipped town. He's still too much of a boy, too unsure of himself, of who he is or what he wants. At one time, Lily thought she was going to be the one to help him find himself. Maybe this Ciara has simply taken her place. The idea of him running away with this girl, whoever she is, seems more likely than him going alone.

And so maybe that's it. Maybe the truth is that he dumped Lily and ran away with this other girl.

She rubs her cheek. But that doesn't explain—

"Who's Eli?"

"What?" Allan says, startled by the break in the silence.

"Why's he looking for Peter?"

"Jesus Christ," Allan grumbles.

Lily squints at the blasphemy like she's adjusting her eyes to harsh light, but she stays focused. "If Peter just ran off with some girl, then why is Eli looking for him?"

Allan doesn't reply, but Lily keeps staring at him, waiting for an answer. Finally, he tells her, "The only thing you need to know about Eli Buck is that you don't want to know anything else about him."

"Buck is his last name?" she says. "Eli Buck?"

Allan frowns at his slip of the tongue. "Just forget about him, Lily."

She crosses her arms and turns toward the window.

"Okay?" he says.

She stares at her own reflection in the glass.

Allan says, "And now you're not going to reply at all…"

"You want a reply?" she asks, turning back to him. "Here's a reply.

First off, you shouldn't take the Lord's name in vain. How's that for a reply? Maybe you don't care, but I'm pretty sure the Lord doesn't appreciate you turning his name into a cuss word."

Allan stares at the road in wonder. "I could be at home watching TCM right now," he marvels. "I'm missing a Myrna Loy movie for this."

"And the second thing," she says, "you don't have to warn me that Eli's a scary guy. I'm five months pregnant, and he climbed on top of me like he was going to beat me to death. I'm plenty scared of him already."

Allan grimaces. "Okay. I get it."

"No, you don't get it. Because if Eli would get that mean just looking for Peter, what's he going to do if he actually finds him?"

Allan chews on his upper lip.

"I understand," he says finally, "why you're worried. And that is why I'm trying to help you. But what you need to understand is, if I don't want to talk about Eli, it's only to protect you. And to protect me. It's better for both of us if you forget about him. What you really want is to find Peter, right?"

"Of course."

"Then let's go find Peter. The rest is just a distraction. Let's find Peter."

Lily crosses her arms. She still wants to pursue this question, but for now, she decides to give Allan some space. She doesn't want to spook him into throwing up his hands and turning the truck around, deciding he's through with the whole affair.

"Okay," she says.

After a few minutes of awkward silence, Allan turns on the radio. The Wolf 105.1 , "Arkansas's home for country legends," the announcer declares. The next song the station plays is Reba McEntire's dead father ballad "The Greatest Man I Never Knew."

Lily doesn't know the song, but Allan mutters, "Great, now Reba's trying to kill me. I can't catch a break."

For a while they sit quietly, the buzz of the road passing beneath Allan's tires drowned out by the thrum of old secular songs Lily doesn't know. She glances out Allan's driver's side window at Lake Conway. It looks more like a swamp than a lake, with gray cypress trees spearing up through murky green water spotted with lily pads. As she looks out his window, she can't help but regard Allan himself.

He's as large as any man she's ever known. His bald head is dotted with brown moles and a faint grayish fuzz in the back. He looks like a man who would drive a big truck like this, but even in repose his face is thoughtful, his dark eyes always focused on something beyond what he's looking at, weighing some distant idea. Without quite knowing why, Lily feels like he has things to teach her.

She says, "So...I guess we're related."

"I guess so."

"When did you find out...?"

"About which part?"

"About...who your real father was," she says. "Did you know about it when you were growing up?"

"No, but when I was in fifth grade, some bully told me I was adopted. He misunderstood the gossip from his parents, I guess."

"Did you ask you parents about it?"

"Yeah. That night. My mom started crying, and my dad just walked outside and started mowing the lawn in the dark. Eventually, Mom dried her eyes and told me about it. She told me she'd had an affair once, and I was born. That's how she put it. 'I *had an affair*.' Like we were on *Knots Landing* or something. Then she told me she loved me, and so did Herman. And that was that. We didn't discuss it again until she got sick. That's when she told me that my biological father was a Pentecostal preacher named William Tackett. Herman and I never really talked about it, even after Mom died."

"She passed away."

"Yeah, not long after I got out of college. Cancer."

"I'm sorry."

Allan nods politely to acknowledge the condolences. "Since we're finally talking about this, what did Peggy say about it? The affair, I mean."

"Not much at all. Grandpa died before I was born. I always knew he had been a preacher once, but whenever I asked why he stopped preaching, my parents would get really vague. Momma sat us down just the other day and told us."

"Does she hate my mother?"

"Of course not," Lily says, though, as she says it, she realizes she's not sure if it's true. "I just think the whole thing makes her sad."

"Well, for what it's worth, my mother was sad about it, too," Allan says. "She and Herman managed to salvage their marriage because they both trusted the same kind of unhappiness, but they probably shouldn't have stayed together. And she certainly shouldn't have had me."

This statement stuns Lily.

"I bet she was happy she had you," she manages to say.

He shrugs. "Two different things can be true at the same time. My mother could love me and still know that her life might have been happier and more fulfilling if she hadn't had me."

Lily sits with that, saying nothing.

"You gotta understand," Allan says. "I come from a long line of mistakes. My grandparents only got married because they got pregnant with my mother. Then my mom got knocked up while she was having an affair. I think God made me gay just to break the cycle of unplanned pregnancies."

Lily looks over at him. "Do you really think God made you gay?"

"It was a joke."

"I know. But I'm just wondering."

"I don't believe in gods."

"Not gods, God."

"Dropping the s doesn't make the idea any less goofy."

Lily realizes that this might be the first time she's heard someone articulate an actual heresy. She's heard plenty of sloppy blasphemies shouted up and down the hallways of her high school, but she's never had a serious conversation with someone—much less someone she's related to—who rejects the entire basis of her faith.

"If I didn't think Jesus was real, I don't know what I'd do," she tells him. "Especially right now. I think I'd roll up and die."

Allan ponders that for a moment before he replies.

"I guess I can understand that," he says finally. "We were Southern Baptist when I was growing up. When I was a little younger than you, I was actually pretty devout."

"What happened?"

He shrugs. "Jesus and I had a falling out."

"About what?"

He looks over at her. "What do you think?"

"You ever miss him?"

"You know what? This is going to sound flippant, like I'm making a joke, but I'm not. It's like remembering someone you used to be in love with. I don't miss Jesus, but I do remember what it was like to love him. I remember how I used to feel about him."

"Did you want to be gay when you were my age?"

"*Annnnd* you ruined it," Allan says, grimacing like he tastes something sour. "Look, Lily. I'm not here to be a stand-in for all the gays, okay? You ain't Kimmy, and I ain't Titus."

"What does that mean?"

"Do you even own a television?"

"No."

"Of course not. What was I thinking?"

They pass a sign that announces North Little Rock.

They're getting closer.

She says, "Can I ask a question?"

"Not if it's another 'what's it like to be gay?' question."

"It's not."

"Okay."

"Did Peter ever talk about me?"

"Sure."

"No, I mean, did he talk about me and him in an intimate way?"

"You mean, like, sex stuff?"

"Yes, that's what I mean."

"No, of course not. Why do you ask?"

"That man at the hotel..."

"What man?"

"The creepy little man you were working with yesterday."

"God. Dillard."

"Dillard?"

"Dillard Sweet III, to be precise."

"Well, he came up to me as I was leaving, and he said that Peter used to tell him stuff about me. Intimate stuff."

"Bullshit."

"Really?"

"Yeah, that's total bullshit. I guarantee you that never happened. Peter wasn't that kind of guy."

"Maybe he told Dillard."

"Please. Besides being the dumbest human being I've ever met in my life, *Dullard*'s an asshole and a creep. Peter didn't like his inbred ass any more than I do. And I can promise you they weren't hanging out swapping sex stories. Dullard's never seen a naked woman who wasn't on a laptop. What would he have to contribute to that discussion?"

"Okay. But he also told me that Peter was coming down to Little Rock for sex. And now you're driving me down here to meet some girl."

Allan glances at her and then turns his eyes back to the road.

Ahead of them, a raggedy old Ford is barely doing forty-five, its rattling rear bumper held together by bailing wire. A Tyson Foods freight truck blows past both vehicles, and Allan merges into the passing lane behind it.

"Well?" she says.

"I don't know what to tell you, Lily. If Peter is down here, you can ask him yourself."

She turns her face back to the window.

"I will," she says.

CHAPTER 15

When the interstate finally swings into North Little Rock, Lily is aware of the city as she's never been before. After passing Verizon Arena, the truck crosses the I-30 bridge into Little Rock, and for a place so notoriously beset by crime and violence, from where she's sitting it doesn't look so bad. The revitalized River Market district is bustling with families, strollers, tourists. Up by the statehouse, a cluster of tall, glassy bank buildings and upscale hotels reflect the shimmering blue of the sky, while sloping lawns running from the park down to the Clinton Presidential Library give the muddy Arkansas River the complexion of a ripe olive. With its carefully curated blend of tree-lined walking paths and memorial gardens, the riverbank has a green luster that shocks Lily.

When Allan turns off the tangled interstate highways and onto narrow streets and narrower backstreets, the luster quickly dies away, though the green does not. Even as the houses and the businesses and the streets themselves grow more decrepit, lawns and trees are everywhere. It's as if, even in the most urban areas of the city, nature is never far away.

Lily takes in all of this changing scenery, but she's ashamed of herself for the thing she notices most. The changing faces, grower darker with every street. People stepping out of houses or working on cars, kids in playing in yards. It occurs to her that while she's grown up around Black people all her life, she's never been in an all-Black neighborhood before.

The fewer white people she sees, the more conflicted she becomes. She's conflicted because she's been taught that racism is a sin, that the ground is level at the foot of the cross, that Christ died for everyone. She's been taught that she shouldn't be racist.

But she's also been taught, more indirectly but more persistently, that Black people are dangerous. Virtually every white person she knows seems scared of Black people. She knows very few white people who would proudly claim the mantle of a racist, but she knows even fewer who would be comfortable in an all-Black neighborhood.

"Where are we going?" she asks.

There must be an edge to her voice because Allan says, "This isn't a bad neighborhood."

"You sure about that?"

"It's just a neighborhood. People live here."

"You think Peter is *here*?"

Allan says nothing to that. Instead, he pulls into the short gravel driveway of a small, brown brick home. A maroon Toyota parked in the carport. Trees in the yard. To one side of the house is a red brick home with a car up on blocks in the front yard. To the other side is an empty parking lot with crumbling asphalt.

"Okay," Allan says. "You stay here. I'll go check it out."

"No," she says, taking off her seat belt. "If he's in there, I'm coming with you."

"Lily," he says. "Really, just let me check, and I'll be right back." He opens his door.

Lily pulls herself out of the passenger side of his truck and follows him.

He stops and looks at her. "For real?"

She keeps walking. Now he follows her.

Just before they reach the house, the front door creaks open and a man steps outside. He's dark-skinned and tall, though not as tall as Allan. He's wearing a long white t-shirt and jeans with no coat. He's also wearing the brightest orange sneakers that Lily's ever seen.

Allan says, "Hi. Hello. I was wondering if Ciara is here."

The man is not so old, perhaps only thirty or so, younger than Allan by at least ten years. He has a small undergrowth of beard below his chin and jawline. Tattoos cover his forearms.

He simply stares at both of them.

"Who're you?" he says finally.

"Does Ciara live here?" Allan says.

The man frowns and lifts his index finger as if to raise a point of order. "Ain't polite to roll up on somebody's property and start answering questions with questions."

"I'm sorry," Allan says. "You're right. I'm Allan. This is Lily. We're looking for Ciara."

"How come y'all looking for Ciara?"

"I drove her here. A few months ago? She and I used to work together at the Corinthian."

The expression on the man's face doesn't change.

Allan says, "If she's inside, I'm sure she'll tell you I'm telling the truth."

The man looks at Allan, then turns to Lily, glancing down at her belly.

"How come you looking for her, though?" he asks.

Allan says, "I hope you don't mind, but I think that's probably something I shouldn't discuss with someone I don't know. I didn't catch your name…"

The man's face is impassive, but Lily can almost feel him thinking.

"Jarell," he says finally.

"Nice to meet you," Allan says. "You're her brother, right?"

Jarell barely—almost imperceptibly—nods. But it's something. Allan takes it.

"If I could talk to Ciara for just one second, that would be great, and then we could get out of your hair. Or maybe you could go talk to her or call her or whatever to check out my story? We can wait."

Jarell scratches his nose with his thumb. "Take a minute," he says.

"We'll wait."

Jarell nods and turns around. The door closes behind him. The curtains are pulled, and they can't see inside.

Lily rubs her lower back, just above her right hip.

Allan says, "You want to sit down? We can wait in the truck."

"Not really," Lily says, kneading the spot on her back with her knuckles. "I'd just as soon stand. Kind of helps me to stretch out." She watches the curtains and frowns. "Why did you ask to talk to Ciara instead of Peter?"

"It's Ciara's house. Seemed polite to ask for her first."

Lily says, "Okay," but her expression doesn't change.

Almost as one, she and Allan turn and notice that down the street a couple of teenagers on bicycles are standing in another driveway, staring at them. One kid says something to his friend, and the two of them ride away.

"So," Lily says, "if her brother is Black, I guess Ciara is Black?"

"Good guess."

"You didn't tell me."

Allan glances at her.

"I'm not being racist," Lily says. "I'm just surprised."

Allan raises his eyebrows.

She looks back at the curtains. "How long does it take to ask someone if they want to talk to us? Do you think that means Peter's here?"

"I don't know what it means."

Lily glances down the street again to see if the teenagers on bikes have returned. They have not.

She turns to tell Allan, "I'm not prejudiced, you know."

He shrugs again. "C'mon, Lily," he says. "I thought you believed in sin. We're all prejudiced. Just like we're all selfish. The key is to try act better, not to act like you were born perfect. Can't turn from your sin if you won't admit you're a sinner in the first place."

The door opens, and Jarell leans out.

He shakes his head.

Neither of them is sure what this means. Allan asks, "She's not home? Or she doesn't want to see us?"

"Same thing either way," Jarell says.

He begins to close the door, but Lily steps up to the door. "Please, sir, I really need to speak to her. I swear I wouldn't bother y'all if it wasn't important. I just need to ask her one question. Please."

Jarell shakes his head. "Sorry. Can't help you."

Gently, the door closes and a lock clicks into place.

Lily turns around and looks at Allan.

As big as he is, he looks small. "Sorry," he says. "We tried."

For a moment, Lily stands still. Allan lifts a hand to her, as if to help her off the steps. She ignores the gesture and steps down on her own. As they walk back to the truck, her stomach feels heavy, like it's dragging her to the ground.

Lily glances back. She doesn't know why. But when she does, she sees the curtains jerk shut.

She spins around and stalks back toward the house with Allan following and grabbing at her arm.

"Peter Cutchin," she calls out. "Are you in there? Come out here and talk to me. Right now."

A moment passes, but then the door of the house opens, and a woman steps out. She is young and small, dark-skinned like her brother.

She's also pregnant.

With her hand on her belly, she says, "I guess you're Lily."

CHAPTER 16

Lily is sitting on a couch. She's lightheaded, her vision slightly blurred. She doesn't quite remember how she got here.

But Allan is sitting beside her, huge and heavy, sweating. His solid presence is reassuring, and she leans against him like a wall to get her balance. A television is on somewhere else in the house. A game show. People are clapping and cheering and laughing.

Jarell is slouching in the doorway between the living room and the kitchen, hands in his pockets.

Ciara is sitting across from her. She's Lily's height, but she's a few years older. Further along in her pregnancy, she's wearing gray stretch pants with a hunter green hoodie unzipped to reveal a white scoop neck t-shirt stretched taut against her belly. She sits forward, hands clasped in front of her, her face somber.

"Peter isn't here," she tells them.

Allan asks, "*Was* he here?"

Ciara shakes her head. "He never stayed here, if that's what you mean." Like Allan's, her voice retains the off-duty echo of calm professionalism; they both have the voice of someone who answers the phone for a living.

"So you haven't heard from him."

"Not in a couple of weeks, no."

Ciara turns back to Lily. The younger woman is staring at her. Ciara says, "Do you want to ask me something?"

Lily swallows hard. She nods at Ciara's belly and says, "Is it his?"

"Yes," Ciara says.

Lily feels so uneven she has to close her eyes, like she's been hit in the head. When she feels steady enough, she opens them again. "It's Peter's baby."

"Yes," Ciara says.

"I knew," Lily says, shaking her head. "I knew when I saw you."

Ciara says nothing to that. Everyone waits. Allan sweats.

Lily says, "I don't understand."

Ciara starts to say something to that but catches herself.

"Did you…?" Lily shakes her head again and puts her face in her hands. "I'm sorry. I need a second."

Allan asks Ciara, "How far along are you?"

"Thirty-nine weeks," she says.

Lily says, "I'm twenty-five weeks."

"Yes," Ciara says. "He and I…it happened before y'all got together." She pats her large round belly. "Obviously."

Lily asks her, "That's why you quit the hotel?"

"No, but it was at the end of me working there."

"Do you love him?" Lily asks.

"No," Ciara replies.

"Did you?"

"No."

"Did he love you?"

"No."

"Then why?"

"Just happened," Ciara says. "My car broke down. Sometimes people from work would give me a ride home. Allan did once. And Peter did a couple of times. The second time I invited him in, and one thing led to another. And that's it. That's all there was to it. It just happened. One time, and I got pregnant."

"It 'just happened'?" Lily says.

"Yes."

"I don't know what that means."

"Which part?"

"Having sex with someone just happens?"

Ciara tilts her head slightly, "How'd you get pregnant, Lily?"

That stops her for a moment. Finally, she says, "I was in love him."

Ciara nods. "Well, I hope you can hear this, but that doesn't have a thing to do with me. You love him, I don't. After Peter and I hooked up that one time, that was it. I didn't want a regular thing with him. I was kinda interested in somebody else at the time. And Peter didn't want a regular thing with me. Right after that, he started dating you. So it really was just a one-time thing."

"He didn't tell me about you," Lily says.

Ciara glances at her brother. "Yeah, we kind of figured that."

Jarell nods.

Lily rubs her eyes. She looks at Ciara. She asks, "Does he know you're pregnant?"

"Yes."

"What did he say?"

"He asked me what I wanted to do."

"What *do* you want to do?"

"Have the baby."

"Why?"

Jarell shakes his head. "That's a fucked-up question," he says.

Ciara asks Lily, "You trying to talk me into an abortion?"

"Of course not," Lily says. "Of course not. I just don't know why you'd want Peter's baby if you don't care about Peter."

"It's *my* baby. Besides, I thought you were Pentecostal."

"I am," Lily says, feeling dizzy again. This is too much. She clutches the arm of the couch and closes her eyes to regain her sense of balance.

Ciara tells her brother, "Got a Holy Ghost woman sitting on my couch trying to talk me into an abortion. That's a new one."

"Signs and wonders," Jarell says.

Keeping her eyes closed while her head spins, Lily says, "I'm not trying to talk you into getting an abortion."

Ciara tells Lily, "It's my baby growing in my belly. You're not the only one who can feel the life inside you."

But Lily can't feel the life inside her right now. She just feels a heaviness pulling her down.

Ciara turns to Allan and asks, "So where did Peter run off to?"

"We don't know," Allan says. "That's why we're here."

"You thought I had Peter hiding in the closet or something?"

Allan spreads his hands. "I didn't know what else to do."

Jarell says, "How about nothing? Nothing's usually pretty good."

Allan glances at Lily, who is still sitting with her eyes closed, trying to regain her equilibrium.

He tells Jarell, "You have to understand, she thought he was missing. She even went to the police." He tells Ciara, "She even came up to the Corinthian and started asking questions…"

Ciara opens her mouth, then shuts it again. She turns to the girl. "Lily."

Lily opens her eyes.

Ciara says, "I haven't heard from Peter in a couple of weeks. Until you showed up on my doorstep, I thought he was still up in Conway."

"No one knows where he went," Lily says. "His mother, the people at my church, nobody."

Jarell says, "Sounds like he just run off."

"Sounds like it," Ciara agrees. After she says it, her gaze drifts to the bare coffee table. "I guess he's gone."

Lily asks her, "You think this is why he left? He got us both pregnant. You think that's why?"

As if she's just been asked the stupidest question she's ever heard, Ciara looks up and says, "What do you think?"

Shame comes down on Lily like a movement of the Holy Ghost. Everything she thought about Peter was wrong. Momma, Daddy, Adam, Fiona, the Drinkwaters, the police—everyone has been right. He's no good. He got another girl pregnant. Lily's just some girl he had sex with. A silly, stupid girl.

But she doesn't cry, doesn't scream, doesn't collapse. She sits up straighter.

"Okay," she says.

Ciara and Jarell watch her.

Allan asks her, "Maybe we should go?"

"Yes," Lily says.

As they're about to get up, however, she remembers something.

"Wait," she says, "what's Eli Buck got to do with all of this?"

At the mention of the name, Ciara turns to Allan.

"Are you out of your fucking mind?"

"I didn't tell her shit," he says.

"That's true," Lily says. "He didn't tell me anything. But now somebody should."

"Eli's just a guy," Ciara says.

"He's not 'just a guy,'" Lily replies. "He's looking for Peter. He broke into Peter's house while I was there alone, and he assaulted me."

"What do you mean he assaulted you?"

Lily tells her what happened, and Ciara quietly takes in the information. Her brother watches her, waiting for her to give him a sign. Should he throw these people out? Allan glances back and forth between Lily and Ciara.

Lily leans forward and stares at the other woman.

"Please help me," she says. "I just need to know what's going on."

Ciara rubs her mouth. "Eli is looking for Peter..."

"Yes."

She nods and sucks in her lips. Jarell is still and silent. Allan rubs his earlobe and looks back and forth between Ciara and Lily.

"What did Peter tell you about the Corinthian?" Ciara asks.

"Not much. He didn't like to talk about work. I'd ask him about it, and he'd just say it was boring, or he'd complain about some guest. I don't think he liked the boss, Mr. Baker, but he didn't say a whole lot about him."

Ciara looks over at Allan.

"We got to tell her," Ciara says. "Better to tell her than to have her traipsing all over hell and Arkansas asking questions."

For a moment, Allan says nothing and makes no move. Then he sighs and lets go of his earlobe. "Look," he tells Lily, "what we're about to tell you is some serious shit, okay? We shouldn't tell you. We should all keep our mouths shut." He wipes his sweaty face. "But here we are, and I guess we're at the point where it will just make it worse if we don't tell you." He nods, takes a deep breath, and says, "Mr. Baker, has this... arrangement with Eli."

"What kind of arrangement?"

"Women." He looks at Ciara. "Well, girls."

"Pretty young, most of them," she agrees. "Eli brings them up from Little Rock. Originally, the girls are from Louisiana or Texas? Louisiana, I think. But now they live in Little Rock."

"Prostitutes," Lily says.

Allan exchanges a look with Ciara. As much to her as to Lily, Allan says, "At first, honestly, I just figured they were regular sex workers. I mean, you work in the hospitality industry long enough, you get used to that sort of thing."

Ciara nods.

"There are a lot of underground economies going on in a hotel," Allan continues. "Private escorts and that kind of thing aren't unusual. Men and women with personal agency doing a job for money. I don't judge that kind of thing."

"People got to make a living," Ciara says.

Allan nods. "That's right. But…"

"But what?" Lily says.

"But…I'm not sure that's what we're talking about in this case."

"Then what are we talking about?"

Again, looking to Ciara for conformation, Allan says, "I don't know, but I think we might be talking about sex trafficking."

Ciara nods. "That's what I figure." She looks at her brother.

"From everything you told me, it sounds like he's running a ring," Jarell agrees.

Lily absorbs this information soberly.

She asks Ciara and Allan, "What did y'all have to do with it?"

"Peter and I didn't even know about it at first," Allan says. "It happened gradually. Every so often, on nights when we weren't working, the girls were brought up for 'private accommodations' in the back wing. The annex, we call it. That part of the inn is weird. It's an addition, an extra building that was built years after the rest, during a period when somebody was flush with cash and thought they were going to really expand the place. You have to go down a long hallway past all the other rooms, past the exercise room, past the boiler room, then you have to go outside under the back portico, and there's the annex. Eight rooms, four on bottom, four on top. It has its own little parking lot back there, and it looks out on a field and some trees."

"It almost feels like a separate inn," Ciara says.

"That's right," Allan says. "Mr. Baker books all the private accommodations himself. Then Eli brings some girls up in the back of an old moving truck." He asks Ciara, "You and Dillard were working the first night, right?"

"Yeah," Ciara says. "We got an extra twenty dollars each. Just for being there. It was like a gratuity. We just went about our jobs like usual and stayed out of the annex 'til morning. Didn't see nothing, didn't hear nothing."

Allan says, "A week later the same thing happened, but this time it was me and Peter working the desk. Mr. Baker called us into his office and said that there were going to be private accommodations in the annex that night. And that was it. Peter and I both got an extra twenty bucks just for being there. We didn't see anyone, didn't talk to anyone. We were just up front doing our regular jobs. The private accommodations were all off the books and out of sight."

"But y'all knew what was going on?" Lily asks.

Ciara shrugs. "We ain't stupid."

"We put it together," Allan says. "Every week or so, Mr. Baker would tell us it was a private accommodation night. That meant he'd rented out the annex as a block, like you'd reserve rooms for a wedding or something. Maybe these guys, the clients, knew each other, or maybe Mr. Baker bundled them together like that to contain it. I don't know. But these weren't guys off the street. The whole thing was done in a low-key kind of professional way. And like I said, for a long time, I just assumed we were talking about professional sex workers. No big deal."

"But then what happened?" Lily asks.

"But then one night, one of the girls came up to the front desk. Eli and Chance always hung out under the back portico after they parked the truck, but I guess she must have slipped out of the room without them seeing her somehow. She was an average-looking girl, kind of pale. But younger than I expected, about your age. Maybe younger. She wasn't dressed like a prostitute in a movie, you know, with the high heels and halter top or whatever. She was wearing a t-shirt and a short jean skirt and some flats. Looked like any other girl walking down the sidewalk. She came up to the front desk and asked me and Peter to use the phone. I guess she didn't want to use the phone in the room, and she didn't have one herself. She wasn't running or crying or anything, just walked in from the annex like she was any other guest of the inn. I wasn't even sure she was with the group in the back until Eli came stomping down the hall. Rough-looking guy. Well, you've seen him, so you know. When she saw him, she just put down the phone. Just like that. No big scene. They didn't say a word to each other. She followed him back to the annex like she'd been caught doing something wrong. It was weird. After a while—once he'd left her with Chance, I guess—Eli came back up to the desk to talk to me and Peter."

"What'd he say?"

"He told us it was nothing, a misunderstanding. Told us if we had any problems, we should talk to Mr. Baker."

"What'd you do?"

"What could we do? We didn't do anything."

"You could have called the police."

Ciara raises her eyebrows. Jarell shakes his head.

Allan says, "You think the cops would do anything?"

"Yes."

"I don't know about that," Allan says.

"You think they're in on it? The chief?"

"I don't know, Lily. I really don't. But I'll put it this way. The cops usually swing by the hotels at night. Just quick drive bys, part of the loop around the all-night places just off the interstate. The hotels and motels, the gas stations, the MacDonald's. But on the nights when we have the private accommodations, the cops never come by. So…I don't know."

"They *have* to know," Ciara says. "They *never* come around when the private accommodations are going on."

For the first time, Lily sits back on the couch. Her back hurts, so she arches it against the cushions. She places her hands on her knees. Her hands have no nail polish. They're just hands, young hands, strong hands. She squeezes them into fists.

"You said these girls…they're in Little Rock?"

"I…think so?" Allan says, looking at Ciara.

She nods. "Eli stashes the girls in a house over on Baseline behind the Soap-N-Suds. Eli ain't there much. His girlfriend Harper runs the girls."

"You've been there?" Lily asks.

"Fuck no, I ain't been there."

"Then how do you know so much about it?"

Ciara glances at Jarell.

He waves his hand. "Never been there myself," he says, "but I know a couple guys who have. Leave it at that."

Lily turns back to Ciara. "Eli is looking for Peter, which means it must have something to do with this business at the Corinthian. Why else would he care if Peter left town?"

Ciara says, "Yeah, but Peter didn't really have anything to do with the business. You know what I mean? He was just a guy who worked at the hotel. He didn't know any more than the rest of us. Eli's got no reason to care if he skips town."

Lily thinks about that. Then she grimaces, remembering a thought she had on the drive down here: *Peter wouldn't run off by himself.*

"Maybe Eli isn't looking for Peter at all," she says.

Ciara's eyes widen. "Maybe Peter ran off with some of Eli's… property."

Lily leans over and presses her palm against her eyes. She's not crying, just taking a moment. Slowly, she rubs her temples, then her eyes.

When she sits back, she shakes her head and smiles, the kind of disgusted smile that often precedes the throwing of a punch.

"Another girl," she says.

CHAPTER 17

As Allan pulls into traffic, Lily puts a hand on her belly because her bladder suddenly feels as tight as a fist.

"I need to go to the bathroom."

"I'll stop at the next station. I need to get gas anyway."

In the quiet hum of the truck, Lily feels the baby moving, stretching.

My poor baby.

She thinks of Ciara standing in the doorway as they left, one hand resting gently on her own swollen belly, her face still inscrutable.

When they see an Exxon, Allan stops and pumps gas. Behind the station, Lily finds a single filthy bathroom that smells deeply, permanently, of urine. The walls sport crude graffiti, mostly of a profane or racist nature, but in the midst of these inky belches, one philosopher has written: *HEALTHY IS JUST THE SLOWEST WAY TO DIE.*

Lily walks back to the truck with her hand on her belly. As she climbs into the truck, she tells him, "I'm hungry. Can we get something to eat?"

"Really?" He seems surprised that she could be hungry, as if he expected her to be too upset to eat.

She shrugs. "I don't decide when I have to eat. Once the hunger pangs start, the nausea and headaches aren't far behind."

He picks up his phone. "We can eat first. I mean, I'm not in a hurry to get back to Conway. We can grab something on the way or…"

"Can we stop somewhere? I can't really eat in the car right now."

"Sure." He searches on his phone for a moment. "Looks like Subway is the nearest and easiest."

"That's fine."

He gets the address, and he's about to put the truck in drive, when she puts her hand on his forearm.

"Wait. Can you pull over, over there?"

"Over where?"

"To the side of the parking lot."

"Are you going to be sick?"

"No, I'm fine. Please just pull over for a second."

Allan drives to the edge of the parking lot and puts the truck in park next to a muddy field of brown grass.

Lily turns to him and says, "I need to ask you something, and I want you to tell me the truth."

"Okay."

"Why did you bring me down to Little Rock?"

He blinks. "To see if we could find Peter."

She stares at him, hard. "But you knew Peter wouldn't be at Ciara's."

"I what?"

"When we got there, you asked to talk to Ciara, not to Peter."

"I was just being polite."

"No, you didn't expect him to be there. You only took me there because you wanted me to see *her*. You wanted me to know about Ciara."

Allan stares at her.

"Did you know she was pregnant?" she asks.

"Lily..."

"Did you?"

He sighs. "I suspected. It's not like Peter and I talked about it, but I suspected."

"And that's why you brought me down here, so I'd think Peter ran away because of me and Ciara."

"Lily, I swear to God that as far as I know, that *is* what happened."

"But you didn't want me asking questions about the Corinthian. You thought if I saw Ciara, I'd stop asking about Eli and the hotel."

"I'll admit that I didn't want to talk about the Corinthian. I still don't. And now you know why."

She sits back. "I'm sick and tired of other people deciding what I need to know," she says.

"Well, congratulations, now you know the truth."

"No, I don't. Not all of it."

Allan doesn't know what to say to that, so he says nothing.

"So, who is she?" Lily asks. "This girl he ran away with."

Allan sighs and stares down at his steering wheel.

Lily says, "There is another girl, right? Just be honest with me."

"Look," he says, "all I know is, one night, Peter went back to the annex. I know he met one of the girls, talked to her for a while. I don't know what happened after that, but maybe it led to something."

She shakes her head. "Well, that's an important piece of information, don't you think?"

"Not necessarily."

"Yeah, that's why you're trying to hide it from me."

"I wasn't hiding it from you."

"Do you know her name?"

Allan wipes the back of his neck.

"I should have stayed a counselor for troubled teenagers," he grumbles. "You know I used to be a counselor in a treatment center for fucked-up teenage girls? Terrible job. Horrible job. I quit because I got tired of being kicked and spit on, and now this is where I wind up."

Ignoring him, Lily repeats, "Do you know her name?"

"Tisha. Her name is Tisha. And I am not saying he ran off with her. But Tisha is the name of the girl he met that night."

"He had sex with her?"

"No. He just talked to her."

"I'll bet."

"I'm serious. That night, there was a problem with her client or john or whatever you call him. I'm not sure what happened, but I guess Eli and Chance had to, uh, escort the guy off the premises. Took a while. While they were tied up with that, Peter went back there to check things out. That's when he met Tisha."

"What did they talk about?"

"I don't really know. But Eli came back after a while and found them together. He got pissed and told Peter he'd kick his ass if he ever found him talking to one of the girls again."

He puts the truck in drive.

"What else?" she asks.

"That's all I know. Everything I just told you is everything Peter told me about it." He turns to her. "Really."

She says nothing, weighing what he's told her, as they merge smoothly back into traffic. Once Peter met this girl Tisha, could they have found a way to stay in contact? Could they have run away together? That would certainly explain why Eli broke into Peter's house.

When they get to Subway, Allan and Lily order their sandwiches, chips, and drinks. They sit down, and Allan opens his footlong meatball sub and takes a large bite. Lily, still pondering what she's been told, nibbles more slowly at her turkey sub.

They eat most of the meal in silence. Allan turns to face the front window, chewing and blankly taking in a view of the parking lot. After a while, he realizes Lily is staring at him, judgment in her eyes.

"Do you always stare at people?" he asks.

Brushing crumbs off her hands, she says, "I can't figure you out."

"Join the club."

"You seem like a decent man. You worked at that place for troubled girls, you said. And I know you tried to help me. So why did you keep working at the Corinthian once you knew what was going on?"

He picks up a napkin, his dark eyes narrowed on her. He wipes his face, then balls up the napkin and throws it on the table. Sitting back in his chair, he tells her, "I needed the money, Lily."

"That's it?"

"'That's it?' is the kind of thing you say when you've never had to pay a bill before. It's twenty extra bucks every time they do private accommodations. Two or three times a week, it starts to add up. I'm taking care of a broken-down old man at home, and our bullshit insurance is worse than having nothing at all. I'm forty-two years old, and I'm still paying off student loans from twenty years ago. I need money *constantly*.

"The truth is, I never even thought about quitting. I found out a long time ago that if you're not hot or rich, you damn well better be useful. So, I kept my head down and I did my job. I just went along. When you work in the hotel business, you learn real fast that there's all kinds of shit going on up in the rooms. You're used to looking the other way. This situation came from the top down, so I did what I was told." He places his hands flat on the table. "That's not a flattering answer to your question, but it's the only answer I have."

Lily doesn't look convinced, but she doesn't contradict him either. "Are you ready to go?" she asks.

"Sure," he says, still irritated.

They throw away their trash and each use the restroom. When Allan comes out, Lily is waiting outside with the same troubling look on her face.

"You okay?" he asks.

She nods.

When they get into the truck, however, she turns to him and says, "I need to know if he ran away with this Tisha girl."

"Yeah," he says with a shrug. *Well, what can ya do?*

"We need to find out for sure."

He pauses with his keys in his hand. "And...how do you think you're going to find out for sure?"

"We can go to that house behind the car wash and see if she's there. Tisha's the only girl that we know Peter had contact with. If she's still there, then obviously she and Peter *didn't* run away together. But if she's gone..."

"Going there would be insane, Lily. Like, literal DSM-IV certified insanity."

"No, it's not. I have to know for sure if he ran away with her, and they're the only ones who can tell me."

"You really want to see Eli again?"

"You heard Ciara, Eli isn't there much. The place is run by some woman named Harper."

"Lily, no—"

"Yes, Allan." She nods and crosses her arms. "I've made up my mind."

"Lily," he says, still calm, "your determination is impressive, and one day it may lead you to accomplish great things, but one thing it will not do is convince me to take you to that house behind the car wash. The *best* case scenario is that it's a de facto brothel. At worst, and far more likely, it's a place where underage girls are being held in sexual bondage. Do you understand what that means? That's interstate sex trafficking, maybe kidnapping. Those are federal crimes, and these are very scary people we're talking about. So this is not somewhere I'm going to take you. And that's that. The only place I'm taking you is home."

He starts the ignition and puts the truck in drive.

"Stop the car," she says.

"Please, this is a truck. One of my few assertions of traditional masculinity. Don't insult it by calling it a—"

"Stop the truck," she demands. "I'm serious."

Instead, Allan pulls onto the street, merging into the light flow of traffic. "Sorry. Can't do it. I know you're going to be pissed at me all the way back home, but I did my part. I gave you more answers than you got from anybody else. Especially from Peter."

"I'm serious, Allan."

"I'm serious too, Lily. Just sit there and watch me being serious all the way back to Conway."

She says nothing to that, but when they stop at the next stoplight, Lily takes off her seatbelt, and climbs out of the truck. Allan screams at her, but she keeps going, crossing the street and walking down the sidewalk in front of a busy Kroger.

He drives past her and pulls off to the side of the road. Jumping out of the truck, he tromps through the grassy ditch and intercepts her on the sidewalk. "What the fuck are you doing?"

She walks past him. "I'm going to the Soap-N-Suds on Baseline."

Following her, he says, "I am not going to take you to a whorehouse, Lily. Understand? You can throw as big a fit as you want, but I am not going to take you there."

"Okay."

"Okay, what?"

"Okay, don't take me there. I'll go on my own. Thanks for nothing."

He shakes his head in disbelief. "Lily!"

"Allan."

"This is ridiculous. How do you think you're going to get there?"

"I have some money. I'll take a bus. Or a cab." Her eyes light up. "That cab right there." She points to a dirty yellow taxi pulling out of the grocery store parking lot.

She waves at it. The driver, seeing her, pulls over.

"I never hailed a cab before," she tells Allan. "This is a big day."

All he can do is grab her arm, a thin but strong limb that disappears into the grip of his huge hand, and physically hold her in place while he yells, "Lily, do you not understand what kind of people these are? What do you think's going to happen when you get there? They're not just going to start telling you everything they know."

His desperate face is flushed and sweaty. Cars pass them, people looking. If a police cruiser were to come by, what would the cops make of this enormous, middle-aged man manhandling a pregnant teenaged girl?

Lily can almost read this fear on his face, the fear a good man has of being perceived as a bad man. She slowly, gently pulls her arm out of his hand. "I'm going to the house behind the car wash," she tells him coolly. "I'm going to ask for Tisha. I'm just going to ask if I can talk to her. I'm not some cop kicking down the door with a machinegun. The worst thing that's gonna happen is they'll tell me to get lost. If they do, I'll leave. But I have to try to find out where Peter is."

She pats his big arm and starts walking toward the waiting taxi.

Exasperated, he calls out, "After everything he's done to you, why are you still looking for this boy? You wouldn't have to chase after him like this if he really loved you."

She turns around as if he's just thrown something at the back of her head. "Are you serious?" she asks. "I don't need him to love me. I need him to marry me. If we get married, maybe my dad can keep his job and maybe we can keep our insurance and our house. If we get married, my son doesn't have to grow up without a father. I won't have to walk around with my head hung down in shame in front of everyone I know. I don't need Peter to *love* me. I need him to do the right thing. That's why I need to find him. If I can find him, I can bring him back and *make* him do the right thing."

"You can't make people do the right thing, Lily."

She shows him her empty hands. "What's my other option? Go

home and watch my life fall apart because I didn't try?"

He's about to say something else, but she goes to the taxi and opens the door.

He hurries after her and grabs the door. "Lily…"

The taxi driver is a tall Black man with black-rimmed glasses and gray hair who has been calmly watching them fight. He looks over his shoulder at the girl. "This guy bothering you?"

"Yes," she says, climbing in.

The driver says, "Hey, dude, let go of my door."

Allan is still looking at Lily, but she takes the handle and pulls the door shut.

He stands there, hands at his sides, cars passing by, as he watches the taxi pull out of the parking lot.

CHAPTER 18

She tells the taxi driver she wants to go to the Soap-N-Suds on Baseline.

"The car wash?"

"Yeah."

"Why you taking a taxi cab to a car wash? Planning on taking a shower?"

"Actually, I'm trying to find a house behind the car wash."

The driver glances up at her in the rearview mirror.

"But I don't know the address of the house," she explains. "So just take me to the car wash."

The driver looks back to the street, ever so slightly shaking his head as he merges into traffic.

After a moment, he asks, "That guy back there, is he the, uh, father?"

"What? No. Lord, no."

The driver stops at a red light.

Lily says, "I guess it must have looked that way."

The driver shrugs. When the light turns green, he tells her, "Wouldn't be the first time I picked up some girl fighting with her baby daddy. Been driving a cab damn near twenty-five years. Seen just about everything at least twice."

"Really?"

"Oh sure. Picked up a girl a couple years ago running away from her boyfriend in the middle of the night. What do you think he did to that poor girl, in addition to beating on her like a dog? Took all the doors out of the apartment, including all the closet doors. He even took out the bathroom door. Didn't want to give her a place to hide, he said. She couldn't even relieve herself in private. If you'n believe that. So, yeah, I know the look of a girl who's running from something."

"I'm not running from anything."

He lifts his eyebrows. *Yeah sure.*

"How did the girl get away from him? If that guy was keeping such a close eye on her?"

"She hit him in the head with a cast iron pan while he was sleeping. He'd already got rid of all the knives in the kitchen, but I guess he didn't think about the pans. She said she only hit him once or twice, but he ended up brain damaged, so they suspect it was more like three or four times. Did you see it on the news? I was interviewed."

"I didn't see it."

He shrugs. "You know what the worst part of that whole story is? At some point, them two thought they loved each other. Makes you wonder, don't it? Every romance is one iron skillet away from attempted murder."

"I'm on her side."

"Oh, sure enough. Got to be on her side in that deal. But I reckon he thought he loved her, anyways. For some folks, love is just the fear of losing the other person, you know. Don't make it right, but it makes you understand how some people go wrong."

After a few minutes, over the driver's shoulder and through the windshield, she sees the Soap-N-Suds. It's larger than she expected. Eight roll-through blue stalls flanking a small white booth. From the booth's window a bald man in a navy-blue uniform sells cloth wipes and car fresheners.

The driver pulls up and puts the car in park. Turning around, he says, "You said you were looking for a house behind the car wash, but you didn't know the address?"

"Yeah. I guess I'll go back there and see if I can find it."

The driver nods. He tells her, "You know…I've brought people over here before. To this part of town. Sometimes they want to go to a, uh, *specific* house behind the car wash."

"Yeah?"

"Yeah. Usually, though, them people are men."

Lily stares at him. "I think that's the house I'm looking for."

In a small cluster of rundown homes at the dead end of a residential street, the taxi drops her off in front of a small two-story house. Lily can still see the sign for the car wash over the trees circling the back yard. Chance's truck is nowhere around. Smoking a cigarette on the sagging front porch of the house is a girl about the same age as Lily. She's wearing a gray sweatshirt, red sweatpants, and black sneakers. Her clothes hang off her skinny frame and her dirty blonde hair spills out of a sloppy bun held together by a rubber band. As Lily crosses the yard, the girl watches her, stepping from one foot to the other like she might run away.

"Hi," Lily says.

The girl twitches, glancing at the front door. Lily can't tell if she wants to bolt back inside or if she's afraid of what's in there.

"Are you Tisha?"

The girl sucks on her cigarette and stares at back her, smoke absently flitting out of her mouth.

The front door of the house opens, and the girl steps out of the way. Two young men in jeans, t-shirts, and ballcaps walk outside. They glance at Lily. They don't look at the girl on the porch at all. They hurry to an orange Dodge Ram parked in front, climb inside, and drive away.

The door of the house screeches open again, and a large woman steps out. Tall and heavy, with broad shoulders and broader hips, she wears black stretch pants and an olive-green t-shirt.

Without taking her eyes off Lily, the woman tells the girl, "Inside."

The girl does as she's told, slipping past the larger woman as quickly as a frightened cat.

"Well?" the woman says.

"I'm Lily. I talked to Eli the other day. He tell you about me?"

The woman has pale skin with diaper-rash-red splotches on her cheeks and chin. She wipes sweat from her forehead. "You're Lily," she says. "Okay. So what?"

"You're Harper? Can I talk to you?"

"Looks like you already are."

"Right. Well, I wanted to ask about—"

"Wait," Harper says scanning the street, "you're really about to ask me about shit standing in my yard in the middle of the motherfucking day?"

"Well, I just had a question."

Harper looks Lily over for a moment, noting her pregnancy, and nods to herself. "Come on inside for a second, you wanna talk."

Lily hesitates as Harper goes to the door and opens it.

"Well, come on if you're coming," Harper says. "One question or ten, I ain't standing outside yacking in the yard for God and the whole world to hear."

Lily takes a deep breath. "Okay."

She walks up the front steps and follows Harper into the house. Harper closes the door behind them.

They're in a den with bare walls and a couple of ratty couches. A thin pink bedsheet hangs over the window. Two Latinx girls Lily's age or younger are sitting on one of the couches, watching *Ellen* on an old television with a cracked screen. One girl wears black shorts and a t-shirt with an American eagle on it. The other girl has dyed blonde hair with long black roots and wears Razorback sweats. On her left hand, she's missing her pinkie finger.

The air in the room is warm and thick, with a burnt, metallic odor that Lily finds overwhelming.

"Go to your room," Harper tells the girls. "Stay down there."

The girl in the eagle t-shirt stands up and takes the hand of the other girl. The blonde girl blinks, looking as if she's on the verge of either waking up or falling asleep. She says nothing, seems to absorb nothing, as the other girl pulls her down the hallway.

To Lily, the room smells dusty, but, even without sitting down, the furniture seems sticky. On the cracked television on the floor, Ellen DeGeneres and Carrie Underwood are sitting in neon-pink armchairs discussing corrective plastic surgery.

"The fuck you coming around here for?" Harper says.

"Did Eli tell you about me?"

"You're that Peter boy's little girlfriend," she says.

"That's right."

"You know where he is?"

"No. That's why I'm here. I'm looking for him."

"Well, Jesus Christ, girl, he ain't here."

"Is there a girl named Tisha here?"

Harper stares down at Lily for a moment. "Tisha who? I don't know no Tisha."

"You don't?"

"Little girl, don't you know it's a goddamn stupid idea to come in here asking me about shit?"

I think Peter knows some girl named Tisha who lives here."

"Who told you that?"

"I figured it out."

Harper crosses her big arms across her chest. "And just how did you figure it out?"

"Look, it's none of my business what y'all are doing here. I just want to know if Peter ran off with this girl."

"What do you mean 'what y'all are doing here'? Nobody's doing nothing here. I done told you I don't know no Tisha. And now you better leave my house."

Lily can tell this horrible woman is lying, which, at this moment, is just as good as if she were telling the whole truth. She stares at the floor. She's not going to get any more from Harper. Without looking up, she says, "I see."

"Yeah, you see."

"I'll go."

"Yeah, you do that. And let me tell you something, girl. Your ass'd be in a whole motherfucking world of trouble if Eli was here. You understand?"

"Yes. I understand."

"Now you best get on out of here and don't come back. You want to help that baby, go on home and pray."

Lily stares at this big woman standing in her dank cave, orchestrating the sexual bondage of young girls and issuing vague threats. Harper's eyes are empty of everything but avarice and meanness. Much later, Lily will look back on this moment, and contemplating the person of Harper, she'll wonder how such a person came to be. *What kind of world*, she'll wonder, *makes such people? Does the world turn people mean or does the meanness come from somewhere else?* One day, she'll ponder these questions, but at this moment, all she feels for this woman is hatred. It's a new emotion for her, one of the emotions that she's been taught all her life to repress in the name of Christ. But right now, at this moment, her hatred feels as pure as baptismal water.

Saying nothing, she follows Harper to the door, but before Harper can reach for it, the front door opens.

They both back up as Eli Buck walks in.

CHAPTER 19

It doesn't take Allan long to walk back to his truck and decide to follow the taxi to Harper's brothel, but in the few minutes it does take, the cab is out of sight.

Cursing, he types Soap-N-Suds into his GPS and finds the address.

This is what you get for trying to do the right thing.

He was just trying to keep the girl out of trouble, to distract her away from the Corinthian by taking her to see Ciara. But this goddamn pigheaded child just charged on ahead, rushing into the dark, looking for the idiot father of her child. Allan doesn't know her enough to know if it's pride or pure stubbornness that keeps her going. Or, hell, maybe it's actually what she says it is. Maybe she thinks she can save herself and her family by finding this boy.

And now here you are, trying to save her from getting hurt.

He puts his foot to the gas, hurrying to catch up to her.

You haven't learned yet that you can't save people?

FIND HIM

He worked at the Home For Youth the winter he moved back from Chicago. He'd returned home from college with nothing but an undergraduate degree in psychology and forty-five thousand dollars of student loan debt. He tried not to see it as a defeat. He looked for a job, any job, that he might get with this degree, and what he found was the Home For Youth, "a residential mental health facility for troubled adolescent girls." He applied for a job as a residential treatment counselor. He was swiftly hired, his supervisor barely pausing to look at his resume. On his first day as an RTC, he realized why.

Home For Youth was a meat grinder. The residents were a dozen deeply troubled teenage girls ripped out of the most horrific circumstances imaginable and locked up together in a cinder block facility on the lonely outskirts of Little Rock. The place smelled of sweat, blood, and piss. When the residents weren't forming short-lived factions or raging against each other, they were trying to hurt themselves. The RTCs were either overwhelmed novices or slightly sinister burnouts. None of them did any actual counseling. They just tried to keep the girls from fucking or killing each other. The residents met with a psychologist—an overworked, sad-eyed woman everyone called Dr. Jo—but she was only there for a few hours a day, meeting with the girls one-on-one. The rest of time, RTCs babysat the girls and tried keep them from slashing their wrists until they could make it to their next fruitless appointment with Dr. Jo.

At the end of his first day on the job, he drove home and cried. By the end of his first month of being an RTC, he'd developed a harder shell. He'd been bitten, scratched, kicked, and spit on. Whenever he arrived at work, he would stay in the truck a minute or two after he'd shut off the engine, gathering his strength to go inside. One day, he had to straddle a girl's back and clutch her head with both hands to stop her from smashing her face into the floor. He went home that night and ate a pizza and watched *The Apprentice* as if nothing had happened. When he went to bed, though, he couldn't sleep because all he could think of was the girl's twisted, broken nose, and the almost serene look on her bloodied face when she finally passed out.

He worked the job for as long as he could. He wanted to help these girls, but defeat was inevitable. There was no way to help them. They'd all suffered too much damage for too long, usually at the hands of their closest family members. By the time he finally quit, Allan had long since stopped crying about the misery he saw. All he could do for these damaged girls was to try to keep them relatively safe.

Then, a girl named Robyn tried to kill herself in the common room. She was sixteen, the daughter of a crack addicted mother who had regularly rented out Robyn to pedophiles for drug money. The mother had been busted in a federal sweep of child pornography rings when she started recording these rapes of her child and selling them over the internet. The girl was shuffled between different foster homes, but after getting violent with her last set of foster parents, Robyn had been sent to Home For Youth.

Despite years of abuse, Robyn was brighter than most of the other residents, and Allan would sometimes give her books to read. She liked him for that, though she never managed to finish a book before one of her demons took over. Any modicum of improvement one moment would invariably be lost an hour or two later, a day at most, lost either to despair or to rage, the twin demons of her soul. She tore up the books, wrecked her room, tried to hurt herself.

Then came the day she learned that her mother had died in prison, possibly of suicide. Robyn climbed on a table, pulled a fluorescent tube out of the ceiling, broke it against the wall, and tried cut her throat with a shard of the glass. As Allan pulled her down and restrained her, Robyn kicked him in the teeth. He could taste his own blood the rest of the day.

After work, he walked out to his truck, got in and looked at his busted upper lip in the rearview mirror. It was not the first time he'd seen a girl try to self-harm. Nor was it the first time he'd been physically assaulted. It was, however, the first time he'd been kicked in the mouth. Something about that made this time different.

He bared his teeth to the mirror. They were all still there.

And that was it. Knowing that he was probably going to have PTSD after working in this hopeless pit of trauma was bad enough, but he told his reflection, "I am not going to lose my teeth for this."

On the drive home, he called his supervisor and tendered his resignation.

"I was wondering why you hadn't quit yet," she told him.

He moved on, got a job in the hotel and hospitality business. Sign people in, sign people out. Much easier. Much less stressful. He did his job and went home and fed the old man and tried not to blame himself for abandoning Robyn and the other girls.

That worked for a while.

Until now.

A few homes, nice once, gone to ruin now, dot the narrow streets behind the car wash. He's turning down one street when he sees Chance Berryman's blood-red Ford Raptor heading down a dead end called Dodson Court. Allan turns around in an empty driveway and creeps toward Dodson. He rolls past, looking down the street in time to see Eli getting out of the truck in front of a dilapidated two-story. Allan turns around in another driveway and heads back. Dodson Court is a cul-de-sac of six formerly nice houses with badly kept lawns and the kind of brickwork that was fashionable in the eighties. Now the hedges all need trimming, and the brick needs to be power sprayed. Some of the houses look abandoned. Everything feels exhausted and ignored.

Chance is sauntering across the front lawn of the two-story house while tapping something on his cellphone with both thumbs. Finally, he finishes and slips the phone in his pocket. He doesn't look back as he steps up on the porch and goes inside, but through the open door,

Allan catches a glimpse of Eli. And, for less than a second, he sees Lily.

He cuts his engine and rolls up behind Chance's Raptor. He stares at the front door of the house for a moment. Shaking his head, he opens the center console next to him and reaches inside.

CHAPTER 20

Eli looks surprised to see her.

"What are you doing here?"

Behind him, Chance steps in. When he sees Lily, his mouth opens, but he quickly closes it and shuts the door.

Harper crosses her arms like a teacher who's taken an unruly student to the principal's office. "She was asking about Tisha," she says.

Eli glares at Lily. "Who told you about Tisha?"

She hasn't seen him since Peter's house, and her blood is beating in her ears. Worse, the baby starts squirming as if he's twisting in sheets. She puts her arms around her belly.

"I think I ought to leave."

"Oughtn't to have come here in the first place," Harper says.

"I asked you a question," Eli says. "Who told you about Tisha?"

A knock on the door stops Lily from answering.

Eli nods at Chance.

Stepping to the door and peering through the peephole, Chance says, "It's her uncle. That big fucker from the hotel."

Lily is quick enough to say, "I told him I was coming here. He must have followed me."

Chance looks at Eli.

Eli nods.

When the door opens for him, Allan takes in the whole scene in a glance. Chance, Eli, Harper, and in the back, Lily, her eyes already locked on his.

Eli says calmly, "Chance, get out of the way and let him come in."

Chance opens the door and Allan steps inside. Chance closes the door behind him.

Allan calmly walks over to Lily and takes her arm like a pissed off father, "Go out to my truck. I'll deal with you later." He nudges her toward the door, but Eli holds up a hand in front of her before she gets there.

"Hold on."

Allan says, "She doesn't need to hear any of this, does she?"

Eli spreads both his palms. "Well, she's here already, ain't she?"

"Yeah, looking for her baby daddy. Let me get her out of here, and you don't have to worry about her anymore."

"But how come she's *here*?" Eli says. "If you didn't tell her about this place, who did?"

"And she was asking about Tisha," Harper reminds him.

"*And* she was asking about Tisha," Eli says. "You been talking about shit you shouldn't have been talking about, Allan."

Lily stops everyone by speaking up.

"Peter told me," she says. "He told me he met a girl named Tisha. He said she lived down here in the house behind the Soap-N-Suds on Baseline. I came down to see if they were together."

Later, she will debate the ethics of her decision to lie at this moment, but in the moment itself, she has no such reservations. If Eli thinks Allan is the one who told her about Tisha, there's no telling what he'll do. But since it now seems clear that Peter and Tisha are together, what does it matter if Eli thinks Peter is the one who told her? In time, Lily will question whether she has culpability in the fallout to come, but for now, with Eli staring at her and the baby starting to kick her insides, telling the lie comes as easily as opening a door.

Before the others can respond, Allan addresses her again like an angry father, "Well, they clearly aren't here. So let's go."

Eli shakes his head. "Hold on, man. You don't decide shit around here. I decide shit around here."

"I'm not deciding anything, I'm just saying—"

"Go back to your room!" Eli yells.

The blonde girl Lily saw before scurries away from the doorway and back down the hall.

"Don't nobody come out here 'til I say," Harper yells down the hall.

"We're gonna go," Allan says.

Eli turns around and locks the front door. "Not yet," he says. "Chance, go over there and get on his left. We gotta find out for sure what he told her."

"Wait a minute," Allan says, raising a hand. "Y'all just hold on."

But Chance, like a good attack dog, does as he's told. He starts moving toward the left while Eli moves to the right.

Harper moves out of the way, toward the hallway, to give them more room.

Allan reaches back. Lily thinks he's going to shove her in a certain direction. Instead, he reaches under his shirt and pulls a sleek black gun from a holster he has clipped to his belt.

Lily can't breathe. The baby kicks. She leaves one arm over her belly and puts her other hand on Allan's back. She can't see his face, just his long arm outstretched, holding a gun that looks large, even in his enormous hand.

For a moment, no one speaks, until Eli says, "You're pulling a gun on me?"

"Harper," Allan says without looking at her, "get away from that doorway, come over here, and stand with these two."

"You must be out of your goddamn mind," Harper says, walking over to Eli and Chance.

"Must be," Eli agrees, hands at his sides. "You're not doing nothing but making this worse on yourself. We was just going to give you a beating."

"Nobody's giving me a beating. Ever. All I'm doing right now is defending myself and the girl. Any of you got a gun on you?"

"Maybe," Eli says. "I'll tell you one thing: if I pull a gun, I'm gonna shoot somebody. Can you say the same thing?"

"Only if you make me," Allan says. He gestures at the couch with his free hand. "Now all y'all sit down. There on the couch. All three of you."

They do as he tells them, squeezing awkwardly against each other on the cushions.

Eli says, "The fuck you think is going to happen now?"

"We're going to leave."

"Just like that?"

"No reason why not. Nothing's happened here—"

"You pull a gun and say nothing's happened?"

"The girl just wanted to find the father of her child. Now she knows he's run off with another girl—"

"With a thieving whore," Eli says.

"—the search is over. Wouldn't you say the search is over, Lily?"

"Yes," she says.

Eli glowers at Allan. "Don't change the fact that you pulled a motherfucking Glock on me."

"You'll get over that. I'm just defending myself and the girl. Can't hold that against us. You let us get out of here, then we're out of your hair for good. No harm, no foul. We're gone."

Eli shakes his head calmly. "No, Allan. No, man. You pulled a gun on me. Don't you see that changes things? Don't matter now if y'all go. You're a fucking dead man. Just so you understand. No matter what else happens, you're a fucking dead man."

Allan's mouth hardens. His grip on the gun tightens as his knuckles whiten. Lily sees it. All three people on the couch see it.

"Eli," Allan says, "you must have been scaring the hell out of strung-out fifteen-year-old girls for so long you started to believe your own bullshit. I got a gun and I outweigh you by a hundred and fifty pounds, so if you want to start some shit, come find me. In the meantime, I don't want you talking to this girl again. You got problems with Peter, you take them up with him. Otherwise, leave me and the girl out of it. We're going now. Lily, go on out to the truck."

It takes her a moment to process the command, but then she moves past Allan toward the door. The three on the couch watch her. Eli sits with his elbows on his knees, staring at her. There's no anger in the way he watches her. He simply seems to be taking her in. When she fumbles with the lock on the door, his expression doesn't change.

Allan has his back to her, his face and gun still pointed at the people on the couch. "Take a breath," he tells her quietly.

She takes a breath. Closes her eyes for a second. Then she opens her eyes, unlocks the door, and steps outside. Rushing across the lawn, one hand on her belly, she watches her step.

After a moment, Allan follows her out into the yard, looking over his shoulder, the gun pressed against his leg, his finger behind the trigger. He unlocks the door with the keyless remote. As Lily climbs into the passenger side, he climbs into the driver's side, the gun in his hand. He locks the doors, starts the truck, and pulls out onto the street, steering with his left hand because the gun is still clutched in his right.

Once they're out of view of the house and the car wash, he pulls over and tries to unclip the holster from his belt. His hands are shaking, though, so it takes a moment to free the holster. "Fuck," he grumbles. Then, "Fuck!" When he finally has it loose, he slides the gun into the holster and returns them to the large center console.

"I didn't know you had a gun," Lily says.

"I'm a gay man in Arkansas," he says. "You're goddamn right I have a gun."

For a moment, they sit quietly. Cars pass them.

Allan opens and closes his fists, stretching out the shakes.

"Jesus Christ," he curses.

Lily wraps her arms around her belly and closes her eyes.

Jesus Christ, she prays.

Finally, Allan puts the truck in drive.

For a while, each of them sits with a stunned expression turned to the world. Occasionally, Allan's face will tighten as he drives, navigating them in and out of traffic, but then his muscles will slacken, and he'll stare ahead like he's looking for something small and specific far down the road.

With her eyes closed, Lily rubs her stomach, listening to her own breathing, searching for the right way to feel.

Eventually, she opens her eyes and tells Allan, "Thank you."

He lifts one hand off the steering wheel with a self-mocking air on nonchalance. *Oh, don't mention it.*

"Really, Allan," she says. "Thank you. And, I'm sorry. I know I shouldn't have gone there. I just…I had to try."

He glances at her and sighs. "I know you did."

"Are you going to be okay?" she asks.

"We'll see."

"We should go to the police."

"I'm not sure that's a good idea."

"That man threatened to kill you."

"I know he did."

"So why not tell the authorities?"

"I don't trust the authorities, for one thing. I don't know that Jeff Reid isn't mixed up in this somehow."

"Maybe he's not."

"Maybe is a mighty shaky foundation."

"Could you go to someone else? The state police?"

Allan seems to chew on that for a moment. "It's possible. But I don't know that they wouldn't protect Reid. Like I said, I don't trust the authorities. The good ol' boy network in this state has covered up all kinds of shit, so I'm not sure that one Arkansas lawman isn't as crooked as any other. They look out for each other. But even if I find someone who'll listen, what will I tell them? That I aided and abetted a sex ring?" Hearing the words, he has to shake his head. "Damn it."

"So what are you going to do?"

"I'm going to quit my job. That's the first thing. Get as far away from this mess as I can. Then, we'll see. I have no idea what Eli will do. He said he's going to kill me, but he's a sex trafficker and a pimp. I'm not sure he has the balls to step up and become a murderer."

"He seemed serious."

Allan stares at the road. "I know."

"I'm just worried about you," she says. "I feel guilty for getting you in this mess."

He shakes his head. "No. You need to go ahead and let that guilt go. I'm a forty-two-year-old man. I make my own decisions. I'm in this mess because I went along with a bunch of shit I shouldn't have gone along with in the first place. That isn't your fault. All you did was push me out of my complacency. Understand?"

"Yes."

He nods.

They drive a few more miles before he turns to her and asks, "How about you? Are you okay?"

She doesn't stop staring into some middle distance, but she rubs her belly and says, "I'm alive. I felt the baby moving earlier, agitated, and now I can feel him settling and sleeping. Other than that…" She closes her eyes. "I really don't know."

CHAPTER 21

Eventually, they're back in Conway. Allan glances at the time. "You can still catch the bus home from school," he says. "Or do you want me to drop you somewhere?"

"School," she says.

He drives her to the school, where the buses are already lined up, waiting for the final bell. He pulls to the edge of the parking lot.

She opens her door, but she stops and looks at him. "You sure you're going to be okay?"

The bell rings, and a moment later the doors fling open and teenage bodies begin loping into the schoolyard and parking lot.

"I'll be okay, kid," he tells her. "Don't worry about me."

She nods. "Okay," she says, stepping out the truck.

"Hey, Lily," he says.

She holds the door. "Yeah?"

"For what it's worth, I'm sorry about Peter."

"Yeah," she says. "Me too."

She closes the truck door and walks toward her bus. Allan watches her for a moment, then puts his truck in drive.

She drifts toward her bus in a kind of emotional fog. She's unsure what she's feeling until someone catches her by the arm.

"When did you get back?" Fiona demands.

Lily jerks her arm back. "Don't touch me," she snaps.

She's never yelled at Fiona before. She's never yelled at anyone in public. She's shocked at herself. Maybe that's why she said it. For a moment, the fog clears from her mind. She's angry. Truly, deeply angry. It doesn't feel good exactly, but it does feel clarifying. She doesn't want to talk to Fiona, doesn't want to answer a single question, doesn't want to be here at all. She just wants to go home and scream into a pillow.

Stepping back to find her balance, Fiona looks like a cartoon of someone who's been stunned. Her eyes bug out, her mouth drops open. She looks so ridiculous, it makes Lily angrier.

Everyone around them has stopped, collectively responding to the same primal schoolyard instinct.

Are the Pentecostal chicks about to fight?

Lily shakes her head and stalks off to her bus.

When she steps onboard, she tries not to look for Fiona, but she can't help but see her through the window, hurrying away. Lily already feels guilty for what she said, but the guilt vanishes when she sees Fiona's stride. That's not the walk of a girl who's upset because her friend snapped at her. It's the hustle of someone who can't wait to get home and tell her parents what happened.

Lily slumps down in her seat as far as her belly will allow. Two younger boys see her trying to hide and they begin to laugh.

Lily ignores them. She knows that when Fiona gets home, she'll tell her parents what happened today. *Lily skipped school with some guy to go to Little Rock and look for Peter. Then when I saw her after school, she yelled at me in front of everybody. I don't know what happened to her.* Lily isn't sure if Fiona's parents will call her parents to share this information out of concern or call someone else in the church to gossip first. The one thing she knows they won't do is keep it to themselves.

But Fiona's bus ride home is longer. She lives further out. Which means Lily will get home first.

She's shaking. She knows both her parents will be home. Do they already know? Maybe the school called them today. Maybe they just know, the way that parents sometimes do. Like with the baby; she was still trying to figure out how to tell them when her mother walked into her room one day, closed the door, and said, *Are you pregnant?*

When she gets home, her father is at the kitchen table eating an apple. Her mother is at the sink. She hears her brother down the hall in his room.

Lily walks in and stands before them. "I skipped school today to go to Little Rock and look for Peter," she says.

David puts down the apple. Peggy turns around.

"I found out where he went," Lily says. "He ran off with a girl, a girl he met at the Corinthian."

Her chest rises and falls against her shirt. She's breathing like she's been running.

For a stunned moment, her parents struggle with how to respond.

David says, "Should you sit down?"

"I'm okay."

"Please sit down, honey."

She sits. Peggy watches her from the sink.

David says, "How did you get down to Little Rock?"

"Allan Woodson."

"What?" Peggy says, stepping toward her daughter.

"He works at the Corinthian."

The idea that Lily went to Little Rock with him, of all people…

"Why would he take you down there?" her mother demands.

"I asked him. He didn't want to, but I told him I was going to do it anyway. I was stubborn. I didn't give him much of a choice. You shouldn't be mad at him."

"Don't you tell me how to feel," Peggy snaps. "You run off to Little Rock with some...some man you don't know, and you tell us we should be okay with it?"

David is staring at his daughter. He has none of Peggy's anger. He just looks worried, almost scared.

"So, he drove you down there and then what happened?"

She lies. Some are lies of omission. She does not mention Ciara or Jarell by name. She does not mention the other baby. She does not mention anything about the house behind the car wash. She knows these things would only freak out her parents, but more than anything, she's ashamed of the blunt, ugly truth.

Instead, she gives them the sanitized version. She tells them that Allan took her to a house where she met a girl who used to work at the Corinthian. The girl, Lily tells them, informed her that Peter has run off with another girl named Tisha.

It's enough of the truth for now. Peter's gone. That's the important thing. Saying it out loud brings the weight of all her own troubles crashing back down on her. He's really gone.

She tells her parents, "I'm so sorry."

Then, the tears finally come. They tell the truth that she cannot bring herself to otherwise speak. She is sorry, sorry for so much. It's not a religious guilt. She's too furious at God to wonder if she's offended him. She feels regret. Deep, helpless regret that can only come out in weeping.

Peggy walks over and puts her arms around her daughter, which has the effect of making Lily cry more. David stands up and, not knowing what else to do, places one hand on his daughter's back and one hand on Peggy's back.

None of them say anything as Lily sobs. None of them pray.

But then Lily begins to speak in tongues. She doesn't anticipate this, and she cannot stop it. Her head tips back, and the holy sounds erupt out of her mouth like a volcano, continuing to flow out of her like a foundation, an expulsion of glossolalia that is equal parts fire and water, anguish and joy.

When it is finished, when her soul has finally wrung itself dry, all of them are shaken. Her astonished father bends down to kiss her forehead, a stunned expression on his face as if this is the first time he's ever seen a movement of the Holy Ghost. Her mother dabs her own cheeks and gently strokes her daughter's hair. Lily looks up. Standing in the kitchen doorway is Adam, regarding them all, but mostly regarding his broken-hearted sister, and even his eyes are full of tears.

CHAPTER 22

About the time that Lily is speaking in tongues at her kitchen table, Allan is having his own revelation. He arrives home, still shaking as he parks the truck and walks up to his apartment, one thought running through his head.

What the fuck did I do?

He stays up most of the night with the gun beside him on the couch, tucked under a pillow so the old man won't see it if he rolls out into the living room. Staring out the windows, watching night turn into day, Allan contemplates the possibility that men might be coming to kill him.

He tries to reassure himself. He tells himself Eli is a pimp, and pimps are just cowards and bullies. He tells himself Eli has other things to do. Eli has money to make; and since coming after Allan won't put a single dollar in his pocket, maybe he won't come at all.

But, then again, guys like Eli Buck have their own logic. Allan pulled a gun on him, and Eli said he'd kill him for it. Can he afford not to follow through on that threat? His crew might only consist of one meth head girlfriend and a dipshit with a truck, but can Eli afford to be humiliated in front of them? And what about those girls cowering in the back rooms? Can Eli afford for them to figure out that he's not all powerful?

The girls in the back rooms...

Now that there's no doubt about those girls, now that he's sure they're being trafficked, now what?

Eventually, with daylight breaking, exhaustion overtakes him. He rechecks all the locks and goes to bed. He sleeps with the gun on his nightstand.

When he wakes up late the next morning, he stumbles out of bed and finds his father already awake and watching television.

Allan pads into the kitchen in his boxer shorts and puts on the coffee. As he often does, he leans against the counter, staring at the maker, quietly listening to it percolate. His father knows to leave him alone during this ritual.

When it's done, he pours a cup for himself and one for the old man. They both take it black. He walks in and hands the cup to his father. Often, he'll sit down on the bed next to the old man and sip his coffee, staring blankly at the TV as the day's talking points are being rolled out on *Fox & Friends*.

This morning, though, as he hands his father his coffee, he just asks, "You okay?"

"Yeah," the old man says.

Allan nods and walks back to his bedroom. It's as ramshackle as the rest of the apartment. Many images adorn his walls—studio portraits of the Irish stage legend Micheál Mac Liammóir, postcards of paintings by Egon Schiele and Ivan Albright, film stills of the 1950s B-movie star Peggie Castle, an entire corner dedicated to the changing hairstyles of Reba McEntire, and a single image of Allan himself, a pencil sketch done six years ago by an ex-boyfriend one Sunday afternoon in Eureka Springs. Books crowd his dresser and bedside table. The autobiography of Elsa Lanchester. *White Girls* by Hilton Als. Two volumes of Micheál Mac Liammóir's published diaries. He's also still making his way through *Modernism: The Lure of Heresy*, but he's recently gotten sidetracked by *Backwards and In Heels*, TCM host Alicia Malone's history of women in film. At least he *had been* reading it, until he got sidetracked, yet again, by his crazy young niece.

He hopes she's okay. After what they went through yesterday, he has to fight the desire to call her and check in on her. But he reminds himself she's got a family around her. She'll be fine.

What about you? he thinks. *What are you going to do?*

"I need to quit," he answers aloud to his room. "That's the first thing to take care of." He hates the idea of being suddenly unemployed and looking for work, but there's no way around it.

Time to go see Mr. Baker.

Allan finds him in his office. Sitting behind a desk covered two inches deep in years of order forms, receipts, and invoices, he's leaning forward, staring at a paleolithic PC looming in the center of the clutter like a glowing monolith.

When Allan walks in, Mr. Baker sighs and leans back in his creaky chair. He slips his glasses on and says, "Close the door and have a seat."

Allan closes the door and sits down across from him.

Mr. Baker is a small man with basset hound cheeks, short-sleeve shirts he wears too tight, and graying hair he wears too long. He's been in the hotel business his entire life, starting as a teenage bellboy in Houston back in the early '70s. Now he owns his own place, but he still wears cowboy boots to give himself an extra inch or so.

"You went down to Little Rock?" he says.

"I did."

"Wanna tell me why on earth you'd do that?"

"Peter's girlfriend—excuse me, his *pregnant* girlfriend—is my niece. She's looking for him."

"What'd you find?"

"I'm sure Eli told you. Peter ran off with one of Eli's girls. I don't know if he was trying to rescue her, or if he fell in love, or if he just wanted to get the fuck away from my niece. Maybe all three. You know Peter got Ciara pregnant, too? Yeah. So, he's got *two* girls knocked up, and now he runs off with another girl..."

Mr. Baker is obviously surprised by this last piece of information, and maybe even a little impressed. "I'll be goddamned," he says. "I didn't know that little fucker had it in him. Thought he was a good church boy."

"A lot of time they're the worst."

"Find out where he run off to?"

"Who the hell knows? I hope he went to fucking Alaska. He comes back here, he's liable to get his ass kicked, or worse, by Eli and them."

Mr. Baker shrugs. "Speaking of Eli, he wants me to fire you."

"You don't say."

"Well, it was a compromise. He *was* talking about killing you."

"Yeah, he mentioned something about that to me, too."

"You really pull a gun on him?"

"He and Chance were about to double team me. Was I supposed to turn the other cheek?"

"You ever pull a gun on someone before?"

"Of course not."

"What did you plan to do with it?"

"If he tried to touch me or the girl, I planned to blow his brains out. He doesn't seem to have much use for them, anyway."

"Well, he's mighty pissed about it. I tried to talk him down, but if I was you, I'd lay low for a while. Which brings us back to the whole question of whether or not you need to keep working here."

"Don't bother to fire me. I came in to quit. I don't need this shit anymore."

Mr. Baker raises his eyebrows. "I see." He spreads his hands. "Well, I hate to see you go. You're a good man at the desk."

"You hate to see me go? I hate to have to go look for another fucking job. I got a sick old man to take care of, and now I gotta go out there and hustle up another hotel gig. I don't really need this shit right now."

"No one told you to get involved in Eli Buck's business, Allan."

Allan leans forward, staring hard at the little man across the desk. "*You're* the one who got me involved in Eli's business. You made everyone who works here an accomplice in Eli's business."

Mr. Baker wets his lips and spreads his hands out, as if to plead for clemency. "Look around, man. This dump is struggling. Has been since the day I took it over. I been robbing Peter to pay Paul for fifteen fucking years. It's a fucking curse. But it's mine, the only ship I got. And if it goes down, I go down with it. So, yeah, I made some arrangements to bring in some extra money. So what? If I didn't, wouldn't none of us have a job."

"You know these girls are basically slaves?"

"*Slaves*. They're hookers. Eli's a pimp. That's all. It ain't pretty, but it ain't slavery."

"Is that what you tell yourself? Or is that just something you're telling me?"

"Hey, this gal Peter ran off with, she seems free enough. Free enough that she and Peter just up and left, according to Eli."

"I don't care what Eli says. I don't want any part of it. The whole thing makes me sick to even think about."

"Well, then," Mr. Baker says, "I guess it is better if we go our separate ways."

"Okay, then my question is, what kind of severance package are you offering?"

Mr. Baker chortles at that. "Only severance package I offer is a fond fare-thee-well. *Vaya con dios*, good luck, and don't let the door hit you in the ass. You expecting money or something?"

"I don't want any more of your money. What I need is help. Make sure Eli is off my back. Soothe his wounded ego or whatever, but convince him that coming after me will just be messy."

"I'll try. I'm gonna shoot you straight, though, I don't tell Eli what to do. Nobody does."

"Fair enough. And now that I have to go look for new employment, I want a *glowing* letter of recommendation when I start looking for another job. 'Allan Woodson is the finest front desk manager I've seen in forty-five years in the business.' That kind of thing."

Mr. Baker picks up a pen from the clutter and tilts all the way back in his chair, so that his feet no longer touch the floor. Tapping the pen against his chin, he stares back at Allan a moment before a grin cracks his lips. "Actually," he says, "I've been in the business *forty-six* years. You believe that shit? I've been doing this longer than you've been alive."

"And I ain't no spring chicken."

Mr. Baker scratches his head. "Texas. That's where I started. And that's Texas in the seventies, mind you. Talk about the wild west. Those were the oil boom years, when the energy crisis sent prices through the fucking roof, and every coked-up shitkicker in the state thought that being in the right place at the right time meant he was some kind of genius. Everybody ran around living like kings. Hotel business was crazy then. If I wasn't rounding up hookers for orgies with oilmen, I was out scoring Mexican blow for congressmen. It was like doing hospitality service in hell."

"Yeah."

"But then the eighties rolled around and the boom went bust and most of them guys lost their asses. Remember *Dallas* and J.R. Ewing? That show barely scratched the surface. Fortunes were made and lost. Fucking shit was insane. Even I made money."

"And now you're in Arkansas."

"Exactly. Must have been out of my mind to move up here and buy this place. That was the nineties. I'd moved into management by then and I did well with some oil stocks, so I had a nice little nest egg saved up. I was smart. I didn't piss it all away like some redneck Caligula. But what did I do instead? Moved to Conway fucking Arkansas because someone offered me a sweet deal on the Corinthian. In my mind, it was gonna be the flagship location of a chain of inns, and I was gonna be Conrad Hilton. Some guys blew their fortunes on coke and pussy; I blew mine on a dream, which might be worse because at least coke and pussy are fun. I ended up pouring my whole life savings into this dump, along with every dime I could borrow, and now I'm gonna die broke. Meanwhile, you know what happened? About six years ago, they had another oil boom in Texas. If I would have stayed put down there, I'd probably be retired by now."

Allan nods, waits, letting Mr. Baker stew in his regrets.

Finally, the old man pushes up his glasses and pinches his nose. "Anyway..."

Allan asks, "We got a deal? A letter of recommendation, and Eli off my back."

Mr. Baker shrugs. "Sure. And, Allan, I'm sure I don't got to say this, but what I'm buying with this, uh, severance package is a vow of silence."

"You know I know to keep my mouth shut, Mr. Baker," Allan says, standing up and going to the door. "You just be sure and tell Eli that. Square me with him, and I won't screw it up."

"Okay. Fair enough. I'll make the call now."

Allan walks out, passing Dillard at the front desk checking in an elderly couple from Missouri.

"It's all yours," Allan tells him.

As he's pulling out of the parking lot, he releases a deep breath. It's an odd feeling, this overwhelming sense of relief. He's going to hate looking for a new job, but he's surprised by how happy he is to leave the Corinthian. The place weighed him down more than he realized.

Maybe, he reflects, that's another reason why Peter ran away. Maybe once it became clear what was happening in the annex, leaving was the only thing to do. Ciara had certainly gotten out while the getting was good, and now she's working down at the Capital City Hotel in Little Rock.

There's a thought. Maybe he should try there first for a new job. Always helps to know someone.

He stops at a red light and looks back at the Corinthian. But even if he secures a new job, then what? Can he really just drive away from here and act like there's not something horrible happening in the back annex? What about those girls?

CHAPTER 23

Before the meeting at church that Friday night to decide their fate, the members of the Stevens family stay in their separate rooms.

Behind their closed door, David and Peggy are talking. Lily's not at all sure what they're talking about. Her? The church? What they'll do if Daddy is fired?

Adam is in his room thinking about whatever it is Adam thinks about. God's eternal judgment, maybe.

Lily, meanwhile, sits in her room and thinks about sex.

She can't help thinking that every problem she faces is because she and Peter had sex. Her pregnancy, the implosion of her grades, her obliterated hopes of going to college, the very real possibility that her family will lose their home tonight. All because she and Peter had sex.

She's ashamed of that fact, and even more ashamed of how quickly it happened between them. After all, she had been taught chastity her entire life. What a vile, sinful girl she must really be, deep down, to have succumbed so easily to lust. Peter didn't seduce her. He didn't have to. It just happened. She bristles to remember Ciara's words, but those words ring with clarity and truth. It just happened. The first time Lily was alone—really alone—with Peter, they had sex, as if they'd both been waiting for it, waiting for the first opportunity. Afterwards, they held hands and prayed together to beg God's forgiveness. For a few weeks, they would repeat the cycle of clumsy sex, instant guilt, and groveling prayer. Finally, overcome with guilt, she resolved they would not do it again until they got married. Peter still wanted her, but she'd made up her mind, and so the sex stopped. But it was already too late.

Now she knows that Peter had already had sex. He'd already gotten someone pregnant. It all makes her feel like an even bigger fool. It all makes her hate him.

She wants to know where he is right now, not because she still loves him, not because she still wants him to be a father to their child, but because she wants to ask him, *Why? Why did you do this to me? Why did you ruin my life?*

When she walks down the hall, she finds her family gathered together.

"I'm sorry, were you waiting on me?" she asks.

"No, dear," her mother replies. "You're not late. Ready to go?"

"Yes."

Adam has his hands in his pockets. "We good to go, Dad?"

David has his Bible in his hand, like always when he's headed to church. "Mine hour has come," he says with a grin. He pauses, though, stops grinning, and then he does something that surprises his wife and children. He lays down the Bible on the coffee table.

"Let's go," he says.

They follow him across the yard, Peggy holding his hand, Lily and Adam walking behind. The air is cool, chilly when the wind blows. High above them, the church steeple juts like a nail into the redeeming sky.

They're greeted politely but not warmly by a few church members lingering at the front door. Inside, the church is as full as it's ever been while David Stevens has been pastor. Adam, noting the robust attendance, leans over to his sister and whispers, "Public executions always draw a big crowd." As they make their way down the aisle, their mother and father receive meaningful handshakes and prolonged hugs, expressions of Christian love and respect that seem a little too deliberate to Lily, and she's reminded of Christ being welcomed into Jerusalem by the same cheering crowds that would be screaming for his death a few days later.

Scanning the congregation, she sees Fiona, whom she has not spoken to since their altercation, sitting with her parents in their usual spot. Fiona, spying Lily, leans over and whispers something to her mother. In front of them sit the Drinkwaters, side by side, holding their Bibles. And near the back sits Sister Cynthia, alone, like some Catholic saint devoted to her own suffering and isolation.

The front row is empty, reserved as always for the Stevens family. They sit down as David takes the stage.

Sister Drinkwater pokes her husband, and Brother Drinkwater stands up and walks down the aisle. The church falls silent as he climbs the stage.

In a breach of decorum, he begins the service instead of Brother Stevens. "Brothers and sisters," he says, "thank you for all coming to this business meeting tonight. This is not a night that anyone here has been looking forward to, but we—"

"I wonder, Brother Drinkwater," David interrupts, "if I might be allowed to say a few words first. Still being pastor of the church."

"Of course, Brother Stevens," Brother Drinkwater replies. "I was only going to suggest that we begin things with a prayer."

"By all means, Brother, please lead us in prayer. Then, if you don't mind, I would like to say a few words to the church. Then you can lead the meeting."

Brother Drinkwater appears flustered at the soft rebuke, but he bows his head and prays. It is a short prayer for guidance. The church assents to it with a unified *Amen*.

Then David says, "Thank you, Brother. You can take a seat, please."

Brother Drinkwater, clearly expecting to do more speaking, looks a little confused, but there's nothing else for him to do but go back to his seat. When he retakes his place beside Sister Drinkwater, she begins to whisper in his ear, but he shushes her.

David tells the church, "As you all know, the purpose of this meeting tonight is to take a vote to decide if I should continue on as pastor. For nine years, I've led this church. With God's grace, I've done my best in that capacity. I've been blessed by each and every one of you. I've been allowed into your lives to minister to you, and, certainly, many of you have prayed for me and supported me and my family. I think it's safe to say that, as a church, we've been through a lot together.

"One reason we named this church the Redemption Tabernacle is that each of us, each in his or her turn, we all need redemption. That's as true for a pastor as it is for a truck driver or a waitress or a cashier at Dollar Tree. Each of us is purified by the Lord as we go along. We're all working out our salvation as we go along.

"But I'm not here today to ask you for your forgiveness or your forbearance. I'm here to tell you that I need to seek my redemption elsewhere."

Lily turns to look at her mother. There's a soft smile at Peggy's lips, a calmness in her expression.

"And so," David says, "after discussing this with Sister Stevens, we've decided to step down as the leaders of this church." He glances at Lily and gives her the briefest smile. "Let me say, I am not stepping down because of anything to do with my daughter. I have been deeply honored to be the pastor of this church, but that honor could never compete with the honor of being the father of my beautiful children." Turning now to address those children, he says, "Lily, Adam, I love you. I'm proud of you, proud of who you are, proud of who you will be. Always remember that with the grace of God, redemption is assured.

"And I hope the rest of you will remember that as well. I love this church, and I pray that all of you will continue to seek out the Lord Jesus, to seek his redemption. Please pray for my family and me, as we move onto a new path. A new life. God bless you all."

David Stevens nods to himself, satisfied with what he has said, and leaves the stage to sit down next to his wife and children.

And, like that, Lily Stevens is no longer a preacher's daughter.

When they get home, she goes to her room and closes the door. She sits on her bed to take off her shoes.

Before she can get them off, there's a knock on the door.

When she opens it, she finds Adam, as serious as she's ever seen him.

"Can I talk to you?" he says.

"Yeah."

He follows her in and closes the door.

"That was wild, huh?" she says.

"This is your fault," he says.

"What?"

"You heard me."

"Adam..."

His face is calm, but his voice quivers. "If you hadn't gotten in trouble, this wouldn't have happened. First, you get in trouble with Peter, then you go down to Little Rock with Allan Woodson? What is that? And what did all that have to do with Chance Berryman? I think you're still not telling everything."

"I've told everything that needs telling," she says. "Not that you have any right to know anything about it. Because you don't. But I've told everything that needs telling."

"Doesn't really matter," Adam says. "Because now Dad lost his job and his faith because of you."

"Adam," she says, stunned. "That's a horrible thing to say..."

"The Bible has worse things to say about a woman like you."

He turns and walks out, leaving her door open. She hears him stomp down the hall and shut his door.

She stares at the empty hallway.

Then, quietly, she walks over and closes the door.

She goes back to her bed and sits down. With her eyes peering into some middle distance, she rubs her belly and thinks. Curiously, she's so numbed by Adam's bludgeoning words that she's able to examine her own emotions as if they were items laid out on a table. She knows that she could dissolve right now into shame and guilt, could condemn herself for being a backslider and whore. That's what Adam wants her to do.

Or she can refuse to do that. Flawed human sinner that she is, she can keep her head above water, keep breathing for herself and for her child to come.

She makes her decision.

Taking a deep breath, she whispers to the baby, "You know what? Screw him."

CHAPTER 24

Allan spends the next week getting adjusted to his new job. Regally ensconced downtown near the River Market, the Capital City Hotel is old and stately, with a Victorian façade, ninety-five rooms, five suites, three meeting rooms, a rooftop bar, a downstairs restaurant, and a grand ballroom. Because Allan's new, he's been stuck on the graveyard shift as the night auditor, manning the front desk and running the rollover reports, but he actually likes this schedule because he can get home in time to feed his father breakfast.

He enjoys being alone most of his shift. Aside from the occasional late check-in or odd room request, after he runs the nightly audit at three am, he has ample downtime until the morning crew arrives, so he catches up on his reading or watches TCM on his iPad. Nice and quiet.

Of course, these long, silent stretches on the graveyard shift also allow him plenty of time to think about Eli Buck.

Although he still carries his gun in his truck when he drives to work or goes out for groceries, Allan hasn't seen or heard any sign of

Eli. No threatening phones calls, no blood-red Raptor in the rearview mirror. As near as he can tell, Mr. Baker has made good on his promise to negotiate a peace. If that's the case, maybe Eli is through with Allan.

But Allan is not through with Eli. He keeps thinking about the girls in the back room of Harper's house. While he's not sure he can trust the cops in Arkansas, sex trafficking is a federal crime, so he figures there must be some way he can leave an anonymous tip with the FBI, to at least point them in the direction of Dodson Court. With anonymity in mind, he decides not to search for the information on any of his own devices. Instead, one morning when he gets off work, he goes home, has breakfast with his father, and then heads to the public library. The bank of computers is sparsely populated. One man is filling out online job applications. Another man, much older, is trying to covertly look at porn. Sitting next to a homeless woman researching information on how to acquire and care for exotic birds, Allan Googles the website of the FBI's Little Rock field office. He had assumed the FBI would have a place where he could leave a tip, would have some kind of form to fill out, but instead all he finds is a number to call for a national hotline and another number to talk to an FBI agent. He's not sure what to do. Talking to someone means getting involved, really involved, means opening himself up to his own possible legal problems. He's not sure if he can do that yet.

He goes home that day without calling the FBI, but the idea keeps bugging him. At the same time that he's considering what his next move should be, he occasionally wonders if he and Lily really got the whole story of what happened with Peter. The kid just up and vanished with Tisha? While that makes sense in one way—Peter's got lots to run from—there is something about the story that sits wrong with him. He can't quite put his finger on it, but something bothers him about it.

It's almost as if he can hear Lily saying, *But Peter wouldn't do that.*

Allan shakes his head. For all he knows, that might be true, but there's nothing he can do about it, either way.

This morning, with his shift winding down and the sun just starting to warm the front bay windows of the hotel, the first members of the day crew to arrive are the uniformed bellhops, a couple of affable metalheads named Dani Carson and Reed Hardy. Allan is fascinated by them. Dani is a tatted-up, richly pompadoured butch who spends her weekends as the screamer in a lesbian grindcore band called Manslaughter. Reed, whom everyone just calls Hardy, is a big, bearded guy who plays drums in a sludge band called Nutsack. They are, Allan thinks, soulmates of a peculiar sort. They're both quick on their feet and friendly with customers, always competing to see who can get better tips. In between unloading vehicles and carrying luggage, they spend their every free moment discussing horrible music.

They wander by the desk and wave at Allan. A few minutes behind them, the front door slides open and Ciara walks in carrying a small cup of coffee from McDonald's.

"Morning," she says, still bleary-eyed. She's cut back on coffee, especially in these last weeks of her pregnancy, but she hasn't given it up completely.

"Morning," Allan says.

"How was it last night?"

"Quiet. That annoying couple on the fourth floor checked out early, so you don't have to fool with them this morning."

"Okay."

"Only problem is that the toilet in 313 is broken again. I had to move the woman in there down to 225."

"And you put in the work order for the toilet?'

"Yeah, but you might mention it to Brett when he comes in."

"I will."

"I think that's it."

Ciara nods. She's silent as she follows Allan to the breakroom. He clocks out. She clocks in. As Allan gathers his things from his locker, she walks back out to the front desk without saying anything else to him.

As he's passing through the lobby on his way out, though, he stops to talk to her.

"Hey," he says.

"Hey."

He leans against the desk, his eyes closed for a moment. "I need to talk to you about something," he says.

Ciara doesn't blink, as if she's been waiting for him to stop by and tell her they need to talk.

"Okay."

"Something important," he says.

"Okay," she says again. "But now doesn't seem like the time for a talk about something important."

"No," he says. "Can I come back on your lunch break?"

The phone rings, a call from one of the rooms.

"I eat at one thirty," she tells him. She pointedly doesn't ask for more information. She just picks up the phone and, in a voice of smooth professionalism, says, "Front desk, this is Ciara speaking. How may I help you?"

Allan nods and leaves.

He goes home and makes breakfast for himself and his father. Bacon, scrambled eggs, toast with butter and blackberry jam. They sit and watch *Fox & Friends* together. Allan tells his father that the show's hosts are two used car salesmen and a beauty pageant runner-up. His father responds that Allan is a fool who does not recognize good journalism.

After breakfast, he gives his father his morning pills, loads the dishwasher, and goes to his room. He strips down to his boxers and flops on the bed with a fan oscillating over him. After reading less than a page of Mac Liammóir's *All For Hecuba*, he falls asleep.

He awakens at noon and staggers out to find his father watching

Law & Order: SVU. Once he's had his fill of Fox in the morning, Herman watches the same old police procedurals he used to sleep through beside his wife. It's too much to say that he has developed a love of watching television, but it's really all he does anymore, a sad state of affairs the old man himself finds pathetic.

Wiping his eyes, Allan yawns and tells his father, "I'll get you lunch."

"Okay," Herman says.

Allan makes him a turkey sandwich with a side of Nacho Cheese Doritos and a glass of Diet Pepsi. He sits on the bed while the old man eats.

During a commercial, the old man looks over at Allan. "You ain't eating?"

"Not hungry."

"That's a first."

"Thanks, Dad. I love you, too."

"Anything wrong?"

Allan looks at him. "That's an uncommonly sensitive question, old man."

Herman waves him away. "I can't win with you. Tease you a little, you get as pissy as a woman. Ask you if everything's okay, you bite my head off."

"I didn't bite your head off. Everything is okay. I'm just not hungry is all. But, listen, I need to go back up to the hotel this afternoon."

"What for?"

"A meeting."

"They gonna make you come in for a meeting on your afternoon off? Don't hardly seem fair."

Allan shrugs. "What can you do?"

When he looks up, Herman is smiling at him the same way he would smile at a precisely cut piece of drywall.

"You're a hard worker," the old man says.

Allan blinks at his father a moment. "Did you just give me a compliment?"

The old man grimaces. He turns his attention back to the television, picks up his sandwich, and takes a huge bite.

They watch the rest of the show in silence.

Allan drives back up to the hotel a little before 1:30. He's walking across the parking lot as the front doors slide open and Ciara walks out. Allan gives her a small wave.

She holds up her lunch bag and nods at a bench in the shade.

He sits down next to her as she unpacks her bag. A bottle of water, and a Tupperware container of pita bread, hummus, and raw vegetables.

Without saying anything, she begins to eat.

As a nice breeze stirs the treetops, the freckled sunlight and leafy shadows flutter across Ciara's face.

"Well?" she says.

"That good hummus?"

"It's okay. Ain't the best I ever had, and it ain't the worst. You come up here to ask me about my hummus?"

Allan rubs his knees. "No. I guess didn't."

"What is it, then?"

"It's just… I'm not sure if I should say something, or if I should keep my mouth shut."

"Well, you didn't come up here to keep your mouth shut, either."

"No, I guess not."

She nods and dips a baby carrot in hummus and eats it.

Allan says, "I'm going to call the FBI and tell them about Eli."

Ciara dips another carrot into the hummus and eats it, chewing slowly.

"Well?" he says.

"Well what? Do what you think you need to do. Eli finds out, he'll kill you, but maybe the feds will lock him up before he can."

"Yeah."

"You gonna leave an anonymous tip on some hotline or something?"

"No. I thought about it, but I think the direct way is better. When this thing blows up, I want to be on the record. Looking in my mirror is unpleasant enough. I don't need to add guilt to the equation."

"You thought about what you're gonna say when they ask you why you took money from a sex trafficker for months and months before you called someone?"

"I've been pondering that very question."

"Better make sure you got your answer ready before you call."

"I will. But, listen, the reason I'm talking to you is because I didn't want to catch you off guard. I wanted to give you time to get an answer ready to the same question."

"I don't need an answer to that question, because I'm not going to call and snitch. If they come to me and say, 'Hey, did you know about this?' Imma shrug and say, 'I don't know nothing. Shit goes on in hotels. Always has. I knew there was private parties in the back, but I never went back there. Wasn't my job to doublecheck Mr. Baker's private accommodations. That's on him.' Which it is."

"Okay."

"That it?"

"Yeah, that's it," he says, starting to get up.

She stops him. "I assumed you wanted to talk about Peter."

He settles back down beside her. "Peter? Oh. Uh, no."

She takes a sip of water and holds onto the bottle. "Let me ask you a question, then. After y'all left my place, did you and Lily go over to that whorehouse behind the car wash?"

"Yes. How did you know that?"

"Jarell works construction with some guys that buy pussy there. *Apparently*, the girls were talking about some big white guy and a pregnant girl that come around looking for one of the girls." She stares at him and asks, "You really pull a gun on Eli Buck?"

Allan glances around the parking lot like Eli might be there waiting for him. "Is he still pissed about it?"

"Hell if I know. Probably. He don't seem like the forgive and forget type. But the way I heard it, he's mostly pissed at the girl that run off, Tisha. And Peter, too, of course."

"Mr. Baker said he'd get Eli off my back."

"The same Mr. Baker you about to rat out to the FBI? That Mr. Baker?"

Allan nods and checks the parking lot again. "Good point."

Ciara says, "Whatever you do, you best be smart about it. If you tell the FBI and they start sniffing around Eli, he's gonna assume you put them on his ass. And then he's gonna come after you for sure."

"Yeah. I know." He takes a deep breath. "Well, I think that brings us up to date. Peter and Tisha ran off, Eli's pissed at me, and I'm trying to figure out how do the right thing without getting killed. It's a whole mess of trouble."

Ciara twists her mouth. "Yeah," she says, "except that doesn't exactly bring us up to date."

"Why not?"

She takes a deep breath. "Because I found out where they went, Peter and Tisha. And I think I know where they're staying right now."

CHAPTER 25

Eli Buck steps into the doorway, and the girls in the back room all look up. Two mattresses lie on the floor, a dirty sheet on one, the other bare. There are no customers right now, and the girls are sitting on the floor with their legs crossed, passing around an old magazine and whispering. There's cardboard taped to the windows, one naked lightbulb in the ceiling.

"What are y'all doing?" he asks in a tone so casual it's almost nice. He always comes in this way, with a veneer of contingent friendliness.

The girls are slow to answer, never sure what the right answer might be at any given moment.

Ximena, at seventeen, the oldest of the current girls, says, "Nothing. Looking at this." She tentatively holds up a year-old issue of *People* with Madonna and her four adopted kids on the cover, as if submitting it for inspection.

Britt, the blonde, fidgets and says, "Eli, when—"

He stops her. "I know you ain't about to ask me for ice."

Ximena and Lena lower their heads, trading glances. This is how quickly his moods can change, how quickly Eli can go from nice to mean.

"You get the ice when you work," he tells Britt. "Hell, you ain't worked at all today."

"Nobody come by yet today."

"What are you talking about? Harper said two come by first thing this morning."

"But they wanted Ximena and Lena."

"Whose fault is that? You're the only white girl here and you can't get guys to call dibs on you? What does that tell you?"

"I been sick."

"And I'm sick of you being sick."

"Please, I just need a little, Eli."

"You work, you get your ice." He jerks his head at the door. "In the meantime, go on down the hall. See if Harper can put you to work cleaning that filthy-ass kitchen."

He doesn't care about the state of the kitchen, which has counters sticky with ancient grease and walls and floors covered in the guts of squashed cockroaches. He just doesn't like when the girls spend more than a few minutes alone together. Especially since Tisha ran away.

Britt gets up in a hurry, but he stops her at the door. He asks all of them, "Y'all ain't been talking to the customers, have you?"

"Talking about what?" Ximena asks.

"Anything."

"Just about what they want and how they want it," Lena says.

He nods. "Good. That's all you need to talk to them about." He looks at Britt. "Right?"

"'Course, Eli."

"And you'll let me know if anyone wants to talk about anything else."

They all agree. Of course. They'll tell him if anyone comes around acting weird, asking questions. They know they're supposed to keep their mouths shut.

He knows they're lying, of course. He's never met a whore who didn't lie. For that matter, he's never met a john who didn't talk too much. No, that's not true. There are plenty of guys who slap down their money, fuck, and then leave as quickly as possible. But Eli's known way too many of the other kind, guys who seem to want more than pussy, even from a whore who's only supposed to be selling pussy.

He walks out on the porch and surveys the neighborhood. Things are dead, but that can always change. Like that big fucker Allan Woodson. He seemed to show up out of nowhere.

Baker was adamant on the phone the other day. *Look, for my sake, don't touch Allan. I made a deal with him. We can trust him. Just let him go away, and we won't have to worry about him.* But Eli doesn't like the messiness of it. First, Tisha runs off with that little prick from the hotel. Then Allan and the pregnant girl come here, right here, and walk in the front door. It's messy, and it's dangerous.

He scans the street again.

Baker trusts Allan, even likes him, but Eli doesn't give a shit about any of that. The fucker pulled a gun on him, right here. The girls all act stupid, but they know what happened. And if they know what happened, then that means everyone knows what happened.

Eli lights a cigarette. The world feels smaller. Like things are pressing in. He can't see it as he looks up the road. No sign of cops, no unmarked vans with dark windows, none of that. But he can feel it, the slow, sick sensation of encroaching walls, like prison.

He grew up hard from day one, but, at least by his own reckoning, he didn't have hate in his heart until he got sent away for the first time. He hated everyone inside. The stupid, degenerate prisoners, gnawing at each other like rats at the bottom of a sewer. The dead-eyed guards who either treated inmates like names on a clipboard or like rabid dogs that needed to be put down. Even the wives and mothers and girlfriends who came by to cry and bitch on visitation days—they never did anything but make a man feel weaker. By the time he got out, he had hate to spare for everyone he met.

A truck starts to turn down Dodson, but the driver thinks better of it and keeps going.

What's that about?

Maybe nothing.

Maybe something.

Eli shakes his head and drags at his cigarette. He needs something to run at. He'd kill somebody right now if he knew who to kill.

Allan Woodson certainly has it coming. But he's a big fucker. He's got a gun. Doesn't mean much, of course. Eli's got a gun, too. Hell, everybody in Little Rock's got a gun. Don't mean much next to the will to use it. Eli has the will to use it.

But if Baker made a deal with Allan to keep quiet, then Allan can wait. Let him get comfortable, then Eli can drop by and see him one night when he's not expecting it. The more pressing problem is Tisha. Having that bitch running around free is the biggest problem Eli has. She could be talking to the cops right now. Hell, even if she's not, just letting her get away sets a bad example for the others. He questioned them, slapping around Ximena, who's the strongest, and buttering up Britt, who's the weakest, with sweet talk and ice. But they don't know anything. As near as Eli can tell, Tisha just walked right out the kitchen door one night, ran through the woods to the car wash, jumped in a car, and was gone.

He drops his cigarette into the mound of butts in a charred soup can on the railing.

Where are you, little girl? You and your little boyfriend...

CHAPTER 26

"I asked all of you to come here today," the old guidance counselor says, "so that I might deliver this dire word of warning in person, the better to underscore its urgency."

He nudges his office door closed with the rubber tip of his cane and slowly treks back around to his desk, letting Lily and her parents wait for him to continue.

Matthew Massing has been a high school guidance counselor longer than all of his current students, and most of their parents, have been alive. In this shabby office, his own tiny realm, he pursues his work of shuffling student schedules with the solemnity of a man handling nuclear launch codes. On his wall are framed pictures of Robert E. Lee, Orval Faubus, and every Republican president since Richard Nixon, as well as a photograph of Mr. Massing shaking hands with Arkansas Senator Tom Cotton. There's also an American flag, before which Mr. Massing stands each morning when he arrives at work and pledges his allegiance.

Sitting down across from the Stevens family, he puts his elbows on his desk and laces his fingers together. He wears a faded red bowtie and matching suspenders over a blue oxford shirt with threadbare cufflinks and a green pack of Pall Malls in the breast pocket.

Addressing Lily directly, he says, "You are in imminent danger of flunking out of school. After consulting with your teachers, I've determined that if you stay on your current downward trajectory, you will not be able to graduate in the spring."

Lily sits up straight with her hands on the arms of her chair. "I can turn things around."

"I certainly hope so," he says. "You've always performed well academically in the past," he nods at her parents, "and I know you two have always been proud of her, which is why I thought we should have this meeting today. Her teachers and I hate to see her stumble this close to the finish line."

"Is there a way to avoid that?" Lily's father asks, fidgeting in his seat. He's already glanced at the clock on the wall twice—distracted, his daughter knows, because he needs to get back to work.

"Yes, sir," Mr. Massing says. "Renewed focus and dedication."

Her father looks at her. "Hear that?"

"Yes, sir."

Looking fretful, Lily's mother turns and regards her daughter, saying nothing.

"I hope you understand," Mr. Massing tells Lily, "how important it is for you to graduate. For an unmarried teenage mother not to have her high school diploma... It can deliver an absolutely fatal blow to her future. And to the future of her child."

"I understand," Lily tells him. "I'll work as hard as I have to. I am going to graduate."

"I'm pleased to hear you say that," Mr. Massing says, unscrewing the cap on a small bottle of nicotine lozenges, "because your current grades don't reflect that same level of passion."

"I've been distracted lately, but I'm ready to refocus."

Mr. Massing leans forward and pushes a lozenge into his mouth, nearly biting the yellowed tips of his fingers in the process.

"Yes, well, pregnancy presents quite a few distractions, doesn't it?" He addresses her parents when he says, "I do wish young people would take that into consideration *before* they get into trouble." Returning to Lily, he says, "What we need to consider, however, is the reality that you'll have to miss much, if not all, of the last semester of school when your baby arrives. This is something we should begin preparing for now. If you get your grades up in English and history, which I believe is in your power to do, I think you can still pull through in those classes. You're so far down in calculus and physics, however, that both look out of reach. And those are tough subjects for you, anyway."

"Could she retake those classes in summer school at the end of the year?" her father asks.

"Yes, sir."

"And if she did, she'd still be able to graduate?" her mother asks.

"Yes, ma'am. Of course, she wouldn't be able to walk at graduation with her class, because she wouldn't technically be a graduate yet."

Lily rubs her belly. "I don't care about walking with my class," she says. "I'll buckle down and study, pass what I can in the time I have left, and make up the rest in summer school."

"I see," Mr. Massing replies. "Well, a diploma's a diploma."

"Yes," she says, "it is."

In the car on the way home, none of them speak. The silence is becoming a habit for the Stevens family.

Her brother hasn't spoken to her since that night in her bedroom, and her parents have both staggered through the week in a kind of numbed shock. After quitting his pastorate, David Stevens talked to his boss at the icehouse and was able to switch to the day shift, so now he leaves in the morning to go to the shed in the woods to pack ice from eight to four. This is, for the time being, his full-time job. In the eyes of his children, it's a humbling—maybe even humiliating—comedown from the exalted position at the church. Neither of them has ever conceived of a job more impressive, more admirable, more profoundly important, than being a pastor. To see their father reduced in this way is bewildering.

David, as always, keeps his own counsel. There's been no talk of him getting another church, at least not yet. He simply goes to work at the ice shed in the morning and comes home at night. He works on things around the house for Peggy, and he reads. Sometimes he and Peggy go for long drives, discussing the future and looking for a new place to live, but Lily and Adam have no access to these discussions and deliberations, whatever they may be. This is not surprising. While she's heard of families where parents and children address each other on equal terms, in her family, there has always been a clear, bright, unmovable line between the two. The role of the parent is to teach the child the truth. The role of the child is to believe that truth and live by it.

For Lily, however, these days have produced a strange new realization. It has not come quickly, as revelations and prophesying do in the church. It's come gradually, as she watches her parents struggle to begin their new lives in the shadow of the church next door. Stripped of their titles, they are now simply David and Peggy Stevens. This time next year, her father could be an insurance agent or the manager of a store somewhere. Her mother is already applying for jobs as a cashier or a waitress. It's never occurred to Lily that her parents could stop being Brother and Sister Stevens because it's never occurred to her that her parents could change. Now, change seems inevitable.

FIND HIM

Peggy drops Lily off at the house and then runs David back to work. Of course, Peggy could just let David take the car, but Lily assumes they want a little time together. As she closes the front door behind her, she finds her brother on the couch with his Bible. Without saying a word to her, he stands up and walks down the hall to his room.

When she hears his door shut behind him down the hall, she thinks, *He likes this. He actually likes treating me this way.* Sure, he seems mad at her. Sure, he blames her for their father losing his job. But this is something else, too. His ability to hurt her gives him some kind of jolt of pleasure and power.

It reminds her of something from a long time ago, something she wishes she could forget.

When they first took over the church from the previous congregation, Lily's father bought a machete to clear away the brush that had accumulated behind the building from years of Baptist neglect. One day when Lily was twelve and Adam was ten, they came upon the machete hanging on the wall in the carport and, on an impulse, carried it out to the yard to hack at some bushes in the ditch at the edge of their property. Only a few seconds into their labor, they discovered a brown-shelled turtle crawling in the weeds. The turtle withdrew into his shell. Without discussion, Adam turned the turtle on its back and Lily struck it with the machete. Then she handed the weapon to Adam and he struck the turtle again and again, until, much to her surprise, they saw blood. In an instant she knew that the turtle had been a living thing and that they had killed it, for no reason, at the prompting of some innate meanness. While Lily cried, Adam watched her. Eventually, they returned the machete to the wall and buried the turtle in a shallow grave in the woods. They did not tell their parents what happened that afternoon, and, to this day, neither of them has ever spoken of it. Lily doesn't know if Adam even remembers it, though the secret memory is vivid and disturbing enough for her that she needs to think of it in theological terms. It is all the proof she'll ever need that she was born into sin and that sin is indeed her natural state. Not even her unexpected pregnancy provided the same kind of proof, because her sexual sin, at least as she adjudges it, was a transgression of God's rules for sex, a misapplication of the godly inclination toward procreation. What drove her to kill the turtle, however, is an uglier mystery. She did it simply to exert brutal dominion over a lesser creature. Cruelty is the ugliest pleasure, as ancient as the world itself. Her greatest sin, she thinks, was introducing it to her brother.

The phone rings.

She walks into the kitchen and picks up the cordless sitting on the counter. "Stevens residence," she says. Everyone in her house answers the phone with the same formality, a holdover from the formality of being the family of a pastor.

"Uh, hello," a deep but gentle voice says. "May I speak to Lily, please?"

"Speaking," she says.

"Lily, why do you answer the phone like a housewife in the fifties?"

"It's good to hear from you, too, Allan."

"Can you talk? Is now okay?"

"Yeah, for a minute."

"Okay. I'll make it quick. Is there any way you can meet me tomorrow?"

"I have school tomorrow."

"Can you meet me after school?"

"Yes."

"I could pick you up, if you want."

"No, it's fine. I could just meet you somewhere. I can ask my mom if I can use the car."

"Okay. Do you know where Strong Coffee is?"

"Over by Hendrix?"

"Yeah. Tomorrow at, what, four?"

"Okay. I'll see you then."

"Lily?"

"Yeah?"

"You haven't asked me what I want talk to you about."

"I know what you want to talk to me about," she says. "What else could it be?"

CHAPTER 27

Lily parks in front of Strong Coffee the next day at two minutes after four. The café is a converted garage, with the big bay doors rolled up to the roof and antique lamps casting soft light on caramel-colored walls.

She gets there before Allan. A few people sit at small wooden tables with mismatched chairs, reading books, working on laptops, sipping coffee and pecking at cellphone screens. The barista is a college girl with pink hair poking out from under a ballcap embossed with the words WORLD'S GREATEST GRANDPA. She smiles when Lily walks in.

"Hi."

"Hi," Lily says. "I'm supposed to meet someone. I guess he's not here yet."

"No problem," the girl says. "You want something while you wait?"

She looks up at the menu board, which looks like it's written in a foreign language. "I don't know. I've never been in here before. I don't really drink coffee."

"You like sweet stuff?"

"Sure."

"Try an iced chai latte. It's sweet, but not too sweet. You'll like it."

"Okay."

"Awesome," the girl says. Over her shoulder she yells, "Iced chai latte!"

"Iced chai latte," a skinny boy wearing a vintage Pac-Man t-shirt yells back at her.

In less than a minute, the drink is in front of her

Lily finds a table and sits down, sipping the drink.

"This is so good," she calls over to the barista.

The girl smiles and spreads her arms. "See? Now you'll be back."

While she waits for Allan to arrive, Lily sits and observes the other café patrons. Under a sign that says STRONG COFFEE: WE ROAST IT SLOW AND SERVE IT FAST, a woman in a tank top and stretch pants is reading a Jojo Moyes novel. A couple of men at another table are leaning over big mugs of coffee and showing each other pictures on their phones. At a table by herself in the corner, a large woman with facial piercings and a crewcut is typing furiously on her laptop.

Lily sips her drink. She doesn't recognize the music playing on the speakers mounted to the wall, but it's certainly not holy music. Nothing about this place is holy, and yet this small coffee shop located just a few miles from her home, her school, her church, is like a portal into another world. It doesn't seem coincidental that Strong Coffee is located just down the street from the redbrick buildings of Hendrix College. Hendrix looms large in Lily's mind. If all institutions of higher learning—with the exception of the Oneness seminaries—are viewed with suspicion by her church, Hendrix College is viewed with the most suspicion because it's so close. In Arkansas, it's *the* private liberal arts school, words that essentially translate to *secular*.

She's been told her entire life that the secular world is a place of sin and anguish. What she's seen of Eli Buck and Harper and learned about the goings on in the annex of the Corinthian Inn would seem to confirm every bad thing she's ever heard. In fact, what she's learned has actually surpassed what she was warned about. But sitting here in this quiet café, watching people go about their lives, this part of the secular world doesn't seem like such a hellscape.

Allan's truck pulls into the parking lot, and he gets out. Much to Lily's surprise, the passenger door opens, and Allan helps Ciara climb out.

When they walk in, Allan apologizes. "There was a wreck on I-40 as we were leaving Little Rock," he explains.

"It's okay," Lily says, standing up but not looking at Ciara. "I just got here."

"I'm going to get something," Allan says, glancing at the counter. He asks Ciara, "You want something?"

"No, thanks."

Allan heads to the counter.

They stand there a moment before Lily finally says, "Want to sit down?"

Ciara nods.

They sit, saying nothing, quietly observing the other's body language.

Ciara is wearing a tight gray maternity shirt with a scoop neck. She's still wearing stretch pants, but her hair is fixed up. Even though her baby must be due soon, she still looks pretty, which makes Lily feel even more homely in her mother's old maternity clothes. Who knew you could look cute when you were pregnant?

Finally, Lily can't stand the silence. "How's your baby?" she asks.

Ciara allows herself a small smile. "Everything is fine," she says. "He's healthy."

"He."

"Yeah, it's going to be a boy."

Lily nods.

Ciara says, not unkindly, “That upset you? To know that I’m having a boy?”

Lily clears her throat. “No. I mean, maybe. I guess it all upsets me. You know. But I’m happy your baby is healthy. Really.”

“Thank you. What about you?”

“I’m having a boy, too,” she says. As she says this, she feels a pang of guilt. She doesn’t know why, except that she’s not past the point of always feeling guilty about her pregnancy. She’s tried to do everything the doctor and her mother have told her to do to protect the baby and prepare for his birth, but in some deep, fundamental way, as she’s dealt with the back pains and the hunger-induced headaches, with the roiling in her belly and the late-night trips to the bathroom, she’s barricaded her mind against the reality of the baby himself. People ask her about him constantly. *How’s the baby? When is he due? Do you have any names picked out yet?* But thinking about the baby at all already makes Lily feel like a failure.

Ciara nods. “That’s nice. Is he okay?”

“Yeah. Doctor says the baby and I are both healthy. In fact, he said I’m as ‘healthy as a pioneer woman,’ whatever that means.”

“Didn’t pioneer women die of rickets and stuff?” Allan asks, sitting down with an iced chai latte. He nods at the drink. “Yours looked good.”

Lily says, “It is.”

While he sips his drink, Lily waits, looking back and forth between Allan and Ciara.

Ciara draws a deep breath and says, “I know where Peter is.”

Lily’s expression doesn’t change. “Where is he?”

“He’s with a girl named Tisha.”

“We already know that.”

“But I know where.”

“Okay.”

Ciara shakes her head. “I been going over this and over this, all the way up here, asking myself if I really wanna do this. First, I ain't a snitch, and second, I don't know what good it's gonna do you."

"Then why are you here?" Lily asks.

"Because," Ciara says, spreading her hands, "no matter what I think about his father, in a couple of weeks I'm gonna have this baby. And I guess in a few months, you're gonna have his brother. Maybe they're gonna want to know each other one day, and maybe one or both of them will want to know their daddy, no matter what kind of man he is. I don't know. But I didn't want to keep this from you. I'd want you to tell me. Better to know."

Lily nods. Then she takes a deep breath and steels herself. "Where's Peter?"

"West Memphis."

"How do you know?"

"I know a girl who works at the Super 8 there. I won't say her name because it don't matter. But she knows who's doing what. Says there's a whore named Tisha from Little Rock selling pussy at the truck stops on the Arkansas side. She and her guy were staying at the Super 8 until the management found out what they were up to and kicked them out. Now they stay at the West Memphis Motor Inn. Room 15."

"Your friend knows their room number?"

"Apparently, they're not discreet. Which probably means Tisha's taking the johns to the room. We ain't exactly talking about a couple of master criminals here."

Allan mutters, "Jesus Christ. They just living on Tisha turning tricks?"

"I think they're selling dope, too."

"Dope?" Lily asks. "You mean, like, marijuana or..."

"Meth," Allan says. He turns to Ciara. "I assume?"

"Yeah."

"He's using meth?" Lily says.

"Don't know," Ciara answers. "If Tisha's trickin' again, some of the dope she's probably selling to johns, something extra to jack up the price of the trick. Don't really know if her and Peter are using any for themself, though."

Allan asks, "Where'd they get the dope?"

"Well, that's a good question. I'm wondering if maybe they didn't steal some from Eli and them."

"Are they really that stupid?"

"All you gotta be is stupid enough."

"Actually," Allan says, tugging at his ear, "you know what? When we saw Eli, he called Tisha a *thieving* whore. I didn't think about it at the time, but now I wonder..."

Ciara and Allan both turn to Lily.

Ciara says, "I thought I should tell you."

Lily shuts her eyes and rubs her temples.

"Thank you for telling me."

Ciara nods.

She and Allan watch Lily until she reopens her eyes, pushes herself back in her chair, and sips her drink.

"That's that, I guess," she tells them. "The thing I don't understand is, if he wanted to be that kind of guy, why'd he get involved with me in the first place? Why'd he have to pretend to be something he wasn't?"

Allan says, "Most of the time when people tell you who they are, they're really just telling you who they want to be." He draws his own deep breath. "Speaking of which...while I have you both here, I wanted to talk to you about something else. Something related. After we get done, I'm going home tonight and calling the FBI. I'm going to tell them about Eli and Harper." He turns to Lily. "I already told Ciara I was thinking about it, and she knows what she's going to do, but I wanted to tell you, too. I don't know how these things work, but there's a good chance that you're both going to have to talk to law enforcement. I thought you should know."

"Do we need to get lawyers or something?" Lily asks.

"I doubt it. All you did was walk in a house for five minutes. You didn't do anything wrong."

"Failure to report a crime," Ciara says. "They might could charge you with that, if they wanted to be assholes about it. Probably wouldn't get more than a fine or something, but still."

Lily thinks of the girls on the couch, thin and wasted looking. "Call the FBI," she tells Allan. "Tell them I was with you. Tell them why we were there. Tell them I want to talk to them if they think it would help."

"Okay, I will."

Lily pushes her drink away, unable to finish it. "I should go."

Allan asks, "You okay? About the Peter stuff?"

Lily wants to affect the posture of someone who's moved on, but how can she? Peter is gone and she's going to be left to raise his baby and deal with Cynthia. A lifetime of consequences.

She shakes her head.

"Are you going to tell his mother?" she asks Ciara.

Ciara leans back in her chair as if to get a more expansive look at Lily. "I don't know that woman. How am I going to tell her some dark, fucked-up shit like her son's selling meth and turning out his girlfriend?"

"No," Lily says, "I don't mean that. I mean, about the baby. Are you going to tell her she's having another grandchild?"

"That bitch already knows."

Lily almost falls out of her seat. Putting both her palms on the table, she leans forward. "*What?*"

"He told her."

"Peter told her you were having his baby?"

"Yeah."

"I can't...I can't believe he told her."

"Why not? He told her about you."

"Yeah, but I was his girlfriend. Know what I mean? I sat next to them in church every Sunday. There was no hiding it. He *had* to tell her about me. He didn't have to tell her about you, so why did he?"

"You know him better than I do, you tell me."

"Well, that's clearly not true. I clearly don't know him at all. Did he tell you how Cynthia responded?"

"She cried. Tore at her hair, made him get on his knees while she tried to cast the demon of lust out of him. That woman's shit-eatin' crazy, if you ask me. And, I mean, I was never trying to have a relationship with Peter, but when he told me about that, about his mother's reaction, I knew I needed to stay clear of her. She wants to contact me, she can. But I ain't trying to bring that crazy bullshit into my baby's life. I got my own fucked-up mother to deal with. I don't need some crazy old white woman on top of that."

Lily stares at the tabletop, dumbfounded. "Peter…" she says.

"Fuck him," Ciara says. "I don't need his crazy bullshit in my life, either. If he's pimping out his girlfriend and selling meth, I don't want him around my baby."

Allan seconds that with a nod.

Lily isn't really listening. "I guess the thing I can't believe," she says, "is that he didn't tell *me* about you. And neither did Cynthia. She stood on her porch a week ago and basically called me a whore to my face, and the whole time she knew her son had another baby on the way. What kind of person does that?"

Ciara and Allan let the question answer itself.

"She didn't tell anyone," Lily says. "Even at the police station, she kept her mouth shut. She was all like, 'My poor son, he didn't have a father at home to teach him how to be a man, and now he's run away. If only he had met a more god-fearing woman.' Meanwhile, he's lying around a motel in West Memphis smoking meth. Is that how you do meth? I don't even know."

Allan starts, "Well, there're a lot of—" before Ciara places her hand on his and closes her eyes.

"That…*bitch*," Lily spits out. "I hate her." Her small hands clench into tight white fists. "She let the church throw us out of our house, and she didn't say a word."

"Your dad lost his church?" Allan asks.

"Yes. He had to resign. We have to find somewhere else to live. Exactly what I told you was going to happen. He's working at an icehouse now, bagging ice every day. But maybe he could have kept his church if that...if Sister Cynthia would have told the truth about her son and didn't let everybody make it all about me."

"I'm sorry," Allan says.

Lily shakes her head. "I have to go," she says. She stands up.

Ciara and Allan rise and follow her outside.

Lily opens her car door but turns around and walks back to Ciara. Without a word, she gives her a gentle hug, an awkward confection of arms and bellies.

Ciara looks stunned.

Allan asks Lily, "Are you okay?"

She turns to walk back to her car.

"No," she says.

CHAPTER 28

Sister Cynthia doesn't meet her on the front porch this time. Lily parks next to her car in the driveway, walks up the steps, and bangs on the door.

The only response is an empty silence. In the woods behind the house, tree limbs creak and leaves shudder in a cool breeze. Up the street, old Brother Wise sits at his window, sees the pregnant girl knocking on the door of the Cutchin house, and then turns his attention back to the squirrels raiding his birdfeeder.

Lily peeks through the window and sees Cynthia in the den, sitting in her chair, as still as a corpse. Lily raps the glass with her knuckles, but the woman doesn't stir. For a moment, Lily's anger dissipates. Maybe something is wrong.

She goes back to the door and tries it. Surprisingly, it's unlocked. She steps inside.

"Cynthia," she calls out.

She notices Cynthia's jacket crumbled on the floor beneath the coat rack, as if Cynthia missed the hook and just let it stay where it fell.

Walking down the hall, Lily smells something unexpected. In this antiseptic home, she's not used to smelling anything except Cynthia's hairspray and mothballs. But now she smells something oddly out of place.

Food.

Or the remains of food. As she passes an open doorway, she's shocked to discover the kitchen in disarray. A loaf of bread left on the counter beside a package of cheese slices. A fly buzzing around an open tub of butter that's been left to melt. A pan on the stove, blackened with grease. In the sink, dirty glasses, pans, and a plate littered with food scraps from a different meal altogether.

"Cynthia," she calls again. For a moment, Lily wonders if she's dead.

She goes further down the hall and steps into the den.

Cynthia sits in her big flowery chair. Her arms drape the thickly cushioned armrests as she faces a bare coffee table and empty couch. Fully dressed, her hair still coiled six inches high atop her head, she sits as upright as a queen surveying her vacant court.

Lily is surprised when the woman lifts her head and looks at her.

"Cynthia, did you not hear me? I was knocking. I called your name."

"Lily."

"Are you okay?"

"Lily."

"Yeah. Are you okay?"

Cynthia's gaze falls back to the empty couch.

"Me either," Lily says.

Cynthia doesn't register the comment. The flesh of her face sags like a bag that's been emptied of its contents. Looking more closely at her now, Lily notices some things she didn't before. Cynthia's hair is unkempt, her bun loose and messy with wisps, errant strands of hair dangling to her shoulders. And she emits a strange odor, a mix of fragrance and stink, as if she hasn't bathed in a few days and has tried to cover it up with perfume.

"I just talked to Ciara," Lily tells her.

Cynthia blinks slowly.

"You know, Peter's other girl."

No blink this time. Cynthia just stares straight ahead. Lily walks over to the couch and sits down, putting herself in Cynthia's eyeline.

"What about that, Cynthia?" she asks.

The woman looks at her, through her, as if she's still staring at the couch's floral print.

"What about this *other* girl who's going to have a baby by Peter?" Lily says. "You didn't think to mention that? You ran my name down in the church, stood there while they kicked my family out on the streets, and the whole time you knew your son had another baby on the way? That didn't seem like something you should tell?"

Cynthia's bland face stares back at Lily, nothing in her eyes, not even tears. For a moment, Lily's not sure if the older woman understands. Maybe Ciara was lying. Or maybe Peter lied to Ciara about telling his mother. He is, after all, a liar.

But when Cynthia finally draws a deep breath, she manages to say, "Lily." She says it as if she's not quite sure who Lily is, as if might be a stranger who's come to the door to sell something.

Lily shakes her head and stares at the coffee table for a moment. Finally, she looks up. "You know what I want to know, Cynthia? I want to know why you hate me. I never did anything to you. I didn't ruin your son, and you knew that all along. So why do you hate me so much?"

Cynthia stares at Lily as if the girl hasn't spoken a word. Then her attention drifts, first to some empty middle distance between them, and finally to a blank spot on her whitewashed walls.

"Do you know where Peter is?" Lily asks.

Cynthia stares at the wall.

"I know where he is," Lily says.

Cynthia doesn't move, doesn't seem to hear.

"He's in West Memphis with a prostitute," Lily tells her. "He's dealing drugs. That's where he is, and that's who he is."

She feels bad as soon as she says it, ashamed of her own cruelty. But the woman across from her doesn't acknowledge this new information at all. The house is quiet and cool. For a while, Lily stares at Cynthia staring at nothing. And, for a moment, Lily feels the pull of this oblivion, the allure of this stunned nothingness. What if she and Cynthia just sat here until they dropped dead?

She sits back against the couch.

"Cynthia..." she says.

Cynthia just stares at the wall.

Lily says, "All I could think about when I was racing over here was telling you off. But I walk in here and you're staring at the wall like you're in a padded room. I tell you Peter's got another baby on the way, I tell you he's run off and dealing drugs out of a motel room, and you don't do anything. 'Cause you can't. He broke you, too. He broke you worse than he broke me. Now what am I supposed to do? You want me to feel sorry for you? Well, I don't. I don't feel sorry for you. I hate you. Did you hear me, Cynthia? I hate you."

Cynthia says nothing, moves not at all.

Lily hangs her head. For a time, the two women are silent and motionless. Lily doesn't know what to do next. All Cynthia really had was being a mother. Perhaps the reason she clung so tightly to a romantic notion of motherhood was because without it she had nothing to show for all the years she'd lived.

Lily looks up at the broken woman staring at the wall and sighs. Hating this woman is as useless as punching air. She stands up and walks around the coffee table. She takes Cynthia's hand. The woman looks at her with empty, unseeing eyes.

"C'mon," Lily says, helping her up. Cynthia gets up, like a blankly accommodating somnambulist.

Lily leads her down the hall to her bedroom. After sitting her down on the bed, she removes her shoes and then helps her out her clothes. Cynthia stoops over in her slip as Lily takes down her massive mound of hair, pulling out the bobby pins and placing them in a small pile on the bedside table.

Then Lily tucks her into bed, the older woman's hair splayed like a large net across her pillows.

Cynthia says nothing, does nothing to acknowledge this kindness.

Lily leaves her there, locking the front door of the house on her way out.

Before she gets home, she pulls over to the side of the road.

For a long time, she simply sits. Outside are gently creaking trees, the occasional passing car or truck. She doesn't notice any of it.

She's angry in a way that she never thought possible. She's always been taught to repress anger. She's been taught to give up negative feelings to the Lord Jesus, to offer them up like sacrifices laid upon an altar. That's always been easy for her. She doesn't come from angry people. Her parents do not have a particularly querulous marriage, and they've always tried to keep whatever arguments they have out of sight of their children. Adam is a cauldron of anger, of course, but since she's always defined herself in part as being different from him, it only makes the point in a different way. She's not an angry person.

But now she's miles beyond being angry. She's moved through fury to a deeper state of disillusionment. The abandonment by Peter, by the church, by her own brother, has left her hollowed out. Love and God and family are ashes in her mouth.

She wants to be free of all of it. That's the new state beyond anger. She must do something, must find some way to end this feeling. As soon as this realization is clear to her, she knows what she has to do.

She puts the car in drive. Her family's not home. They're in Searcy looking at prospective new homes, planning for the future.

Lily still has to bury the past.

When she gets home, she goes straight to the kitchen and opens the junk drawer. There, among a random assortment of pens, paperclips, mismatched batteries, and old takeout menus, are a pair of scissors.

She takes the scissors to the bathroom and locks the door. Stripping naked, she stares at herself in the mirror. Then she unpins her hair.

The Apostle Paul wrote to the church in Corinth, *But if a woman has long hair, it is a glory to her; for her hair is given to her as a covering.*

You can talk about Jesus and wear your hair as long as you want, Sister Cynthia had told her, *but you ruined my son's life.*

You know, Lily, Peter told her that first night at the church, *I really like your hair.*

She picks up the scissors.

She pulls her hair around to her chest, and it's so long it curtains her bare round belly and hangs to her hips. It fills her hands as she closes the scissors slowly, feeling the soft crunching slice and then the relief of the first heavy lock dropping away. She never realized how much all this hair weighs until she cut it off. She keeps cutting, going up higher and higher. It feels like she's cutting coils of rope. Hair carpets the bare bathroom floor, thousands of strands of it, two feet long or more, an unholy mess.

When she's cut off all the length, she trims her remaining hair, with no real idea of what she's doing. This is, in the truest sense of the phrase, the first real haircut she's ever had. She clips it close, thinking of the woman in the Eurythmics. The short-haired girl staring back at her in the mirror doesn't exactly look like a rock star, though. She is surprised by the shape of her own head, the broadness of her forehead, the way her ears stick out like small pale buds.

What's most jarring is what she doesn't see in the mirror, though. She doesn't see a Pentecostal. For the first time in her life, she just looks like some girl.

She wishes everyone could see her now. Cynthia, the Drinkwaters, Adam, the kids at school. She'd like to show Allan. But there is one person above all others that she wants to show. One person who needs to see it, to see her, to know that she's something new now. She wants to show Peter.

And, it occurs to her, that for the first time in weeks, she knows where to find him.

CHAPTER 29

Eli sits on Harper's couch listening to the moans down the hall. The moans are Ximena's. She always moans loudly to make the guys come faster. Eli can't hear the guy, which isn't unusual. The guys rarely make much noise.

Eli looks at the time on his cellphone. The guy has two minutes left.

Chance wanders in from the kitchen eating a bowl of Coco Pebbles and plops down on the couch next to Eli.

"This place is a shithole," he says. "Never nothing to eat."

Harper lumbers down the hall.

"That toilet's broke again," she says.

"So fix it," Eli grumbles.

"You know I can't."

He waves her away. "Do I look like a fucking plumber to you? The fuck you need with a second toilet, anyway? This ain't a fucking day spa. You got one that works, use it."

"That one's mine. The rest of them use this one down here."

“Well, share yours or fix this one yourself,” Eli says with a shrug. “You can’t bring no plumber in here, and I ain’t gonna fix it.”

“You’re high,” she says.

“Not high enough.”

Harper turns her attention to Chance. “You too? Getting high and eating all my food. What the fuck am I supposed to feed these bitches if you eat everything in the goddamn house?”

“A bowl of cereal?” he says. “You’re giving me shit over a bowl of cereal?”

“Harper, why don’t you go pull that boy out of Ximena?” Eli says. “While you’re in here counting the cereal boxes, he’s back there going over his time.”

Harper grunts and trudges back up the hall to yell at the customer.

Eli shakes his head. “Always something,” he tells Chance. “With a woman, it is always something.”

Chance dribbles brownish milk down his chin and shirt when he says, “Always something with Harper, that’s for sure.”

“Nah,” Eli says, drawing the word out. “It’s all of them. All they do is take. Always want something more from you. You ever hear Harper do anything but bitch and moan?”

“Nope,” Chance says, tipping back his bowl to drain the last of the milk.

“Or them whores in the back? I give ’em a place to live, keep ’em out of the rain, and all they do is fucking cry.”

Chance stares at his empty bowl as if contemplating another round of Harper’s cereal. “Yeah, I guess so,” he says dully.

Eli glowers at the sound of Harper stomping back down the hall. He tells Chance, “I never met a woman I didn’t wind up hating sooner or later.”

Emerging from the hallway first is Ximena, wearing a dirty oversized white V-neck undershirt and Razorback sweatpants. Her hair hangs to her shoulders in unwashed, knotted strands. She takes the bowl from Chance. "Eating all our cereal again?" she asks.

Chance shrugs. "Hungry," he says with a smile.

Ximena grins as she starts toward the kitchen to get herself some cereal.

She stops when Eli, who has been watching this interaction with a sour look on his face, says, "Chance, go on outside."

"What?"

"I said go outside."

"How come?"

"Go on now. I don't want you hanging around flirting with the girls."

"I wasn't—"

Harper walks in with the client. "Chance," she barks, "you go on outside and smoke a cigarette like you was tolt. Eli's in a mood. You need to leave him be for a while."

Chance climbs to his feet, shaking his head in a silent proclamation of his innocence. With no expression, Ximena watches him go, and then takes the bowl to the kitchen.

The john standing beside Harper is a beer-fat redneck in jeans and a black Taco Bell work shirt. Sweat still beads his upper lip. "Eli Buck," he says after Chance closes the front door. "How you doing, man?"

"Kenny Wayne Custer," Eli says. "Sit your ass on down here, boy."

"He's done," Harper protests. "Time for him to go."

"Oh, shut the fuck up," Eli says. "For once in your life. Go on in the kitchen."

Harper starts to move toward the kitchen as soon as Eli tells her to, but she points at Kenny Wayne. "You don't live here. You can sit and visit for a minute, but then I want you out of here unless you're ready to pay again."

Eli's glower follows her toward the kitchen.

"She's a piece of work," Kenny Wayne offers.

"Piece of something," Eli says. "Women. Like I said, I never met one I liked."

Kenny Wayne's missing his bottom two front teeth, a recent enough loss that he can't help running his tongue over his rough exposed gums every minute or so. "Oh, I don't know," he says. "I met some good ones."

"You only think you did," Eli says. "But you wait and see. A woman's always gonna want you to be less of a man. It's the only move they got. We're bigger, stronger, smarter. That means they got to tear us down before they can be anything at all. It's the only way they can move up, if we fall down."

"I guess."

"You got to keep both eyes on 'em."

"I guess that's right."

"Goddamn right, that's right."

"Like Tisha."

"What?"

"Tisha run off, right?"

"Yeah…" Eli says, turning to stare at Kenny Wayne.

"Heard you been looking for her."

"Heard from who?"

"Who you been talking to? You been asking around town the last couple days. People say you're looking for her, and they say she took some shit that belonged to you."

Eli stares at Kenny Wayne, his mouth slightly open, his breath as strong as exhaust fumes. Finally, he says, "You got something to tell me?"

Kenny Wayne leans back a bit into the cushions, crossing his legs and draping his arm over the arm of the couch.

"Maybe."

"What you want?"

"Just paid for pussy," he observes. "I could use my money back. Maybe a little extra on top of it."

"You tell me what you know," Eli says, "and I'll tell you what it's worth."

Kenny Wayne shrugs. "C'mon, man."

Eli yells to the kitchen. "Harper!"

Sticking her head in the room, she answers, "Yeah?"

"Kenny Wayne fucks for free for a week."

Harper almost falls over. "What?"

Eli turns to him. "You fuck for free for a week—*if* you got something worth hearing."

Walking over to the couch, her arms crossed, Harper's waiting.

Kenny Wayne's about to speak when Eli puts a rough hand on his arm. "Hold on," he says. "Ximena?" he calls to the kitchen.

"Yeah," she calls back.

"Go on back there with Lena and Britt."

"What?"

Harper barks, "Go on back to your room."

The girl wanders through the den carrying a bag of Great Value potato chips. She says nothing to any of them, makes no eye contact with any of them, and walks back down the hall.

Harper sticks her head down the hallway after her to make sure the door is closed. Then she comes back in the den. "Okay," she says to Kenny Wayne. "What is it?"

Kenny Wayne looks back and forth between Eli and Harper. "Okay, y'all know I got my daughter living in Marked Tree?"

"You got a daughter?" Harper asks.

"Yeah. Her momma and me split up a long time ago, but we still get along. I get my girl every other week or so. She's eleven."

"What's this got to do—?"

"Well, so, I take her back to her momma's last Sunday, and on the way back I stop in West Memphis to gas up at the Flying J. And who's there working? Tisha."

"No fucking shit," Eli says.

"Working how?" Harper says. "Like working a register?"

"No, man, selling pussy."

"You talk to her?"

"No."

"Then how you know she's selling pussy?" Eli asks. "You buy some?"

"No. Nothing like that. I gassed up, and I'm paying at the pump, and I seen her walking with some guy to a truck."

"What guy?"

"I don't know, just some dude. Maybe fifty or something. The truck was a work truck for a tree and lawn service. Had ladders and ropes and poles and stuff in the back. So I guess he was just like a regular tree guy, like a gardener or whatever."

"Then what?"

"Then they got in the truck and drove off, and I followed them."

"Where to?"

"They went to the West Memphis Motor Inn. They went straight to her room. Before they even get to the room, a dude opens the door. You know, like he was waiting for them. He goes outside and smokes a couple of cigarettes until they finish inside and then the guy with the truck drove away. I stayed there to see if Tisha'd come back out, but she didn't. Or, anyway, I don't think she did. I got tired of sitting there, and I had to work the next day, so I just drove on home."

"What'd the dude in the motel room look like? Like nineteen or twenty? Brown hair?"

"I guess so. Just a guy. Kinda young, yeah. Brown hair like you said, kinda skinny. Didn't look tough or nothing."

"What's the room number?"

"Fifteen. In the back."

Eli stands up, goes to the front door and opens it. Chance is sitting on the porch steps, smoking a cigarette and staring at his cellphone.

"Chance," Eli says quietly, "run up to my place and grab the machete and the big bolt cutters out my toolshed."

"What?" Chance says, a little slow.

"I said, go grab the machete and the big bolt cutters. We're fixing to leave."

He closes the door. Kenny Wayne stands up, but Eli gestures to him to sit back down. Then he sits close to him, hip to hip, and hangs an arm around his shoulder. "I got one more question for you, Kenny Wayne."

"Okay," Kenny Wayne says, glancing between Eli and Harper's scowling face and trying to smile.

Eli smiles and asks, "You didn't fuck her, right? After you seen that other john leave, you didn't go in there and get some for yourself, did you?"

"No, dude. I told you."

"Reason I ask is, 'cause if you *did*, then she knows you seen her. And she'd figure you'd turn around and tell me."

"I didn't go in, Eli, I swear to God."

Eli asks, "And she didn't see you?"

Kenny Wayne's tongue flicks over his red gums. "I don't think so," he says. "I mean, I ain't no superspy or nothing. But I'm sure she didn't see me at the Flying J. And I don't think she seen me outside the motel. That boy with her, the one who waited outside, he couldn't see me where I was parked. Didn't even look my direction. So, I mean, I don't got no reason to think they seen me, no." Looking back and forth between Eli and Harper, Kenny Wayne says, "I swear to God. I swear on my kid. It was just like I told you. I watched for a while, and then I went on home."

"Okay, then," Eli says, removing his arm from around Kenny Wayne's shoulders and patting his knee. "You're a good man, Charlie Brown." He jerks his head back to the hallway. "You gonna go get your first freebie?"

"No," Kenny Wayne says with a performative yawn. "I should go on home. I'm tuckered out. Ximena done drained me dry."

"Yeah, you go on home. Maybe I'll come by Taco Bell tomorrow. You can hook me up with some free gorditas."

"Yeah," Kenny Wayne says, standing up, happy to be leaving. "Yeah, sure, Eli. I'm working tomorrow, come on by."

As soon as the door shuts behind him, Eli tells Harper, "They didn't even leave Arkansas."

"That fucking little bitch," Harper spits out. "She's trickin' too. What you think of that? That's just rubbing it in our damn faces. The fuck she think she is? She was fine 'til she started talking to that boy at the Corinthian."

"No, that ain't right." Eli says quietly. "That time I caught them together at the hotel, I'm pretty sure that was her idea. I don't think *he* was putting thoughts in *her* head. He's just some dipshit. Always looked like he was on his way to Sunday school. It's her. Of all them girls back there, she was always the one that worried me. She was afraid, but she was never grateful. They gotta be both before you can trust them not to run off."

"I tolt you she had a thick head. I didn't make her run off. She's just a sneaky little bitch."

Eli nods. "If she's working for herself, how long will it be 'til she gets busted? And once she gets busted, how long you think it'll take her to talk about this place?"

"You could get her and bring her back here."

"Is that worth the trouble? Keeping them bitches corralled back there is trouble enough. Anyway, that boy could still talk."

"That's true."

"If we shut him up, we gotta shut her up. And vice versa."

Harper is pondering that when the front door opens, and Chance comes in carrying a large red-and-black bolt cutter and a sheathed machete.

"What's up?" he says.

Eli and Harper look at each other a moment before Harper shrugs.

Eli rises to his feet. "We're going to West Memphis," he says.

Chance drives, blasting some metal band Eli doesn't know.

"Turn that shit off," Eli says. "Can't hear myself think."

Chance shuts it off. Eli doesn't like metal. He doesn't like much music at all, truth be told. Slow songs bore him, and the harder stuff makes him jumpy.

He sits quietly beside Chance, the bolt cutter and machete laid across his lap.

They've been driving for an hour before Chance says, "What are we going to do when we get there?"

"Get my shit back."

"The meth?"

Eli stares out, past the headlights, into the dark. He says nothing.

"She probably done smoked it," Chance says. "Or sold it, maybe."

Eli says nothing to that for a while before he says, "That better not be the case."

Chance just nods and keeps driving. Eli stares at him for a while, though.

"Chance," he says finally. "You ready for what we gotta do tonight?"

"I guess so."

"No, man, you can't *guess so* about this. You got to know. You got to prepare mentally for what's about to go down."

"I ever pussy out on you before? You know I'm hard."

"I ain't talking about whipping some kid's ass in parking lot. I'm talking about being prepared to do whatever it takes. *Whatever* it takes. No matter what I tell you to do, you got to be ready to do it."

Chance blinks at that, swallows. He grips the steering wheel tighter.

"You just tell me what to do, Eli. You know I'll do it."

"Good. Those two stole from us. You know what happens to guys like you and me when motherfuckers think they can steal from us?

Other motherfuckers start getting ideas. And the next thing you know, you got every redneck, nigger, and spic in Little Rock kicking down your door trying to take your shit. Bunch of fucking animals. Animals with guns. So, this here is survival of the fittest. Prison yard rules. You got to make examples of motherfuckers like these two so them others don't get no ideas."

Chance nods at this wisdom. "I know that's right."

"Just follow my lead, and you'll be fine. We're gonna get my shit back, and then I'm gonna set these two straight on what I won't tolerate."

They ride along for a while in silence before Chance brings himself to ask one more question.

"But what if they ain't got our shit no more?"

The sheathed machete softly clanks against the bolt cutter as Eli turns it over. "That's something," he says, "I won't tolerate."

It's dark by the time they get to West Memphis. Chance follows the directions to the West Memphis Motor Inn on his truck's GPS. They can still see the traffic on I-40 in the distance, but the streets in this part of town are a shadowy sprawl of broken lamps, closed-up storefronts, and trash-strewn sidewalks.

"This place is a shithole," Chance says. "It's so dark. I wonder if this GPS is giving us the right directions."

Eli nods his head in disgust. "Fucking swamp. Half of Arkansas ain't nothing but a fucking swamp. Full of rats and snakes."

The first light they see in a while is a dull sign sitting atop a skinny twenty-foot pole announcing the West Memphis Motor Inn. In the corner of the sign is a smaller sign lit up in bright neon red script: Vacancy. The place itself a two-story structure with thirty rooms, fifteen up and fifteen down. There's an office with a single light on, but Eli doesn't see anyone at the front desk. Perhaps they're sitting down or maybe they're in the back. There's a car parked in front of the office, which Eli assumes belongs to the person in the office. On the north side of the motel, there are four trucks and two cars parked in front of rooms.

"Fifteen," Eli says. "Kenny Wayne says it's around back. Cut your lights."

Chance's truck creeps around the back of the motel in darkness. Four more cars and another truck. There's no lamp on this side of the motel. The only illumination in the parking lot comes from the red vacancy sign and a sliver of light escaping the clumsily pulled curtains of one room.

Room 15.

"Park at the other end," Eli says.

When they park, he unsheathes the machete and hands the bolt cutter to Chance. Then he pulls a gun from under his seat. He checks to make sure the safety is off, and then slides the gun between his back and his belt.

He glances at Chance.

The younger man's face is fleshy, sweaty, amped. He's slightly rocking in his seat.

"Just do like I tell you," Eli says.

"Yes, sir," Chance says. It's the first time he's ever used the word *sir* with Eli, and he says it the way a football player would say it to his coach.

Eli nods. "We walk on down there. I'll keep out of sight. You knock on the door. Hang to the left. They won't be able to see you very good from the peep hole or the window. Tell them you're the manager and you need to talk to them."

"But they know me."

"They won't know it's you. Too dark out here. Just try to sound official when you talk. 'Front office, I need to speak with you a moment, sir.' Something like that. They'll crack the door to talk to you, then we clip the chain."

"What if they don't crack the door to talk?"

"Then we kick the fucking door in. All you gotta do is follow my lead, okay?"

"Okay."

"You ready to do whatever it takes?"

Chance rocks in his seat. "*Whatever* it takes, man."

"Whatever it fucking takes?"

"That's right, Eli."

"Goddamn right, that's right. And then, after tonight, after what we give these two, ain't nobody ever gonna fuck with us again."

Chance rocks in his seat, the bolt cutters in his hand. "I'm ready."

Eli clutches the machete. "Let's go."

CHAPTER 30

Lily is doubting the wisdom of this idea as soon as she pulls onto the interstate. Her parents and her brother will be home soon. They'll find the hair. What will they think?

She shakes her head.

They'll know, she reassures herself. They'll understand that she had to do something. They'll be upset. Of course. But she'll deal with that later.

She has to do this. Simple as that. She has to finish this with Peter. She has to tell him what he's done to her, to their son. He can't just leave. He doesn't get to do that.

As she drives, she can't stop from looking at herself in the rearview mirror. With her hair this short, it has an almost reddish tint. The whole shape of her head is different, wider in the front and narrow at the neck.

Everybody's going to think you lost your mind.

Maybe. But I don't care. I spent my whole life caring what everybody else thinks of me. She thinks of Momma and Daddy. Adam. Cynthia. Peter. The Drinkwaters. Fiona and her parents. *Even the kids at school. Maybe even especially the kids at school. I acted like I didn't care what they thought of me. I acted like I was living the Holy Ghost truth to show them the way, to be a witness for Christ. That's what I thought. Stupid.*

She shakes her head again. She'd been taught that she was a walking advertisement for the faith. People look at you, she was told. What do they see? Do they see just another girl, or do they see a Ghost-filled woman?

All they ever saw was some girl with long hair and longer skirts. I didn't win anybody to Jesus with any of that.

Jesus. What about Him? All the rest of it is surprisingly easy to let go of. The opinion of someone like Brenda Drinkwater? That weight falls away as easily as another clump of hair. It's a relief to be free of it.

But the Lord Jesus Christ? Will she ever be able to let go of Him? Does she really want to?

"Are you there?" she says aloud, her voice oddly loud in the empty car. "Be honest with me. Talk to me. You've never said a word to me. I've been praying to you every day since I was five years old. And you've never said a single word back. Say something now. Talk to me. Please. I want to hear you. You talked to Paul on the road to Damascus. Talk to me now," she laughs, "on the road to West Memphis."

The only answer to her pleading is the steady thrum of tires on pavement.

"You never say anything. Why is that? I'd do anything you tell me to do, if you'd just tell me to do it. Don't you realize that? If you would just say one word to me—just one—I'd do anything."

She comes up to a car and passes it on the left. An old man and an old woman.

"If you want me to turn around, tell me now. I'll turn this car around right now and go home and start growing my hair back out."

Tires, pavement. She passes another car, an old junker, driven by a tired-looking middle-aged woman.

Lily takes a deep breath and tells the Lord, "Okay. I mean, if you're not going to talk to me now, I guess you're never going to talk to me. It's okay. Really. Either you're there, and you've got your reasons for your silence…or you're not there."

Both hands on the wheel, her face tight, her eyes focused on the road, she breathes as hard as if she's just run up a flight of stairs.

"Are you not even there?"

For a long time, she just stares at the road in silence.

Her vision blurs as tears pool in her eyes. "I don't want that to be true. I don't. I don't know how I'm going to make it without you. But if I have to, I guess I will." She wipes the tears away. "That's up to you. I don't know if anything could be harder than praying and praying for you to do *something*, begging you to show me some kind of mercy and forgiveness, and always coming up with nothing." She wipes more tears away and clears her throat. "If you want me, you know where to find me."

The sky is darkening above the endless soybean fields that stretch between Little Rock and Memphis. This is the longest drive she's ever been on, the longest she's been alone, truly alone, in her life. No one knows where she is. She isn't even sure if God Himself is still watching over her. Cars and trucks pass by, each one seeming foreign and strange to her. The world, as it silently falls into darkness around her, seems new and odd.

It is when she sees the first exit sign for West Memphis that it occurs to her that she doesn't really know where she's going. The West Memphis Motor Inn. But where is that? She can see other motels just off of I-40, but unless she stumbles across the place by accident soon, she knows she should exit and find someone to ask.

When she spots the Arkansas welcome center on the other side of

I-40, she decides to get off the interstate. She doesn't know how many exits West Memphis has left, and she doesn't want to mess around and get stuck on the bridge crossing the Mississippi River into Tennessee.

She pulls into the first gas station she sees. She's got enough gas, so she parks by a construction truck in the front and goes inside. The place is all fluorescence and plastic.

A gray-haired white man in a dirty khaki work shirt is loitering by the counter, eating a Krispy Kreme cherry pie, and telling the attendant, "You ain't ever heard the Stones? How is that even possible?"

The attendant, a young black man not much older than Lily, replies "Heard *of* them. Everybody's heard *of* them. I just ain't never listened *to* them." He turns to Lily. "Howdy."

"Howdy, do you have a restroom I can use?"

"Other side of the drinks and stuff."

"Thank you."

"You're welcome."

She walks to the back and pees next to a condom dispenser inside the small single toilet restroom. When she walks back out, the attendant is stocking cigarettes in an overhead bin. The gray-haired man is finishing his pie and brushing off his hands on his jeans.

"What about The Beatles?" the gray-haired man is asking. "You must have listened to The Beatles?"

"Man," the attendant says, "do you like anything that ain't fifty years old?"

"Women," the gray-haired man says.

The two of them laugh, and it's only now that they seem to notice Lily waiting politely for their conversation to end.

"Excuse me," she says. "Could you tell me how I get to the West Memphis Motor Inn?"

"Dunno," the attendant says. "Sorry."

Taking a bite of another cherry pie, the gray-haired man points out the window of the station. Chewing with one side of his mouth, he says, "You stay on this road here for a while, then take a right at... oh, I forget the road there. But there's a Burger King. Turn right at the Burger King and keep on that road. It's a ways down there. No sure how far, but you'll see it."

"Okay, thank you."

"No problem. You ain't planning on staying there, are you?"

"What? No. I'm just visiting a friend."

"Well, your friend should have picked somewheres else to stay. That place is kinda rough."

"Oh. Okay. Well, thank you."

As she's walking out the door, the gray-haired man takes another bite of his pie and turns back to the attendant. "What about The Beach Boys?"

When Lily gets to her turn, she has her first serious doubts about what she's doing. What, she has to wonder, *does* she think she's doing?

Despite the doubt, she takes the turn. She needs to show him, needs to tell him, *My dad had to quit his job. We left the church. I cut my hair. Because of you. You did this.*

But that's only part of it. The main thing is that she needs to see him with her own eyes. She needs to discover the truth for herself.

She pictures the scene: her pulling in, getting out, knocking on the motel door. Will Tisha answer? Will she be dressed like those girls at Harper's house? In t-shirt and sweats, slightly zoned out, slightly bored looking.

Will she recognize Peter? Will he look the same as he always has, like a boy who can't believe what he's gotten himself into? Or will she finally see his true face, the one that he's kept hidden from her all this time?

The streets grow dark. Boarded-up storefronts. Rivers of trash in the gutters.

She's smart enough to be scared, but she couldn't turn around now even if she wanted to. She knows that no matter what happens at the motel, she will have to look back on this night. One day, the child in her belly will be a grown man, and that man will ask her what happened to his father.

I can't tell my son the truth unless I know what the truth is.

Immediately upon having this thought, she sees, down the road peering out from the dark, the dim sign of the West Memphis Motor Inn.

CHAPTER 31

Ten minutes before Lily Stevens turns into the parking lot of the motel, Ed Greb gets another complaint of sounds coming from room 15.

Greb is fifty-nine years old, too old to be doing this goddamn job. He's been working the front desk at the West Memphis Motor Inn for a year and half. He started working here on the condition that he only had to work days. The manager, a peckerhead young enough to be his son, told Greb that wouldn't be a problem.

Turned out the kid was a damn liar. Greb got stuck on nights about two months into the job. He wants to quit, to tell the manager to go to hell, but where would that get him? He has his daughter and granddaughter living with him, along with the occasional boyfriend the daughter drags home. Greb's the only one in the house working steady. His income, plus a little bit of insurance he collected when his wife Gloria passed away, is the only thing keeping them all alive. So he's stuck on nights.

Working in this part of town, it didn't take him long to buy a gun. One of his daughter's boyfriends, during his brief stay at their house, hooked him up with it. He was a gun guy, NRA membership and all.

Greb, who hasn't shot a gun since he was a boy, told him, "Don't get me no damn cannon. I ain't trying to kill a moose. And I don't want nothing hot."

"I got just the thing," the boyfriend told him. "Smith and Wesson Shield. It's pretty small, just an eight-round magazine, and it's got a recoil soft enough for a little girl. That's what you're looking for, Hoss. I can get it for you cheap, too. Maybe two fifty."

So now Greb keeps the gun loaded and ready in the side pocket of the coat he always drapes over the back of his chair, even in the summer heat.

When he gets the third call about the sounds from room 15, he moves the gun up to an open drawer on his desk.

He picks up the phone and calls 15.

Busy.

Damn it.

He takes a deep breath.

The front desk phone rings again. Room 13.

"I'm telling you," the woman on the phone says, "there's some weird shit going on in that room."

"I tried calling them, but the phone is busy."

"Well, some of us got to sleep. If I gotta go over there and bang on the door and get into some shit with them people, that's gonna be on you. You the desk man, ain't you? You the one supposed to do something about it."

"Yeah, yeah, yeah," Greb says, hanging up.

Room 15. Boy and girl, both white, both barely out of their teens. They've been there a little over a week. Greb's seen plenty of guys going back to the room with the girl in that time, so he figures she's a hooker. He's supposed to do something about that and run off her and the boy, but he keeps delaying it, hoping they'll just leave so he can avoid the confrontation. Besides, she isn't the only one doing it here. Most of the time, it doesn't matter because the guests tend to be transients. They only stay a few days, and if Greb suspects that some of them might be turning a few tricks to raise the cash to move on, what can he do about it? Nobody stays here who isn't flat broke or basically homeless, and it isn't really worth the hassle to call the cops on the kinds of people who are going to be gone in the morning anyway. But Greb *is* supposed to keep an eye on anybody who stays more than a few days to make sure they aren't squatting and turning the motel into their own one-room bordello.

And now he's had three complaints in the last hour about room 15.

What if the boy in there is beating the hell out of that girl?

Greb sighs.

Goddamn it. He can't abide a woman beater. Man that beats a woman is the lowest kind of man. Except for maybe the kind of man that sits in an office doing nothing to stop it.

Greb gets up, checks the gun to make sure the safety is off, and moves the weapon to his right pocket. He can get at it easy.

He'll make the boy leave. If the girl suddenly turns on him and starts defending the boy—which happens about as often as it doesn't—he'll throw both their asses out and threaten to get the cops.

He locks the office door and steps outside. It's a hazy night, with the moon buried under gray clouds.

As he rounds the southside of the motel, his boots clicking against the concrete and his shadow stretching before him in the red glow of the vacancy sign, he hears a car pull into the front parking lot. He's heading back to see who it is, when a doorknob turns behind him. Of the five occupied rooms on this side of the motel all the lights are on, except for the one at the end. There, in the shadows, the door opens to room 15.

As it does, the car rounds the other side of the parking lot, casting two bright lights on the man stumbling out of the doorway haggard, bloody, and carrying a machete.

CHAPTER 32

Lily screams when she sees Eli Buck standing there, squinting against her headlights, blood dripping from his face. She slams on the breaks and the car jerks to a halt. Eli is flustered, dazed by the car lights blasting him in the face and jarred by the sudden appearance of a scared-looking man at the other end of the walkway, near the red Ford. Eli takes a step back toward the door, but then either thinks better of it or bumps into someone else coming out of the room. He staggers back outside, lifts the machete, and runs toward the scared man.

Maybe Eli just wants to frighten off the man so he can get to the truck.

But the man pulls a gun from his pocket and starts shooting. The gun goes off like a string of firecrackers. Chance, stepping out of the room, ducks back inside. When Eli keeps coming at him, the scared man runs the other way, back toward the office. The man disappears, but then Eli stumbles and falls. He drops his machete, and it clatters into the parking lot. Chance peeks out of the room, then runs up to

Eli, yelling and trying to pull him up, but when Eli won't move, Chance runs to his truck and jumps inside. He pulls out of the parking space so quickly and erratically, he scrapes the side of the motel. The metallic scream of the truck against the wall is louder than any of the yelling or shooting. The truck vanishes into the dark and after a moment, as the sound of his escape fades down the road, the parking lot is silent again.

Lily tries to get out of her car, but it lunges forward. It's still in drive. She realizes she's had the brake smashed to the floor this whole time.

She puts the car in park, shuts it off, and gets out.

Eli lies sprawled in the light between motel rooms. He isn't moving. His back isn't even rising against his shirt.

Lily walks toward room 15. The door is still open.

She steps inside. The weak light of the vacancy sign fills the room with a grayish-red glow. From the cracked bathroom door, a crooked beam of orange light falls across emptied suitcases and clothes scattered on an unmade bed. Staring at the bathroom, she tries to call out to Peter, but she can't. It's all she can do to breathe. Her misshapen shadow stretches out before her, reaching the bathroom door as she's lifting her weakened hand.

She pushes the door open.

On the floor, a bloody shower curtain. Splattered ceiling and walls. In the bathtub, one piled atop the other, two decapitated bodies. And in the bowl of the toilet, two heads, one turned to her, his eyes still open.

CHAPTER 33

Inspector Gil Kliner and Lt. Sandra Sortland stand at the edge of the illuminated parking lot of the West Memphis Motor Inn.

Kliner nods at the girl in the back of Sortland's car. "What's her name?"

"Lily Stevens."

"Looks young."

"Eighteen, according to her driver's license."

"What's her connection to this mess in the motel room?"

"Says she was here to see one of the victims. Ex-boyfriend. You can't tell from this angle but she's pregnant. Five months, she says."

"Lovely."

"The baby daddy ran off with a hooker. They crashed here." Sortland turns and points to the body still lying in front of the motel rooms. "According to Lily Stevens, this charmer over here is Eli Buck, pimp of the girl in the bathtub."

Kliner jots down the names in a short, fat spiral notebook. "Go on."

Sortland says, "According to her, the second suspect who drove off was a guy named Chance Berryman."

"That fits. State police have Berryman in custody."

"Really?"

"They found him on the shoulder on I-40. When the trooper gets up to the truck, Berryman's passed out and bleeding all over the place. Shot in the right shoulder. Looks shattered they said. He's awake now, and he won't say shit about how he got shot, but his truck's GPS still had the motel's address entered in, so they called me."

"Unless there were shots fired in the room, which doesn't seem to be the case, the shooter is probably our hero desk clerk, Ed Greb."

"Nobody that works at this shithole is a hero."

"At any rate, Greb says he was responding to noise complaints from the other guests. He was carrying a Smith & Wesson Shield."

"Nice."

Pointing, she says, "He's rounding the corner there when Buck comes out with a machete and, according to Greb and Lily Stevens both, Buck starts charging Greb. Greb unloads the gun on him. Berryman was coming out of the room a few paces behind Buck."

"Shield's got a nine-round capacity. We know where all the bullets went yet?"

"Well, we'll see what Ropes says when he's done with the body, but near as I can eyeball it, Buck got one through the throat—in and out—and two in the left shoulder."

"Berryman was behind Buck to his left, which explains how he caught one in his right shoulder..." Kliner says, tapping his own shoulder.

"Yeah. That sounds right. According to Greb, he had a full magazine and one in the pipe. So it looks like four bullets are in the suspects and," she gestures to the darkness beyond the lights, "five out in the trees somewhere. Greb was also carrying a Ruger in his jeans, but it doesn't look like he touched it. I think he thought he was just going to scare away the old guy with the machete and didn't expect him to pull a gun and start shooting."

Kliner walks toward the motel room. Above them, residents of the motel are standing out on the balcony watching the proceedings. Kliner barks up at them, "Y'all go to bed."

No one moves very far.

"Pretty sure it was one of them called the press," Sortland tells him. "Channel 11 got here first. After that, the rest of the stations came as quick as they could, like a swarm of mosquitoes. The guy from the *Democrat-Gazette* is here too. All of them are already asking about the beheading. It's all they want to talk about."

"Oh, for god's sake. How do they already know about that?"

Sortland shrugs. "When the girl found the bodies, she ran out screaming. Everybody came outside, and she told them what she'd found. Guess some of them told the reporters once they showed up."

"Great," he grumbles. "Well, keep those cameras up there in the front. Don't let them back here."

"Of course."

They step into the room. Sortland gestures at the clothes on the floor and a knocked over chair. A large red-and-black bolt cutter.

"Signs of struggle in here," she says, "but not much blood except for some on the side of the bolt cutters there, like they were used as a blunt force weapon. Maybe to hit the boy when they first came in? Appears the killing was done in the bathroom."

"Looks like they were looking for something."

"Yeah. Some paraphernalia laying around, but no signs of drugs or money yet."

"Need to check Berryman's truck, see if they scored any before the killing went down."

"Okay."

Kliner walks over to the bathroom, takes a breath, and goes inside.

Sortland stays behind in the room, saying nothing, watching the crime scene investigator dusting the bedside table for prints.

When Kliner comes out of the bathroom, he says, "Beheaded them one at a time using the edge of the tub. Tub's hacked up like a chopping block."

"Did they kill them first, you think?"

"I don't know yet, but I think the boy was the first one they beheaded."

"Not the girl? Her head's on the bottom in the commode."

"Yeah, but his body's on bottom in the tub. Maybe they didn't throw the heads in the commode until they were both dead. Plus, the girl's face has an excessive amount of bruising."

"What do you make of that?"

"Well, it would indicate to me that the girl was the main target, and the boy was just here. So my guess is that they killed the boy and beheaded him and made her watch. Maybe as punishment, or maybe to scare her into telling them where she had the drugs or cash hidden. That's my hypothesis, anyway. We'll know more when we talk to Berryman and get the autopsy."

Sortland makes a note about the bruising on the female victim's face.

"We pull the prints off the bodies yet?" Kliner asks.

"Yeah," Sortland says.

"If the girl is a prostitute, she might have prints on file somewhere. We'll see about the boy. What's the girl outside…?" he reaches for her name.

"Lily Stevens."

"Right." He jerks a thumb toward the bathroom. "What's she say this boy's name is?"

"Well, that's the thing," Sortland says, gesturing Kliner toward a table in the corner of the room. On it are two open wallets. One is pink nylon, the other is brown leather. "Got two wallets in the room. The pink one belongs to the girl. Got an expired Louisiana learner's permit from 2015 that identifies her as Tisha McCready, which fits what Lily Stevens told us. She didn't know her last name, but said her first name was Tisha. The man's wallet has a current Arkansas driver's license for a Ryan Vila. But the girl outside said his name is Peter Cutchin."

"So it's a fake ID?"

"Or this ain't her boyfriend in there with his head missing."

"You show her the ID?"

"Yeah, she doesn't think it's him in the picture. Now, she's pretty upset, and sometimes it's hard to tell from a driver's license, but my guess is that the guy with his head in the toilet ain't her baby daddy."

Kliner twists his mouth. "We've extricated the heads from the commode. Got them on a tarp. We could have her see if she could ID them."

"C'mon, Gil. She's eighteen, pregnant, and already in shock."

He shrugs. "Right. 'Course." He asks, "You have the EMTs look at her yet?"

"Yeah. They said she's okay."

"Well, see if they'll take her in for an OB/GYN consultation, anyway. All we need is our eyewitness having complications with her pregnancy because of this horrific shit."

"Okay."

"She got a family?"

"Yeah, I had Cooke call them."

"Okay," Kliner says. "You got her statement. Get anything else you need from her, make sure she gets a clean bill of health, then let her go home. She's had a rough night."

CHAPTER 34

When the call comes in the middle of the night to tell them that Lily has been found at the scene of a violent crime, no one in the Stevens home is asleep. Peggy, terrified since she came home and discovered her daughter's hair discarded on the bathroom floor, is quietly crying on the living room sofa while her son, his arm around her shoulders, tries to comfort her. They can both hear David pacing in the kitchen. He's already called the Starks and talked to Fiona, who hasn't spoken to Lily since their fight at school. He's called Sister Cynthia's house three times, thinking that perhaps there is some news about Peter that caused Lily to act out, but he's gotten no answer each time. He even tried reaching Allan Woodson at the Corinthian, only to find out that he doesn't work there anymore.

When the phone rings, Peggy jumps up. As David answers the phone, she hurries to the kitchen doorway and stares at him.

"Hello," he says. "Yes, it is... Yes, I'm her father. Is she okay?" He listens, sighs, and puts a hand on the counter. He looks up and tells

Peggy, "She's alright. She's okay."

Peggy's head swims, and she has to steady herself against the doorway until David's done talking on the phone. When he finally lays the phone down, he tells her, "It was the police. She's in West Memphis. She was at some…motel, and apparently there was a shooting."

Peggy puts her hand on her mouth. "A shooting… But you're sure she's okay?"

"Yes."

"You didn't talk to her. If she's okay, why didn't you talk to her?"

"She's okay, dear," he says, trying to sound confident. "Completely unharmed, they said. Just shaken up. She didn't want to come to the phone." He rubs his face. "I think it has something to do with Peter."

"Peter was there, at this motel?"

"I'm not sure. I think they're still figuring it out, but she was there looking for him. We need to go get her. We need to get a ride down there because we'll have to drive your car back from the station."

"Can I come?" Adam asks, standing behind his mother.

"No," she tells him. "You need to go to bed."

"How am I supposed to sleep?"

Peggy pats his arm, but she doesn't answer him as she returns to the living room to put on her shoes and coat.

David clasps Adam's shoulder. "You stay here. We'll be back in a few hours. Don't call anyone, but answer if it rings because it might be us, or it might be the police again with more information."

"Who are you gonna call for a ride to the police station at this time of night?"

David unlocks his phone. "Aztec."

One of the more unconventional members of their former church, James Tinson is known to one and all as Aztec Jim, a name he picked up in prison in the 1990s while serving seven years for second-degree manslaughter. Aztec had been a biker and a brawler back in those days, blazing a path of hellraising that ended when he accidentally killed a man in a bar fight. He's never eager to discuss the particulars of that fateful encounter, but he's always quick to point out that it led directly to him finding the Lord Jesus Christ in prison.

When Aztec Jim found Jesus, he also found a post-incarceration career in prison ministry. Now he lives most of the year on the road, sleeping in the back of his van and preaching the gospel to the imprisoned in Arkansas, Tennessee, Mississippi, and Louisiana. With his thick beard, bald head, and tattooed arms, Aztec Jim doesn't look like a normal Pentecostal, but while his appearance and makeshift prison theology don't conform to church dogma in every respect, he does preach the name of Jesus and the redemption of the Holy Ghost to society's castoffs, so the members of Conway Redemption Tabernacle embrace him like something of an eccentric cousin. Because he's so often on the road, he was away when Brother David resigned from his ministry, though he certainly would have voted to allow the preacher and his family to stay. If Aztec Jim believes in anything, it's second chances. Maybe because of this, he is the only one the Stevens think to call.

He picks them up in his beloved van thirty minutes later. It's a white Chevy, spotted with acne-red rust. There's a bed in the back with a shelf of books for a headboard, a hotplate stacked on a little cooler, a box of tools, a spare tire, a sack of clean clothes to be worn, and a sack of dirty clothes to be washed.

Aztec has met enough distraught parents that he knows to be quiet. After effusively thanking him when he picks them up, David and Peggy settle into worried silence. Not only do they not speak to him, they don't speak to each other, each of them trying to hold on to their nerves. Peggy sits on the bench seat between Aztec's bed and the front of the van. Aztec hunches close to the wheel, almost lying on top of it, steering with both hands and forearms. David sits across from Aztec, staring out the window.

For a long stretch of the trip, David closes his eyes. He's not sleeping, just silently praying, asking God for help, unsure if it will come, unaware that his daughter prayed much the same prayer on this very road just a few hours ago.

When they get to the station, Peggy opens the door and climbs out. At this hour, the parking lot is mostly empty, and the station looks half asleep.

David asks Aztec Jim, "Could you stick around a couple of minutes? Just until we know there's no problem getting the car?"

"Of course, Brother. I'll be here."

David thanks him and gets out of the van. He takes Peggy's arm, and together they walk into the lonely-looking police station to retrieve their daughter.

Peggy sees Lily waiting on a bench before Lily sees her. The girl's beautiful long hair, the glory of Pentecostal womanhood, has been shorn off, most of it abandoned on their bathroom floor. What remains is a raggedy chaos. The girl's shoulders are low, her face wan, her arms wrapped protectively around her belly. When Lily looks up and sees her mother, Peggy begins crying. Lily does not. They embrace, but Lily's face stays blank, her skin taut against her skull, as if she's waiting for something else to happen.

While David talks to the police, Peggy and Lily go outside to their car. When David comes out of the station, he walks over to the van first to talk to Aztec Jim.

"There's no problem with the car," he tells him. "I can't thank you enough, Aztec. Driving us all the way here in the middle of the night… Thank you."

"Glad I could help, Brother. Not my first time being at a police station in the middle of the night. Heck, to tell you the truth, it's not my first time being at *this* police station in the middle of the night."

David manages a polite grin at that. "Well, I really appreciate it."

The door creaks as Aztec gets out of the van to give David a mighty hug. "I'll be praying for you all," he promises. "Especially for Lily and that baby."

David thanks him and slaps him on the back. He gives him a final wave as Aztec Jim Tinson drives off into the night, then he braces himself for the long ride home.

Peggy stays in the backseat with Lily. They're both quiet, though after a while, the girl lays her head on her mother's lap and goes to sleep. A couple of hours later, they're still driving when a large diesel blows past them, shaking the car so much it jostles Lily awake. With her head still on her mother's lap, she opens her eyes just enough to see Peggy's hand resting on her shoulder and the back of her father's head over the seat.

"I'll call tomorrow," Peggy is saying quietly, "and see if we can get her in to see Dr. Eljerary."

"Think she'll be up to going anywhere that soon?" David replies softly.

"She needs to be looked at by her own doctor, honey, not just some EMT."

"I know. But she just witnessed a man getting shot. And Peter..."

"We don't know that was him at the motel."

"Well, if it is or if it isn't him, what she saw back there is enough to traumatize anybody."

"That's all the more reason for her to go see her own doctor as soon as possible, to make sure she's alright."

Lily stirs, rising slowly from her mother's lap. "They don't know if it's Peter?" she asks, still blinking the sleep out of her eyes.

Peggy stares at her. "Lily..."

"They don't know if it's him?"

Adjusting the rearview mirror so he can look at his daughter, David says, "They're not sure yet, honey. But they told us they had their doubts."

Lily nods and turns her face to the window, but she doesn't really look outside. "They showed me a driver's license that had some other boy's name and address on it," she says. "The picture looks a little like him if you're not really looking. But it isn't him in the picture."

"Hopefully, that means it wasn't him at the motel," David says.

"I'm sure that's what it means," Peggy reassures her daughter.

Lily gazes blankly at her dim reflection in the window, as if she were drugged. Her father returns his attention to the road and the sunlight just breaking over the trees.

Her mother asks, "Are you okay?"

"No," Lily says.

"Want to lay down again?"

Lily says, "I feel…numb? Like when the dentist gives you a shot? At this very moment, I don't feel anything actually."

Peggy reaches over and takes her daughter's limp hand, but Lily makes no effort to return the gesture of affection.

"It's okay," Peggy tells her.

Lily says nothing to that. Her father drives. Her mother holds her hand.

After a few minutes, Lily says, "It's not Peter."

Her parents exchange a concerned look, and Peggy tells her, "We'll see, dear. Right now, you just relax your mind and try to rest. We'll get you in bed soon. We're almost home."

Lily looks out the car window and watches the murky waters of Lake Conway, still black under the weak light of dawn, passing by.

She stares at them a moment.

"It's not Peter," she says again.

CHAPTER 35

It doesn't take Chance Berryman long to realize that his only hope of avoiding a charge of double homicide is to turn on his former associates. Seeking a plea deal for a lesser charge of aggravated assault, he presents himself as little more than a driver and a gofer in a larger criminal enterprise. Placing most of the blame on Eli Buck is simple enough. While Berryman, twenty-one, has been arrested a few times for public intoxication and misdemeanor assault, his record is relatively clean compared to Buck's litany of charges and convictions. In his twenties, Elijah Jerome Buck served eight years in Tucker, Arkansas's maximum security unit, for manslaughter. A few years after getting out of Tucker, he was arrested again for possession of a narcotic with the intent to sell and contributing to the delinquency of a minor. From 2001 to 2005, he was back in Tucker, this time for the near-fatal beating of a young woman police believed to be a sex worker in his employ. With this history of violence and mayhem, it is easy to accept that Eli Buck was primarily responsible for what happened to the occupants of room 15.

The victims are quickly established to be Tisha McCready, nineteen, and Ryan Vila, twenty. Investigators learn that McCready was originally from Louisiana. She ran away from an alcoholic mother and abusive stepfather when she was fifteen. She started doing sex work within a few months of leaving home, eventually falling under the control of a man named Demarko in Shreveport. Demarko sold McCready to Eli Buck in 2016. Since then, McCready lived and worked at a house on Dodson Court, just off Baseline Road in Little Rock. Ryan Vila, originally from Pine Bluff, worked at the Walmart Supercenter on Baseline Road. Police believe that McCready and Vila met at the Walmart and began to see each other secretly in the weeks before her abrupt departure from the house on Dodson. Text messages taken from Vila's phone indicate that McCready had indeed stolen an unknown quantity of crystal meth belonging to Eli Buck when she fled the house. Police believe the primary motive behind the murders to be one of revenge, with an added goal of recovering some of the missing drugs. No drugs, however, were recovered at the crime scene.

Since Eli Buck is dead, Berryman's defense shifts as much responsibility as possible onto the proprietress of the Dodson Court brothel, Evelyn Harper, forty-nine, claiming that because she and Buck were equal partners, both functioning as his employers, she'd essentially ordered him to accompany Buck to the West Memphis Motor Inn. With Berryman talking and both the police and press investigating, more details about the pair begin to emerge. Harper first met Eli Buck in the winter of 2005, after his release from prison. Harper had been convicted of prostitution twice before, in 1993 and 1998, and had been arrested for, though never convicted of, procurement in 2002. With Buck, she found a protector and business partner. Chance Berryman met Buck and Harper as a repeat customer of their girls. At that time, the girls were still soliciting johns at different car washes and gas stations on Baseline, a sloppy and potentially dangerous way to do business. After one too many of their girls had been arrested, Berryman would tell police, Buck and Harper decided they needed a more controlled space. Harper rented the house on Dodson Court, and business began in earnest.

Within days, these revelations lead to an expansion of the story in the media. The grisly double homicide in West Memphis now leads to a house of prostitution in Little Rock, which, in turn, has ties to a sex trafficking ring in Shreveport, Louisiana. The involvement of one witness in particular, Lily Stevens, eighteen, of Conway, expands the story further, to a hotel in Conway, the Corinthian Inn, and its owner, Harold Baker, sixty-four. Stevens says she was looking for her ex-boyfriend, a former employee of the Corinthian who had gotten her pregnant and left town. She'd been informed by two other former employees that she would find her ex-boyfriend at the West Memphis Motor Inn. She'd also been told that Buck and Harper had been using Baker's hotel in Conway as a base of operations for Central Arkansas.

The cause of death for the victims in the Motor Inn murders is ruled to be exsanguination because both victims apparently bled to death before they could be fully decapitated. Eli Buck, in turn, died of a gunshot wound to the neck, which entered his throat and exited through his third and fourth cervical vertebrae.

These details, among others, dominate the news statewide for weeks. For a few days, the case even goes national. CNN leads the pack with a report called "Death and Decapitation in Arkansas." A stringer for the *New York Times* writes a story entitled "Beheadings in West Memphis Motel Room." Fox News runs a chyron that reads: TWO HEADS IN A TOILET. Several true crime podcasts devote segments to the murders, and the case makes its way into the monologue of one late night host who jokes, "It's a horrible case, but, man oh man, just imagine being the plumber who has to unstop that toilet! 'Ew boy, I don't think Drain-o's gonna work on this one!'"

After a few days of this fevered attention in the national press and media, however, the case is forgotten just as quickly, pushed aside in favor of the intensifying impeachment drama in Washington, the controversy surrounding the release of the movie *Joker*, and the ongoing investigation into the suspicious suicide of billionaire sex trafficker Jeffery Epstein. The national press has bigger, flashier stories to follow, and so the sordid tale of low-rent sex slavery and murder in Arkansas soon recedes from view.

In the statewide press, the story stays hot for a little longer, and for a time the sight of Berryman and Harper being transferred into or out of courtrooms in their prison scrubs and handcuffs becomes a regular television news fixture. Once they are caught in the dry procedural machinations of the legal system, however, their separate cases begin to slow down as news stories, hobbled by a lack of new revelations. No charges have been pressed yet against Baker, and though an official from the Arkansas Department of Health announces that the health officer for Faulkner County will be conducting a thorough review of the Corinthian Inn's business practices, as the weeks go by, the Arkansas press moves on, following other breaking stories. A man in Little Rock murders his fiancée and then leads police on a manhunt across the state for days. A hunter in Yellville is gored to death by a deer he was trying to kill, a macabre twist of karma so explicit it becomes a minor national news story for a day. And, week after week, the Razorbacks play so horribly that one newspaper commentator tells his shaken readers, "Arkansas football fans were put on this earth to suffer."

And so it is that the murders at the West Memphis Motor Inn, though initially a shocking story that makes headlines, becomes just another news item in the unceasing current of scandal, atrocity, and titillation roaring through the media pipeline, the equivalent of a single Styrofoam cup bobbing up from the sewer before being sucked back down again and swept out of sight.

CHAPTER 36

Special Agent Diane Herrera of the FBI's Little Rock Field Office is the most impressive woman Lily has ever met. Fifty years old, with straight, shoulder-length black hair, she smiles easily, but she never breaks eye contact. Greeting Lily and Peggy in the brightly lit foyer of the FBI's offices, she strides up and gives each woman a friendly handshake. Lily notes, however, that Herrera is also wearing a gun clipped to her belt.

"Peggy, Lily," the FBI agent says, "thanks for coming to see me today." She gestures for them both to follow her down a long corridor. "We're going this way."

She shows them back to her office, which faces the building's green front lawn. Beyond the lawn, traffic drifts by on West Shackleford Boulevard. Herrera gestures at a couple of seats across from her desk.

"Please, sit down. Make yourselves comfortable."

Their first interview was at the Stevens' house, the FBI agent sitting with Lily and her parents at their kitchen table, writing down what the girl had to say about Eli and Harper. Now, Lily's fascinated to see Herrera's office, although it's not so different from any other office she's ever been in. Clean, neat, orderly. There's a family portrait on the wall, Special Agent Herrera with a handsome man and two handsome sons. Next to it are a couple of photos of Herrera with official-looking people at official-looking functions. Lily glances at all of them as she negotiates her way back into the chair.

"Is that chair okay, Lily?" Herrera asks. "We could get you another..."

"No, thank you. It's fine."

Lily's now eight months pregnant. Protruding against her sleeveless fuchsia maternity shirt and soft cotton pants, her belly is the exact shape of a large watermelon. The weight of the baby puts pressure on her left hip, so under her clothes, she's wearing a black belly band to help offset some of the pain. Once she's settled into the chair, she breathes deeply.

"Okay," she says, running her hands through her auburn hair. Her mother has trimmed it down so it will eventually grow back evenly, but Lily loves the way the short hair bristles between her fingers.

Peggy says, "Lily's father is sorry he couldn't be here. He just started a new job at UPS, and he couldn't get off from work today."

"That's okay," Herrera assures her. "This won't take long." She glances down at the notes she scribbled at their previous meeting. "Lily, I just have a few follow-up questions about what you saw when you went to the house on Dodson Court on September nineteenth."

"Okay."

"When you got there, you said you saw a girl on the porch. A blonde girl smoking a cigarette."

"Yes."

Herrera slides over a form with a mugshot of Britt on it.

"Is this the girl?"

"Yes, that's her."

"And when you went inside, can you tell me exactly *who* you saw?"

"Well, I saw Harper. I saw this blonde girl. And there were two other girls on the couch. Mexican girls, I think."

Herrera slides over two more pictures. Ximena and Lena.

"I think that's them," Lily says. "I only saw them a second." She points at the picture of Lena. "I think this girl was missing a finger."

Herrera nods. "That's Lena. She's missing the little finger on her left hand. Besides these three girls you've mentioned, did you see anyone else?"

"Well, Harper, of course. Eli and Chance showed up a little later. Eli and Harper were mad that I was there. Like I told you, they were all being threatening. That's when Allan showed up."

"And while you were at the house, did you see anyone else? Either inside the house or outside?"

"No, ma'am," Lily says. She catches herself. "Well, actually, I saw two men coming out of the house when I got there."

"Coming from where?"

"Out the front door."

"Can you describe these men?"

"Mm. Not really. I didn't really get a good look at them. I think they were customers."

"If you didn't get a good look at them, what makes you think they were customers?"

"I don't know...the way they were leaving? Like they were in a hurry. Like they'd done their thing, and they were in a hurry to leave."

Peggy Stevens, staring at her daughter while she describes this scene, shakes her head in quiet horror.

Herrera asks, "Did you see these men exchange money with anyone?"

"No. They just walked outside and got in their truck and left."

"What kind of truck did they get into?"

"A big orange pickup. It looked new. It was shiny. I'm not sure what kind it was."

"A big orange pickup," Herrera says, writing it down. "I don't guess you got a look at the license plate?"

"No, I barely looked at them or the truck. I only saw them for a second before they drove away."

"Try to describe the men for me," Herrera says. "White? Black? Latino? Young? Old?"

"They were white. They were young. Like, in their twenties, early twenties, I guess. They had on jeans and t-shirts. They both had on ballcaps. Just kind of average-looking guys. They walked outside, got in the truck, and left. I saw them for maybe thirty seconds." She watches Herrera jotting this down in her notes and asks, "Is that important?"

Still writing, the FBI agent says, "You never know what's important or what's not. You collect all the information you can, then you shift through it later and try to figure out what's important." She nods and looks up from her notes. "Okay. Other than these two guys who you think were customers, did you see anyone else there? Anyone else who might have lived there or worked there?"

"No."

"Did you see any other vehicle at the house?"

"No."

"Do you recall Eli or Chance or Harper mentioning anyone else? Or mentioning any other vehicle?"

Lily ponders that a moment. "I don't think so."

Peggy asks the FBI agent, "Are you going to ask about what happened at the motel?"

Herrera says, "Well, to tell the truth, Peggy, the incident at the motel is someone else's jurisdiction, someone else's case. What the FBI is looking into is the trafficking of these girls, and potentially others, that Lily saw when she was inside that house. We're trying to find out as much as we can about the operation, including how the girls were transported. Usually, there are three distinct phases of sex trafficking: acquisition, transportation, and exploitation. The person who acquires the victim hands them off to the transporter, who then sells them to the exploiter. This process usually results in the accumulation of a debt that the victim is then told she has to work off, which seems to be the case here, but what's different is that Eli seems to be handling both transportation and, with Harper, exploitation. What I'm doing right now is seeing if Lily can corroborate certain pieces of information we've got about who lived and worked at the house on Dodson Court around the time that she was there."

Lily says, "Allan told me the girls were brought up in a moving truck."

Herrera flips back a few pages in her notes. "He told me that, too, which supports what the girls themselves told me. We're still trying to find the truck, though. Chance has his Raptor, and Harper has a car, an old Taurus, but Eli doesn't seem to have had his name on any vehicle in over twenty years. And none of them have their name on any rental agreements that we can find. So this moving truck is a bit of a mystery."

"You've talked to Allan Woodson?" Peggy asks.

"Yes. He called in the original tip, ironically at about the same time Eli was getting himself shot to death in West Memphis. He's coming in for a follow-up interview, similar to you, as a matter of fact." She turns back to Lily. "But, just to clarify, you never saw a moving truck at the house? Or van? Or anything like that?"

"No."

"And in terms of the girls you saw there: you saw the girl smoking a cigarette on the porch, and you saw the two girls sitting on a couch watching television. Correct?"

"Yes, ma'am."

"Okay." Herrea writes something down. "Is there anything else you think I ought to know?"

"Like what?"

"Anything. Big or little. Never know what might help."

"I can't think of anything. Not right now, anyway."

"Okay. You have my number, so you can call me or text me if you think of anything else. You also have my email."

"Okay. May I ask a question now?"

"Of course."

"Are you looking for Peter?"

Special Agent Herrera glances at Peggy before she answers Lily, already aware of the family sensitivity to the issue of the missing father of the child. "We would like to talk to Peter, sure. Since we know from you and Allan that he had some kind of contact with Tisha McCready at the Corinthian, we would definitely like to question him. But, I will be honest with you, locating him is not a primary concern for us at present. We're more focused on the logistics of how the girls were procured and transported across state lines. I'm not sure he can help us with that."

Lily shakes her head. "I can't believe no one's going to look for him."

Her mother reaches over and pats her hand. "This isn't the place, Lily."

Lily laughs. "If the FBI isn't the place, where is the place?"

Herrera closes her notebook and sits up straighter in her chair. More coolly than before, she says, "I sympathize with your frustration, Lily. My understanding is that the state police are looking for Peter right now."

"I get the same run around from them that I've gotten from everybody else," Lily replies. "Everybody's got a bigger case to work on. You're investigating sex traffickers, the state police are investigating the Conway Police, and the Conway Police say that unless Peter's in Conway, there's nothing they can do. Everyone says, 'We'll let you know if we hear anything,' but no one is actually out there looking for him."

Special Agent Herrera says, "I'm sorry to hear that, Lily, but I can only work on the things that are in my power and purview to work on."

Lily stands up, which takes a while, but when she's up, she says, "I'll call you if I think of anything I can do to help you. I'd appreciate it if you'd do the same for me."

"I will," Herrera says, standing up.

Lily nods and turns to her mother. "You ready, Momma?"

"Go on ahead. I'll catch up."

Lily nods at the FBI agent again and leaves.

When she's gone, Peggy says, "I'm sorry. This is all very stressful for her."

Herrera shakes her head. "No need to apologize. I'm sure it is. I promise I'll let y'all know if we get any kind of information on Peter."

Peggy thanks her, shakes her hand, and leaves.

As Lily is stepping into the empty elevator, she feels the baby move. She's relieved. It's been almost twenty minutes since she's felt him stir. If she doesn't feel him move every fifteen minutes or so, she always notices. If she doesn't feel him move for thirty minutes or more, she starts getting nervous. The doctor says everything is fine, but she worries, anyway. What if she hurt the baby somehow that night at the motel? What if the shock of what she saw somehow affected her child?

She shakes her head. Dr. Eljerary has told her not to worry about this. Her ultrasound is fine, and the blood work looks good. Apparently those nasty-tasting vitamins were the right choice. She's a robustly healthy eighteen-year-old girl. She's never done drugs or had a drink of alcohol or so much as a puff on a cigarette. She eats right, she sleeps on a soft bed with six pillows, and she's not working or going to school. She's fine. And so is the baby.

And yet, she can't help the small voice in the back of her mind that's always praying. *Please Jesus*, it pleads. *Please don't make my baby pay for my sins.*

For the first two trimesters, she had been twisted into knots by shame and guilt. Part of her wanted to wake up every day and forget that she was going to have a baby. As a result, she experienced the early months of her pregnancy almost exclusively as pain and inconvenience, as ache and hunger. Now, however, things have changed. Over the last three months, she's begun to worry more and more about the baby. Now, she thinks about him constantly, relishing every shift and movement in her belly, crying unexpectedly at every mid-tempo song she hears. She's not plagued by shame and guilt anymore—not because those feelings have miraculously disappeared, but because she's more overcome by worry about what life will be like in a month when the baby arrives. While the future is a long road shrouded in fog, about once an hour she thinks, *I'm going to be a mother.*

Rubbing her belly, she thinks, *But where is your father, little boy?*

She's found out so much about Peter, about the life he was living and the secrets he was keeping. Ciara and her baby. The Corinthian. Yet the final question remains.

Where is he?

What will she tell her son when he asks her that question?

She's wondering this as she steps outside the FBI's offices and runs into Allan.

When Peggy walks outside and finds Lily talking to Allan, she can't believe how big he is. They've never spoken but each knows the other by sight. She last caught a glimpse of him a few years ago, passing him in the aisles at Walmart. He had not seen her, but she had recognized him immediately. Even so, she's still surprised by how large he is. He is as tall as their father was but much heavier.

He looks at her nervously, unsure if he should introduce himself. Lily beats him to it.

"Mama, this is Allan."

"Hello," he says politely.

Peggy doesn't look at him. "Lily," she says, "go wait in the car for me, please."

Lily, sensing that this is not a request, pats Allan's arm, "I'll see you, Allan."

"Okay, Lily."

When they're alone, Peggy turns to him and says, "I think we need to talk, Mr. Woodson."

CHAPTER 37

Peggy Stevens sits down with Allan Woodson for the first time two days later at Strong Coffee, the same café where her daughter had met with Allan and Ciara.

As her daughter had done, Peggy arrives early and orders a drink. She gets a cup of hand-bagged mango Ceylon and sits at a table. She looks around at the customers. Two girls not much older than her daughter are having coffee and sharing a chocolate chip muffin. A thin man in his fifties, wearing a purple t-shirt with a pink seahorse on it, sips coffee and reads a book called *Sleep of Memory*. The music on the radio is some kind of hip hop, but it's so staccato it sounds jittery.

The door opens and Allan walks in.

"Hello," he says, extending his hand.

She stands up and shakes his hand.

"Hello," she says. "Thank you for agreeing to meet me, Mr. Woodson."

He notes the formality of her response and asks, "What are you drinking?"

"What? Oh, uh, tea. Mango."

He regards the board over the head of the barista. "I think I'm going for coffee. Just got off work, and I could use the caffeine."

He goes to the counter and orders his coffee from the barista, a short college-age girl wearing a black hoop in her eyebrow and a 1972 Shirley Chisholm campaign t-shirt.

"This place is like a hipster oasis," he says when he returns to the table. "I can feel myself fighting the urge to grow a mustache."

Surprised by Allan's attempt at small talk, Peggy just nods. "I guess it's where the Hendrix kids hang out," she says.

"I guess."

Peggy nods again and takes a sip of her tea. "Yes, well," she says. "I assume you're wondering why I asked you to meet me."

"I did wonder, yes."

"There are some things I want to say to you. I'm not… Most people would consider me a quiet person. I guess I am quiet, but that doesn't mean I don't have my own ideas. My own feelings. And I have some things I need to say to you. I know we don't know each other, but I feel like there are some issues I need to clear up with you."

Allan blows on his coffee, sips it, and then sets the mug on the table. He crosses his arms. "Okay," he says.

"First off, do you know what happened to Peter Cutchin?"

Allan almost smiles at that—at being asked this goddamn question one more time—but instead he feels his own blood start pumping. He glares at Peggy. "No. I. Do. Not," he says.

She's taken aback by the defensiveness of his tone. "You don't have to be sarcastic about it."

"Well, then, allow me to be blunt instead. Your daughter came to my home looking for Peter. She came to my work looking for Peter. I hauled her down to Little Rock and pulled a gun on the worst shithead in the state to help her look for Peter. I feel like I've put in my time on the Peter Cutchin beat, okay? Once and for all, just so we're crystal clear, I don't know where the fuck he is."

"I don't appreciate being cursed at."

Allan actually does smile at that. "You're Lily's mother alright."

"And I also don't appreciate a forty-two-year-old man palling around with my teenage daughter."

"What?"

"You heard me."

"Okay, Peggy. This is going very poorly. I have been nothing but... I saved your daughter from getting hurt by some very bad people. Has she told you that?"

"Yes, but—"

"'Yes, but' my ass. She would have kept bugging people at the Corinthian until Eli Buck went to see her with his machete."

Peggy closes her eyes. "I know how Lily is," she says. "She's headstrong. When she sets her sights on something, nothing can hold her back." She shakes her head and looks at Allan. "I just wish someone had gone to the authorities earlier."

Allan stops himself from pointing out that the authorities were part of the problem. He has to admit that she has a point that someone should have done something sooner. He says, "Okay."

She picks up her tea. He picks up his coffee.

Allan makes a face that Peggy can't quite read.

He says, "The Reverend William Tackett."

She puts down her tea. "What about him?"

"My long-lost father. Is that the other reason we're here?"

"Yes," she says. "I guess it is."

Allan sips his coffee.

"You have something you want to say to me?" he asks.

"Yes."

"Okay."

Peggy takes a deep breath. "What happened between my father

and your mother pretty much ruined my family. It was like our house burned down, but we had to keep living there in the ashes. My mother never got over it. She could never love him again. Couldn't leave him, couldn't love him. And she didn't just lose her marriage, she lost her church, her place in the world.

"I just lost my church recently. I still have my family, thank God, but I think I know how horrible it must have been for my mother to lose her place in the world. I don't have it as bad as she did, but just the taste of it I've gotten has made my heart break for her all over again.

"So, I guess I just want to know something. Did your mother feel guilty? Did she regret what she did to my family?"

Allan says, "You realize this question is messed up, right?"

"Why?"

"It's like you want to hear that my mom suffered so you can feel better. This is my mother we're talking about. You understand that? You know how much you loved your mother? Well, guess what? That's how much I loved mine."

Peggy considers that. She's ashamed to recognize that he has a point. Still, though…

"The affair ruined my family," she says. "I guess I blame your mother for that. I'm sorry, but that's the way I feel."

"Well, *I'm* sorry, but that seems kind of sexist. It takes two people to make a baby, last I checked. And let me say something about William Tackett while we're on the subject. When I was a kid, I found out my dad wasn't my biological father. Turns out, my biological father was some preacher on the other side of town. Sorry, some *ex*-preacher. I'm just lucky that Herman Woodson is a good guy. He didn't have to stick around and raise me as his own, but he did. He stuck around after I came out of the closet, too. I wonder how many guys around here would have done that. I wonder if Tackett would have done that."

Peggy starts to say something, but Allan waves away her defense of her father.

"No," he says, "I already know the answer. He turned his back on me as soon as he was done having sex with my mother."

Peggy can't believe he would say such a thing about her father. She reaches for her purse.

"I have to go," she says.

"Fine, Peggy, but you're the one who called this meeting. Whatever your reasons were for doing that, you want to know why I agreed to see you? Because like it or not, you're the only blood kin I got. Whatever bullshit went down between our parents forty-plus years ago, the one thing I know for sure is that it doesn't reflect on either one of us. It doesn't have to get ugly between us. That's your choice to make."

Peggy gets up without saying another word and walks outside to her car. She gets in, puts the key in the ignition, and looks up. Seeing the back of Allan's head through the coffeehouse window, she pauses and watches him sit there for a while.

Finally, she pulls her key out and walks back inside, careful not to make eye contact with any of the other café patrons, most of whom are trying not to be obvious as they watch her reenter and sit down across from Allan.

"You're back?"

"I'm back."

"Okay."

"I'm not a bad person," she tells him.

"I don't think you're a bad person."

"Yes, you do."

"No. In fact, I was just sitting here thinking that if I was you, I'd probably feel the way you do, and if you were me, you'd probably feel the way I do."

In truth, until she walked back into the shop, Allan was sipping his coffee and thinking she was a bitch. But now that she's back, he wants to stop the fight.

Peggy sits with her purse in her lap, as if she might get up again at any moment, but she says, "I'm just...angry. About a lot of things. I know that my father was just as much to blame for what happened as your mother. I have no right to take it out on you. It has nothing to do with you. And it's not very Christlike of me to take it out on you."

Allan says, "I'm not a bad person, either."

She tells him, "That's what Lily says."

"Smart girl, Lily."

"She is smart, but she's also going to be the death of me."

"Hey, she almost was the death of me."

Peggy nods, putting her purse on the floor next to her chair. "That's another reason I came back. After West Memphis, Lily told us everything that happened. I still don't know if you did the right thing in all of this, but I know you protected her from that man down in Little Rock. And I'm bright enough to figure out that it could have turned out worse if you hadn't been there. So...thank you."

Allan tells her, "Since you walked in here originally to chew me out, I know that must hurt to say. So, you're welcome. And for what it's worth, I'm not sure I did the right thing, either, but I am glad I was there to help her. I don't regret that."

When Allan and Peggy finally leave Strong Coffee thirty minutes later, he walks her to her car. They shake hands, and he goes to his truck.

Climbing in, he feels strangely relieved. He didn't know what to expect going into this meeting. When she'd talked to him in front of the FBI offices, she was clipped and cold, clearly upset. He wasn't surprised when she showed up pissed today. But now? They're not exactly leaving here as reunited siblings, but they're on better terms than before, and it can't hurt to be on good terms with one's closest remaining blood relation, can it?

He's still pondering this question when Peggy drives past him and waves. He waves back and watches her pull out of the parking lot. He's still watching when a U-Haul moving truck speeds through the red light at the intersection and smashes into Peggy. The impact spins her car around until it slams to a halt in the middle of the street.

Allan yells and throws open the door of his truck. He runs across the glass-strewn pavement.

In her crushed car, Peggy sits behind the deployed airbag, her hand pressed against her bleeding nose. As Allan opens the driver's side door, shattered glass spills into the street.

"Are you okay?" he asks.

She reaches out, dazed. He takes her hand.

CHAPTER 38

Five days later, on a chilly Saturday afternoon, Allan knocks on the door of the Stevens home.

Lily opens the door.

"Well, hello," she says.

"Hello," he says. He shakes his head. "Wow. I can't get used to the new you, Lily."

She waves him into the living room, where they share a cumbersome hug that, because of their big bellies, is mostly a squeezing of shoulders.

"Do I look so different?" she asks with a smile.

"A bit. Chopping off two feet of hair makes a difference, I guess."

She touches her cropped hair. "What do you think? It's growing back okay, I think."

"It's very *Be Yourself Tonight*."

"I have no idea what that means."

"Annie Lennox, 1985."

"Okay… So that's a compliment, then."

"It's literally the highest compliment I can give a head of hair. Hair that doesn't belong to Reba McEntire, anyway."

She smiles as she's taking her purse off the coat rack by the door. "Well, thank you, then. Are you ready to go?"

"No one else home?" he asks.

"No. Momma and Daddy are both working, and Adam is over at a friend's house."

She locks the front door behind her and follows him to the truck.

"Need some help getting in?" he asks.

"Yes, please."

He helps her climb into the truck and walks around to the other side and gets in.

"Where are we going?" he asks.

She gives him the address of her doctor's office as he taps it into his phone's GPS.

"Okay," he says, clipping the phone into a holder on the dash. Backing out of the driveway, he says, "And away we go."

"Thanks for taking me."

"Of course. Happy to help."

"Well, we all appreciate it."

"Oh, it's just a ride. Nothing big. How's your mother feeling?"

"For a few days, she had a black eye from the airbag. But that's pretty much gone. Just a little blue on her eyelid. You can't really even tell."

"Well, good. But the car's totaled?"

"Yeah. It sucks. With Daddy and Momma both working, we really need two cars. I think we'll get a used one when we can afford it."

Allan turns onto the interstate and drives to the next exit.

"So this must be one of your last checkups before the big day, right?"

"Yep, three more weeks."

"Do you hate being asked when you're due?"

"I hate being asked by strangers in the checkout line at Walmart. But it's okay if my *friends* ask."

They stop at a red light. Allan checks the GPS and makes a left turn at the next street. As they're turning, he glances at the girl as she stares out the window. She's watching people on the street, looking at every face. Although she's rounded and softened with pregnancy, even in repose something about her remains hard—harder, in fact, than before.

"What?" she asks.

"Nothing. You just seem different to me."

"Less hair? More baby?"

"Sure, but there's something else. You seem…older?"

She turns back to watching people on the street, looking into cars, into windows, searching every face they pass. "I've lived a lot in the last eight months," she says. "That's for sure."

He nods, both hands on the steering wheel. "Yeah. I guess so. You know, the other day I wanted to ask you about what happened in West Memphis, but I thought it was better to give you space. I'm sure the whole world's asked you about it."

"They have."

"Reporters, cops, the FBI."

"The FBI only wants to talk about the trafficking case against Harper."

He nods and stops at another red light. "Herrera was asking me about that, too. Asking about the truck."

"Why is she so hung up on the truck that was used?"

"It helps her make the case against Chance and Harper, I guess. They have to show that the girls were moved across state lines. From what Herrera told me, they're trying to figure out if the truck used to bring them up from Louisiana was the same truck that was used to move the girls back and forth from Little Rock to Conway."

"Was it?"

"How would I know?"

"Did you see the truck when you were working at the Corinthian?"

"A couple of times, always fleetingly in the dark. I didn't hang out back there."

"What did it look like?"

"Are you working for the FBI now?"

"You told me it was a moving truck, right? Like a U-Haul or something?"

He shrugs. "Well, I'll tell you what I told Herrera. It was a twenty-footer. About the size of a truck that would pack up a small home. I think the front was painted white and the sides were stripped bare down to the metal. So it might have been a U-Haul or Penske or Budget at some point. I'm not sure. Maybe it was none of them. Like I said, I didn't get a great look at it."

Lily doesn't reply to this, and when Allan looks over at her at the next stoplight, her face is pale.

They get to the doctor's office, and Allan pulls up to the door. He gets out and walks around and helps Lily out of the truck. She says nothing, and with an odd expression on her face, she walks through the double doors. Allan gets into the truck and pulls into a parking spot.

Thirty-two minutes later, Lily walks back out through the doors. As he helps her up into the truck, she still has an odd expression on her face. She looks as though she's been turning a complicated equation around in her head the entire time she's been inside.

As Allan is walking back around to the driver's side, Lily leans over and takes his phone from the dash. Into the GPS she taps *Tyler salvage*. The address for Tyler Auto-Salvage comes up. It's less than ten minutes away.

"Hey," she says as he's shutting his door. "Could you run me by here?"

He looks at the address. "What's at…Tyler Auto-Salvage?"

"My mom's car. She and I went there the other day to get some stuff, but we forgot a body pillow that was in the backseat. She went to the store right before she met up with you. And the pillow cost, like, forty bucks, so we can't afford to lose it."

"Sure, we can swing by and get it."

"Thanks," Lily says.

Allan asks her about the doctor's appointment. Did everything look okay? She tells him the appointment went fine. All signs are good.

But she's not really talking to him, not really listening to him.

She's watching the road as they leave Conway and head north of town. As they turn onto the red gravel road, she's watching for the break in the tree line where she can see Brother Wise's house at the top of the hill, and then, at the bottom of the hill, Sister Cynthia's house, sitting empty for two months since Cynthia's cousins checked her into inpatient care at the psychiatric hospital in Benton. Allan keeps driving, following the GPS over the hill, to another little cluster of houses, where the Drinkwaters live and where Brother Drinkwater only has to drive a few minutes down the road to work for his brother-in-law at Tyler Auto-Salvage.

It's a two-story building, with a couple of shabby offices above a garage, flanked by a six-foot chain-link fence topped with helical razor wire. Allan pulls up to the main building. Beyond the fence, Lily can glimpse acres of twisted metal and broken glass.

Nodding at the field of discarded vehicles, she asks, "Can you go back there?"

"I don't see a way to go into the back lot." He turns to look at her, and her face is tight and serious. "Someone would have to open the fence."

Lily doesn't move.

Allan puts the truck in park.

"What's this about?"

She turns to him. "Remember I told you that Eli and Chance broke into Peter's house when I was there?"

"Yes."

"Yeah, well, Peter lives right over that hill. We just passed his house a second ago. And the truck you described—an old moving truck that's been stripped down—is the kind of vehicle they have all around here."

Allan glances back at the sprawling acres of old cars and trucks. "That's weird, but it doesn't have to mean anything."

"No, but when they broke into the house, Eli told me they were just in the neighborhood. That's what he told me. 'We were just in the neighborhood.' I thought he was being sarcastic. But what if they *were* in the neighborhood, visiting the salvage yard, when they saw my car at Peter's house and thought it might be Peter?"

Allan looks at the building. "I don't know, Lily. I agree that it's curious, but..." He looks back at her, studying her face. "What? There's something else. What is it? Do you know who works here?"

"Yeah, I do," she says. "And so did Peter."

CHAPTER 39

Four months ago.

Peter is pacing the parking lot, moving in and out of the orange lamplight, his hands clenched into fists. Through the sliding glass doors of the Corinthian, he can see Allan at the front desk reading his book.

Peter turns and walks across the half-empty parking lot to the annex. If Eli is bringing his girls up tonight, the lights and air conditioning need to be turned on in the rooms. Since the annex is hardly ever used for legitimate business anymore, most of the time it sits empty and dark.

He unlocks the doors and turns everything on. In the last room, he stops and looks around. He often wanders through the unoccupied rooms of the inn. They feel strange—small, intimate spaces where travelers stop and live their lives for a few hours, or maybe a few days, before moving on, going back to their real lives. But the rooms of the annex feel different to him. They're ominous, evil. These are no longer hotel rooms. Men come here to use the bodies of young girls and then slip away undetected.

He could never be that kind of man. He doesn't know what to do about Lily and Ciara. But he knows he could never be the kind of man who comes to the annex.

He wonders if that Tisha girl will be here tonight with the others. He feels sorry for her. Maybe he'll see her, and they'll get to talk again. Probably not, though, with Eli around.

Headlights sweep across him through the window. He goes outside, slipping into the shadowy cluster of trees at the edge of the annex parking lot and watches a car approaching. The car doesn't go to the front portico, the way a normal car would. It drives straight to the back, to the annex. It's the clients. Three men.

Assholes, Peter thinks.

The car parks. The men are older and obviously a little drunk, especially the man in the back. The driver and the passenger in the front have to haul him out.

"No one's gonna see us?" the man from the back asks.

"I done tolt you," the driver. "We just stay back here. The girls come to us."

"Okay, then," the man from the back says, breaking into a drunken laugh. He leans against the car in order to stand up right. He keeps laughing, like he can't stop himself.

Peter stays in the trees. He can't see the men very well without getting closer and exposing himself.

Then the moving truck pulls into the Corinthian's drive. The men giggle and slug each other like frat boys. "Here they come," they say, stumbling forward to get a better look, wobbly and pale in the truck's approaching headlights.

The truck glides out of the night and rolls to a stop under the glow of the portico.

He's never gotten a good look at the truck before, never been here when it pulled into the hotel. Once the girls are unloaded, it will be moved to the darkest corner of the parking lot, away from lights and the view of passing motorists on the road. But now, as Chance stays behind the wheel and Eli climbs down from the passenger side to roll up the door in the back, Peter sees the truck fully for the first time.

And he knows in a terrible instant that he's seen this truck before, saw it months ago driving down his road, away from the salvage yard, its silver sides glinting in the sunlight. He knows who owns this truck.

Brother Drinkwater.

CHAPTER 40

Allan unclips his phone from the dash and scrolls to the number he has saved for FBI Special Agent Herrera.

"All she can say is we're nuts and overreacting," he tells Lily.

She stares up at the main building of Tyler Auto-Salvage. "His last night at the hotel, you said that Peter left abruptly, right?"

"Yes," he says, putting the phone to his ear, its ringing audible to Lily. "We'd just had a talk about a lot of things, one of which was how much he hated working at the Corinthian. Then he went outside to get some air."

"Did Eli come up that night with the truck?"

"Yes." Allan stares at her. "Right at that time. The truck pulled in and a couple of minutes later, Peter just got in his car and tore ass out of the parking lot. Didn't say a word."

"Do you think he recognized the truck?"

"It's possible." He lowers the phone and shakes his head. "I'm getting Herrera's cell voicemail. I'll try her office number."

The front door of the garage opens, and Brother Drinkwater walks out. He's a lean man of about sixty, with a creased face and mournful eyes, wearing dirty jeans and a faded work shirt with a name tag that reads: *Tommy Lee*. He walks over to Lily's side of the truck, smiling, trying to be friendly. She lowers her window.

"Howdy there, Lily. Saw y'all from the window. What can I do you for?"

Allan reminds her, "You forgot your body pillow."

Lily shakes her head. "No, I didn't. I just told you that so you'd bring me over here." She turns in her seat and asks the old man, "Brother Drinkwater, do you own an old moving truck?"

"A what?"

"An old moving truck. Allan, describe it."

"A twenty-footer with stripped down silver sides," Allan says. "Something that was once a U-Haul or a Budget."

Brother Drinkwater has salt-and-pepper eyebrows that furrow as he's trying to stay affable. He tells Lily, "I mean, on the lot we got a lot of old vehicles of one kind or another..."

"Let me ask it more directly, then," she says. "Did you help Eli Buck traffic girls?"

The old man swallows hard at that. He's about to say something when the phone in Allan's hand buzzes and glows to life. For a moment, the name of the caller is clear to all three of them, just the way Allan saved it in his phone's contacts: Diane Herrera.

Brother Drinkwater groans in pain when he sees the name, one he clearly recognizes from the news, one he clearly fears. He reaches under his shirt and pulls out an old black revolver.

"Put that phone on the dash," he tells Allan. "Leave it there. Don't answer it."

"Look—"

"You do as I say. Turn off the truck." Drinkwater reaches through the window and opens Lily's door. "Get out, Lily."

She stares at him in disbelief, this man she's known most of her life, this man she's watched receive the Holy Ghost of Jesus.

"Brother Drinkwater, what are you doing?"

"I don't know what I'm doing. I need to think. I need to think, and y'all need to be quiet." He points the gun at Allan. "Turn off the truck, I said, and get out. I need to think clearly for a few minutes, and I can't do it standing around out here with y'all about to drive off."

Allan knows he can't go for his own gun or put the truck in reverse without endangering Lily. Besides, her door is already open. He shuts off the truck.

"Why do you have that gun?" Lily asks Brother Drinkwater.

"Because I'm scared, Lily," he admits. "'The wicked flee, though no man pursueth.' I've been scared out of my wits for months now. Please get out of the truck."

He takes her arm and helps her down from the truck.

"You're not going to hurt me, Brother Drinkwater," she tells him. "The Lord is watching us right now. Me and you. Watching both of us."

"I know he is," the old man says, his eyes already glistening. "I knew it when I saw y'all out the window. I knew that the Lord had brought you here. I just don't know why yet." He keeps the gun on Allan as the larger man gets out of the truck. "Please go inside," he tells them both.

The inside of the garage smells of oil and cigarettes, though Lily sees no one working on cars or smoking. She sees no one, in fact. Just greasy racks of tools, a few posters for cars or equipment, and a wooden flight of stairs going up to the offices.

"Up the stairs," Drinkwater says behind them.

She climbs the steps, Allan behind her, Drinkwater in the rear. They step into a lonely little office where several dismembered newspapers are spread across a desk. Drinkwater closes the door and walks over to the desk, as if to show them the papers.

"I've been trying to find information," he tells them. He gestures at articles on the FBI's investigation of the sex trafficking ring.

"Something that would tell me..." When he looks up and meets Lily's eyes, he slumps against the desk, shaking his head, nearly overcome. "To tell me how close they were."

"Brother Drinkwater," she says, "what did you do?"

"I didn't mean to hurt nobody," he says. He limply holds onto the gun, almost placing it on the desk. "Oh, Jesus..."

Lily can't tell if the man is cursing or praying.

With his free hand, he wipes sweat away from his brow. His hair is thin and gray, his eyes a shallow, watery blue.

Allan reaches for Lily, trying to pull her back.

Drinkwater, in a quiet panic, raises the gun and points it at him.

"Stand still!"

"Okay," Allan says. "Okay. Just take it easy. Whatever it is that you did, you need to understand that keeping us here, threatening us, it's only going to make it worse."

"I want *you* to stop talking," Brother Drinkwater says. Then he pleads with Lily. "I'm a good man. You know that, Lily. You knowed me all your life. Have I ever been cruel to you?"

"No, sir," she says, her arms around her belly.

Again, he lowers the gun to the desk without releasing it. "No, because I'm not a bad man. I just needed some money to keep this place from going under. It wasn't for me. It was to protect Brenda and Gordon. I'm not a bad man. I didn't know what Eli was up to at first. You got to believe that. I knew it was wrong, what he asked me for, but I didn't know it was evil. He wanted a truck that couldn't be traced to him, but he let me think he was moving stolen merchandise. Cigarettes, cell phones, that sort of thing. I didn't know what he was really doing. By the time I got suspicious, it was too late. I couldn't do nothing about it." He wipes tears away. "And I never thought they'd take the truck to the hotel."

Lily leans back as if she's been slapped. "Peter..."

"I didn't mean to hurt him," Drinkwater pleads. "You got to know that. He saw the truck at the hotel, and he came up to my house to ask me about it. He wasn't mad yet, but I made a mistake. I lied. I said I didn't know nothing about it. Once he caught me in that lie, he thought I was in on the whole thing from the beginning."

Lily's mouth opens, searching for words. When she finally speaks, her voice breaks. "Oh god. What did you do, Brother Drinkwater?"

"I didn't mean to hurt him, you got to believe that. But he said the whole church deserved to know about me. I tried to tell him I was desperate. I tried to tell him what I told you, that I didn't know what was going on at first."

"Where's Peter? Brother Drinkwater, where's my baby's—?"

Drinkwater releases his breath in a burst, like his lungs are collapsing. "He's out back. In his car. Under twenty tons of other cars." He rubs his sweaty face. "Oh Lord. What have I done? What am I going to do?"

Allan takes a step forward. "You don't have to do anything. Like you said, you're not a bad man. You don't want to take this thing and make it worse. You said you didn't mean to hurt the boy..."

Brother Drinkwater scowls at Allan.

"You don't *know* me," he says sharply. "You're nothing but a *homosexual* that works at a *whorehouse*. What business is this of yours?" With his gaze turned to Allan, his face changes. He's not looking at the pregnant girl anymore, but at a large man, a man whom he can face not with shame but with superiority, with anger. "You don't know what it's like to face the Lord. I've been sitting here for weeks, trying to gather up the courage to blow my brains out. As much as I want to do it, I'm too scared, because I know I'm gonna burn in hell forever if I do. That's what it's like when a man faces the Lord on the Lord's terms. Who are you to judge me? I been following the word of God for sixty years. I've walked the path of righteousness for sixty years. And I slipped off the path, okay. I slipped off and sinned. But you, you're a *sinner*. Living a life of wickedness and sodomy and then coming in here, leading this girl in here with her mannish hair, pregnant with a bastard, and you look at me with condescension. You two are everything that's wrong with this world and you stomp in here to judge me?"

"Please, we just want—"

Brother Drinkwater raises the gun. *To point? To shoot?* Allan moves without thinking. Gets to him in one big step. The gun goes off like a bomb, as if the windows in the room should shatter. The fear that he's been shot blinks across Allan's mind, but he's still moving. He grabs the gun, gets his hand around both the gun and the man's hand all at once, and wrenches the man's entire body forward, smashing the gun and the hand into the desk. There is another explosion, and the gun is hot but Allan doesn't let go, instead he holds on, takes a punch to the face and then drags Brother Drinkwater across the desk and slams him into the floor and punches him once, twice, three, four times, keeps punching until Drinkwater is bloodied and babbling and too weak to move.

"Stay right there, goddamn you. You just stay right there. Lily, call the police." He turns. "Lily?"

The girl is still standing, but her mouth is open in a silent scream, one hand pressed to her bleeding torso.

CHAPTER 41

She's in his arms, lifted, carried. Her ears ring with the scream of blood. She can't hear, can't speak, can't breathe. Yet she smells everything. His cologne, then the grease and cigarettes of the garage, then the crisp autumn air, then the clean upholstery of his truck.

They're moving. He's explaining that they're going to the hospital. She struggles for breath, but it won't come. She tries not to panic. Her chest feels like it's being crushed.

No. Please, no.

He's on the phone now speeding down the gravel road. 9-1-1. "Listen to me, a man shot a pregnant girl. He's unconscious at the Tyler Auto-Salvage. The girl's in the truck with me. We're only a few minutes away. Yes, she's alive. Yes, she's awake. No. In the chest, I think. I'm not sure if her belly was hit, but there's a lot of blood, and I can't tell. She's having trouble breathing."

My baby.

My baby can't breathe.

Please, Jesus. Please don't do this.

"Jesus…"

"She's trying to talk. I don't know. I think she's trying to pray. Lily, are you okay? Lily? Lily? No, she can't tell me anything. She's just trying to breathe."

Jesus, please don't do this. Please, Jesus. Please don't hurt my baby.

The pedal is smashed to the floor, his palm pounding the truck's horn as he whips around two cars at a stop sign. The ground beneath the truck goes from gravel to blacktop, the smoothness giving way to greater and greater speed.

"Yes, she's still awake. What? I don't have time to drive safely, goddamn it! You tell them we're coming?"

Please, Jesus.

"We're almost there. Lily, you hear me? We're almost there. Hold on. Just hold on a little longer."

And then the truck stops and the door opens and she's in his enormous arms again. She's holding her belly as if she's cradling the baby in her arms, as if it's something she could drop, and he's running, carrying her and the baby both into the bright lights of the hospital and she's crying and trying to find her breath.

Then other hands take her and Allan's arms slip away and she's on her back on a hard-soft surface and she's moving and someone is leaning over her speaking quickly and clearly.

"I know you're having a hard time breathing. We're going to take care of you, but I have to ask you some questions. They are very important. How far along are you?"

"Eight."

"Eight months? When's the last time you ate?"

"I can't…breathe."

"Can you hear me? Can you tell me the last time you ate? Did you have lunch?"

"Break…fast."

"Have you ever had anesthesia?"

"Yes."

"Did you have any problems with anesthesia? Any kind of bad reaction?"

"No," she says, but the word takes the last of her breath and her chest sinks into itself. She claws the air like she's trying to climb out of a collapsing hole.

my baby please jesus my baby

People are yelling, but a woman with iron-gray eyes leans over her and speaks with the calm authority of the Bible.

"You are going to be okay, Lily. Your baby is going to be okay. I need you to be still now and let us work."

The iron-eyed woman gives orders.

Bodies move above Lily. Light. Plastic. Metal. The voices are loud and fast but calm and controlled.

Plastic on her face.

She shuts her eyes. She shuts her ears. She floats away.

No surface beneath her

No gurney

No floor

No ground

No sound

No light

No weight

No body

One last thought

my baby

and then

nothing at all

CHAPTER 42

Conway police dispatch two teams to respond to the 911 call. One team goes to the hospital to question Allan Woodson, the man who carried in a pregnant teenage girl suffering from a gunshot wound. After a few minutes of preliminary questioning, they ask him to accompany them to the station for follow-up questions from police chief Jeff Reid and lead investigator Jamarius Smith. Woodson agrees to go.

The second team is dispatched to Tyler Auto-Salvage where they discover Tommy Lee Drinkwater unconscious on the floor of the office, still limply holding a loaded .38 Smith & Wesson with two spent cartridges. (The gun is later discovered to be registered to Gordon Tyler, the owner of the salvage yard and Drinkwater's brother-in-law. Tyler, who suffers from Parkinson's, is semi-retired and tells police that Drinkwater has been in charge of day-to-day operations at the salvage yard for the last two years.) Drinkwater is suffering from a broken nasal bone, a broken zygomatic bone, a fractured maxilla, and two lost teeth.

When Drinkwater eventually regains consciousness, he will also be questioned by Reid and Smith. With an attorney present, Drinkwater will admit to the officers that he killed Peter Cutchin on the night of September 6, following an argument in the garage of Drinkwater's home. Though he will make a full confession, he will also assert that Cutchin's death was an accident. According to Drinkwater, he was in his garage working on his car when Cutchin arrived and confronted Drinkwater about his connection to Eli Buck and the Corinthian Inn annex. The escalating confrontation became physical, at which point Drinkwater says he inadvertently killed Cutchin with a blow from the handle of his hydraulic car jack.

Claiming he was panicking, he tells the officers he put the body in the trunk of Cutchin's car and drove over to his house. Both Drinkwater's wife and Cutchin's mother were out of town on a church trip, so Drinkwater entered the Cutchin home with Peter's keys, packed his suitcase with clothes and some toiletries, and placed them in the car. Then he drove the car to Tyler Auto-Salvage.

Following his confession, Drinkwater directs investigators to the partially flattened car, buried under 19.4 tons of other discarded automobiles in the salvage yard. There, Peter Cutchin's body is discovered wrapped in a plastic tarp in the crushed trunk of the car. A subsequent autopsy reveals that the body was also posthumously soaked in an industrial-strength chemical agent used for eliminating the odors of dead rodents. (A nearly empty five-gallon bucket of Quality Chemical's Deodorizing Fluid will later be found in the salvage yard's supply shed along with rat poison, and Gordon Tyler will confirm that the poison and deodorizer were purchased the previous summer to fight a rodent infestation.) Despite Drinkwater's claim that the killing was unintentional, and its concealment was done in a state of panic, his seemingly cool-headed efforts to mask his crime and avoid detection eventually leads Conway prosecuting attorney Stephen Kennedy to forego the lesser charge of manslaughter and instead charge Drinkwater with the second-degree murder of Peter Cutchin.

The same week as the murder charge is filed, FBI Special Agent Diane Herrera of the Little Rock Field Office announces that her office is also investigating Drinkwater's connection to a sex trafficking ring operating between Louisiana, Mississippi, and Arkansas. The crushed remains of a moving truck found buried deep in the Tyler backlot is believed to be the same truck used by the late Eli Buck. Further charges against Drinkwater are expected.

As for the shooting of Lily Stevens, while Drinkwater will confirm that he fired the gun in his struggle with Allan Woodson, he will also claim that this was another accident. He had, he will swear, no intention of harming either Woodson, the Stevens girl, or her baby.

CHAPTER 43

Stumbling out of the police station, Allan is in a daze.

Hours before at the hospital, as they hurried Lily away behind closed doors, he collapsed in the waiting room, still covered in her blood, his knuckles busted and bleeding from pummeling that man at the salvage yard office. He knows he must have been a sight to see, a bloodied giant sitting on a bench quietly weeping. But when the police arrived and took him away for questioning, he gathered his strength again and regained his composure. He told all he knew, first to the lead investigator, and then to the police chief, and then to both cops at the same time.

Now he stands in front of his truck, his busted hands trembling. He takes out his phone.

A couple of missed calls from his father, who expected him home hours ago. No missed calls from Peggy.

He scrolls to her number.

He takes a deep breath.

He calls her.

No answer. A few beeps, then a generic voicemail.

"Peggy…it's Allan," he says. "I just got done talking to the police. They said you'd been notified and that you were up at the hospital. I'm sure you're still there now. I hope…god, I hope everything is alright. I just hope she's okay. I'm just calling to say that I hope everything is alright. I'll call and check on you later. Please let me know if there's anything I can do. I'm thinking about all of you. God bless you. I'll talk to you soon."

God bless you? he asks himself. Somehow it seemed like the right thing to say.

Now he doesn't know what to do. He thinks about going back to the hospital, but he needs to run home first and take care of his father—give him his dinner and his pain pills. Besides, it's certainly not a good idea to go back to the hospital still wearing clothes stained with Lily's blood.

Lily…

He reaches for the door handle. He'll drive home, tend to Herman, change into clean clothes, and go back to the hospital to sit with Peggy.

When Allan walks in the front door, his father looks up from his bedroom television. He watches as Allan, saying nothing, heads down the hall to his own room.

"Is that…blood?" his father asks.

Allan doesn't answer. He walks into his room and takes off his shoes. He strips his dress shirt. The t-shirt underneath is stained with pinkish-brown spots.

"What happened?" his father asks from the doorway. He sits up in his wheelchair, his face taut, his eyes worried.

Allan closes his own eyes and rubs the busted knuckles of his right hand.

"There's been some shit going on. I didn't want to tell you about it because I didn't want to worry you."

"Worry me?"

"I just…"

"Does it have something to do with that Tackett girl?"

"Her name's not Tackett, it's Stevens. Lily Stevens."

"You know what I mean. She's the granddaughter of William Tackett."

Allan turns and looks at his father. He's never heard him use the name of William Tackett before. There's so much that hasn't been said between Allan and Herman. Some of it is hard, brutal even, but not all of it. Some of it is simply so tender that it feels fragile, as if it would shatter if ever given voice.

"Yes," Allan says, sitting down on his bed.

Herman rolls into the room and rests his arms on the arms of his wheelchair. "Tell me."

Allan draws a deep breath and tells him everything. Lily and Drinkwater, the Corinthian and Mr. Baker, Eli and Harper, and Peggy Stevens née Tackett. There's a lot to tell, but it's a relief to get it out. Herman, never a good listener, listens, asking nothing, making no comments.

When his son is finished, the old man sits quietly with it all, until he finally tells Allan, "I'm sure she'll be okay."

Allan's voice is very small when he replies, "I hope so."

"You got her there in time. She'll be okay."

Allan closes his eyes. "I hope so," he says again. "I'm just worried that Peggy hasn't called me back yet. I need to go back up there."

"Do you want to try her again before you go?"

"Yes," Allan says, taking his phone from the bedside table.

He calls her, listens for a moment, and says, "Straight to voicemail."

"Maybe she's on the phone with somebody else. Or it's off. Don't mean nothing."

"I know."

Allan gets up and starts getting dressed. As he does, he looks over at his father sitting quietly in the wheelchair.

"What do you think?" Allan asks.

"About what?"

"About what? About everything I just told you."

Herman laces his fingers together on his belly and purses his lips. "Sounds like this Eli character was a bad hombre."

"Okay…"

"And this Drinkwater fella sounds like a damn hypocrite."

"True…"

Herman shrugs. "Sounds like you did the right thing."

"I tried."

"Well, trying is about all you can do sometimes."

"Okay. But what about the rest of it?" Allan pauses. "We never really talked about…" he pauses again to choose his words carefully, "…we never really talked about William Tackett or Mom or any of that. What about that?"

Herman has tired russet eyes that blink at his son for a moment and then seek relief in looking at the floor. He sits quietly until he has chosen his words.

"My daddy used to say, 'Once you shit in my boots, it's done.'"

Having spoken these words, Herman nods to himself and settles back into his wheelchair.

Allan stares at his father. "What?"

"What do you mean, what?"

"For the first time in my life I ask you point blank about Mom and that preacher, and the only thing you have to say is, 'Once you shit in my boots, it's done'?"

Herman makes a *Well?* gesture with his hands and says, "It is."

"Okay…"

"Don't know what else you want me to say."

"I don't know either, Dad," Allan says. "I just wanted to tell you what's been happening."

Herman nods at that. "I appreciate it."

"I hope you don't mind me talking to Peggy."

Herman nods at that too, seeming to consider it a moment before he says, "I reckon she's the closest thing you got to a sister."

"I reckon she is."

Allan watches his father's face a moment, as the old man lowers his head, lost once again in his own thoughts. Seeing his father's head bowed like this reminds Allan of the day his mother died. When Alice Woodson finally stopped breathing in a bed at Baptist Hospital, her husband held her left hand while her son held her right. Both men cried that day. Herman had not seen his son cry in many years. Allan had never seen his father cry.

Herman doesn't cry now, either. He simply nods to himself. Then he tells his son, "Don't forget to fix my supper before you go back up to the hospital. A man could starve around here waiting on you to feed him."

Allan is about to reply when his phone vibrates. He can't find his breath as he looks at the screen.

"It's Peggy."

Herman leans forward and tries to hear as Allan answers the phone.

Drawing a deep breath, he says, "Peggy?"

He closes his eyes, listening. Tears roll down his face.

"Oh thank God," he says.

CHAPTER 44

Lily Stevens holds her son as he lies sleeping against her chest. As of today, he weighs ten pounds and nine ounces. He sleeps on her right side, away from the wound healing in her left breast and the incision across her bruised lower abdomen. His downy head is as round as a peach, his pink skin soft and warm in the daylight streaming through her bedroom window. As he opens his tiny wet mouth to sigh, she breathes with him, her chest lifting his small body, as if he's floating on her breath.

She's named him Peter. He will know who his father is. One day, he will know why his father died, will know the tragedy connected to his birth. She will have to explain it to him. She doesn't know yet how she'll do this, what words she'll use. She only knows that she'll tell him the truth and that the most important part of that truth is that when she awakened from her anesthetized sleep and met him for the first time, she was born again. Nothing that ever happened to her in church was as lifechanging as the moment she saw him, crying and stretching his balled-up hands and kicking his balled-up feet, reaching out, it seemed, to her, *for* her, and when she took him in her arms for the first time, she knew he was hers and she was his. Whatever their future held, she knew in that moment, they would face it together.

Everyone cried along with her and the baby that day. Momma and Daddy, even Adam. Lily and the baby had almost been lost, but then they had been saved, allowed to stay, to return to this world, to live their lives.

"It's a miracle," her brother told her.

Lily said nothing to that.

Once Lily is ready, she calls Allan and asks him to come see her and meet the baby.

He comes the next day, still wearing his uniform from work, lifting the baby in his enormous arms, cradling him.

"Your mother said you named him Peter," Allan says. "I think that's sweet."

Lily watches them a moment, smiling. "I asked her not to tell you his middle name. I wanted to do that."

"What is it?"

"Allan, of course."

Allan holds the child, staring down at his sleepy face. "That's very sweet, too," he says quietly.

"It's the least we could do," Lily says, pushing herself up on her pillows. "You saved us."

Allan says nothing to that, too overwhelmed. Then he smiles. He laughs.

"Peter Allan?" he says.

"Yes…" she says.

"I guess you don't know that Peter Allen—Allen with an e but pronounced the same—was the name of Liza Minnelli's first husband."

"Who's Liza Minnelli?"

Allan closes his eyes and shakes his head. "Jesus take the wheel. You gave this kid the same name as *The Boy From Oz*, and you don't know who Liza Minnelli is?"

"Nope."

Allan tells the baby, "I'll explain later. You'll need to know."

After a moment, Allan's smile turns sad.

"You okay?" Lily asks.

He walks over and lowers the baby gently into her arms.

"Yes," he says.

"What's wrong?"

"Nothing."

"You sure?"

"Sure. I'm happy to see the two of you doing okay. Just reminds me of that day."

"It must have been really scary for you," she says.

He shrugs. "It was worse for you."

They say nothing more about it, but she knows. She and Allan have been through so much together, the two of them. He doesn't tell her that he's had trouble sleeping ever since that day.

Lily doesn't tell him that she hasn't been sleeping either. She wants to rest, of course, to dream new dreams for her child, but every night, when her baby finally falls asleep, her mind reels, shocked anew at the tectonic collision of life and death that she somehow, inexplicably, survived.

The hospital patched up her shattered lung and then split open her belly. They pulled out her screaming baby and then dragged Lily back into the world to stay with him. *A miracle*, her brother said. And Lily supposes it must be a miracle, though now, in a strange way, she's more confused than ever.

She has her baby, but she's lost his father. She hasn't had the strength to really cry about that yet. His remains have been interred in his family plot, alongside the graves of his father and uncle. She'll go there when she's ready. She has things she wants to say to him.

For now, though, it's just Lily and baby Peter. That has its own complications. She loves her son more than she ever thought it possible to love another person, but a love that large casts a terrifying shadow. A love that large feels like fear. And in the face of that kind of fear, the promise of miracles seems too transparent, too false.

She holds her son to her chest. Then she says, "Hey," to the giant man sitting next to her. He looks up. She reaches for him.

He gives her his massive hand, eclipsing hers, his mouth already primed for a joke.

"Is everything going to be okay?" she asks.

Allan's face softens as he looks into hers. Blinking, he smiles and swallows a caustic reply. Then, gently squeezing her small hand, he tells her, "Of course."

When Allan leaves, Peggy comes in to ask her if she wants the baby moved to his crib.

"No," she says. "We're fine right now."

"Okay," Peggy says. "I'm going to go work on the laundry. I'll check in on you two in a while, but call me if you need me before then."

Lily thanks her and asks her to turn off the light as she's leaving.

Now it's just the two of them, mother and son, lying together in the dark, breathing as one. Eventually, Lily drifts off to sleep for a few peaceful moments, but with sleep soon comes dreams of the living and the dead. And then she's awake again with a start, her heart pounding in the darkness, the baby heavy on her wounded chest. Sensing his mother's panic, the child jerks from his own slumber, twisting and crying. She shifts him a bit to cradle him, gives him kisses, rubs his back and his legs. She lets him cry until he has exhausted himself, whispering into his ear the only assurance she has left to give him.

"I'm here. I'm here."

ACKNOWLEDGEMENTS

First, a huge thank you to my agents Nat Sobel and Judith Weber for their invaluable work, first in helping me to revise the book and then finding it a home. Thank you to the whole team at Sober Weber, especially Victoria Dillman and Sara Paolozzi for reading early drafts.

In studying sex trafficking in the United States, I was informed by the work of researchers Louise Shelley, Siddharth Kara, Kevin Bales, Stephen Lize, and Ron Soodatler; investigative journalists Aryn Baker and Ginger Allen; and survivor activists Shandra Woworuntu and Windie Lazenko.

I owe deep thanks to friends who were kind enough to share their hilarious/harrowing/touching experiences of pregnancy with me, including Maureen Brown, Kezee Procita, Adrian Wade-Keeney, and my sister-in-law Amy Bolding Hinkson.

Thanks to Jenny Garnett and Chris McSween for taking time to answer my medical/surgery questions.

Thanks to Stephen Bridges for sharing his experiences working in a facility for troubled teens.

Thanks to Jason Pinter at Polis Books for believing in *Find Him*.

And my deepest thanks to my wife Anne-Sophie Rouveloux, for spending the last couple of years with me while I worked on this book. *Je t'aime.*

CPSIA information can be obtained
at www.ICGtesting.com
Printed in the USA
LVHW011209220922
728893LV00004B/5/J